FLEABAG

– BOOK 3 –

FLEABAG

– BOOK 3 –

SOMEONETOFORGET

Podium

Cover design by J Caleb Design

ISBN: 978-1-0394-5410-1

Published in 2026 by Podium Publishing
www.podiumentertainment.com

Podium

FLEABAG

- BOOK 3 -

CHAPTER 1

"And I'll be sure to name my price for that as well. Farewell, Ironheart," Mirena said through the bugs' clicks and hisses and buzzes, and the moment the call ended, she released her control of the swarm, breathing out a deep sigh as she let the bundled cloud of chitin and wings scatter away from the crystal.

She was getting better at doing that, but progress remained glacial. And unpleasant. She rubbed chitin fingers into the edges of her eyelids, trying to soothe that persistent pressure and stall its inevitable buildup to a migraine.

It was an ability that was barely worth the pain and trouble in her opinion, considering that all it did was make her a range-limited version of Arach and her spiders.

There weren't supposed to be any side effects like a headache, but she'd been an unfinished project when Ghoul and Holocaust got her out, at least according to her file. It was entirely likely that her body wasn't quite at the stage where she should be doing what she was, but Ghoul needed her.

So even if it rankled her to live up to the name Tillenhall had given her, she could endure being "hive controller" if it meant they could keep themselves in the loop. Informants were only as good as their paycheck told them to be.

The Struggler's Mantle were the only ones whose info she could somewhat trust, but for the most part, it was just her and Ghoul gathering intel.

Mostly her.

It wasn't like anyone else could do information gathering like her, not in their group. Holocaust was the exact opposite of "inconspicuous" and currently half comatose, and Ghoul himself was busy all twenty-four hours of the day, every day.

So she would control as many bugs as there were in her range, and use their eyes and ears for their own purposes. She just hoped Ghoul knew what he was doing by telling her to lie to Ironheart. Whatever the hell he wanted a wolf for. She moved a swarm into her work room, keeping only a few fire beetles on Holo's body, both to absorb her heat and to notify her if she started thrashing or waking up again.

Now, she had a "face-to-face" meeting to attend.

She checked her belts and pouches, her grenades, field generators, her enchantments, the body sleeve spider-silk armor, one by one, and then waited for the swarm to settle around her into the most nightmarish image she could come up with. She took her mask off, the falsehood of her humanity, and set it on the table, letting plague and horror make a new one for her.

The Stranger.

A robed, hooded figure, whose face was but a mess of holes and writhing insects with two large black holes for eyes.

A persona that she both felt fondness and bitterness toward.

Gnats and flies and moths and cockroaches and bees and a million other things settled on her, around her, in the folds of her robes, atop her face. Writhing centipedes covered in spikes and glowing green with acid coiled around her fingers. Arrow wasps lined her mandibles.

She closed her eyes.

The swarm mixed and swirled, settling into a shape. The Stranger opened their eyes, fireflies lighting up on the bottom of the insect-formed pits. A million points of view expanded in her mind, each insect's muddled senses, muffled sounds, thousands of them. She was going to have a horrid migraine later, but for now, the Stranger had business to attend to.

"Be good, Holo," Mirena murmured under her new mask, and with a flare of mana, the Stranger teleported out of their base.

Ghoul finally reached the hole in the dungeon's wall, mere innocuous stone and fading cobbles from a collapsed bridge remaining, and for one last time, leapt up with his hands, nearly fifty feet, and grabbed a hold of the protruding brick.

It cracked a little, so he reinforced it with a brief flare of tagma and nimbly swung himself up. Seemingly abandoned, far out of the way of anything else, and without any way of reaching it beyond climbing or teleporting. It was little wonder they had difficulty finding her den.

Elizabeth's pet had given him many boons, thankfully. After all, in the maw of a ghoul, flesh had memory, life force, flesh had inklings of soul. And even if the fuzzy memories would fade all too quickly from his mind, Ghoul knew how to catalog such things in mediums less fickle.

He walked forward in the pitch-black tunnel.

Reality dismissed his very existence as tagma stripped him off the world's mind, his passing leaving neither footsteps nor a brush of wind and breath. A hundred and one eyes swerved, rolling, jerking and racing around the quickly widening tunnel, opening to a vast cavern. Forgotten mining facilities and sparse gutted machinery were sprawled across a hundred feet forward on the path. Abandoned worker suits, helmets, lights, buckets, and carts were sprinkled across the area.

Another eye rolled, glaring into the distance, at a construct of mana, an illusion.

He took the first half of a step.

Reaching into reality's innards with ice-cold fingers, tagma's thick, cloying essence oozed from his frozen heart. His foot and shoulder twisted as he squeezed himself through a fold in space, one footstep to carry him a mile, so long as he could see it. And he had more than enough eyes to keep everything in sight.

He took the second half of a step and saw the illusion shift behind him from the sudden disturbance, the cavern's entrance that he left behind now barely a blink of dim light in the distance. Here though, there was more than enough light. An illusion that hid from the outside and lit up on the inside.

He idly wondered if there was a chance to persuade one of Elizabeth's pets, whichever one made this, to do some work for him.

After this visit, he doubted it.

Thralls lined the outer walls of the colossal manor, their minds as empty as their eyes, their imprints on the human consciousness all but erased. An eye swerved up, past blacksteel spires and half-lit windows, tracing runes and a crafted, simple mind, artificial, hovering in the sky. A mana-detection field that covered the estate, just beneath the illusion. Alarm circuits, mana conduits racing through the air, blind to human eyes.

Convenient, that he did not have mana. Only this bizarre energy he'd dubbed tagma, a strange opposite to qi, and a thing that nobody in the world seemed to know even existed.

He couldn't complain much. Qi was so much louder than tagma. So much harder to hide.

Another eye rolled up, to the right. The buzz and static of a radio connection struggling to connect, its waves whispering of curt words, spread across his sight, each different frequency another shade in a palette of colors that he could not even describe to himself, much less to others.

A forty-foot-tall gate of flower-and-thorn-textured metal stood in his way, flanked by four thralls, both a work of art he didn't care enough to appreciate. Another eye glanced at the electricity racing through each inch of the gates and fences, arcing beneath the surrounding metal's surface. He stared at the double doors far beyond the entrance, past the gate.

Another step, a yank at space as he felt it fold beneath him, and he was in front of the wooden doors.

A kick to the lock sent them inside the manor in the form of a hundred broken pieces, and he allowed the world to notice him again, idly watching the mana signals start to flare along invisible, immaterial lines as they tried to warn their creators of an intruder.

He took a few steps, just enough to be inside the manor itself, and folded his hands behind his back, waiting. A hundred different gadgets, grenades, and artifacts were buried within his new buttoned coat, dimensional storage cuffs and time-freeze bombs, all manner of things that could render this place into rubble within less than ten seconds.

But he wasn't here for that. For the moment, he appreciated the architecture. A long hallway, lined with metal pillars that had been shaped into flower and ocean wave patterns from the top to the bottom, a dark-red carpet in the center of the open foyer, and a staircase that split into two, beneath which were iron doors.

He stared through them, waiting.

It took a mere ten seconds for the first monster to tumble through one such metal door, a hideous thing not unlike a gargantuan bat mixed with a ram and something vaguely muscled and scaled, fur lining most of the creature and scales covering the weak points. Its flat triangle-shaped nose flared as it smelled for him, only to give up when nothing entered its nose but broken wood and the vague scent of blood.

Two beady eyes locked onto him.

It shrieked and dug its wings' claws into the floor to lunge forward, only for the mirror-smooth floor to resist its grip and send it forward in more of a lazy jump. Then it raised its wings off the floor, kicked with its legs, and managed to almost fly for about ten feet.

It was a slow, stupid thing. But it wasn't Tillenhall's. So that left one of his suspicions yet unanswered.

After another few seconds of the bat creature rushing at him, covering the massive distance of the entrance, it finally got close enough and folded its wings in a rough imitation of arms, raising them skyward to smash him into the floor.

Tagma pooled at his left foot, into the ground, anchoring him.

He twisted his waist, idly watching the ton of muscle that was about to hit him, and with a twist of his torso and shoulders, kicked with his right.

With speed that most wouldn't see with the naked eye, his leg slammed through the leg-thick wings, through the left side of its chest and shoulder, the point of his foot digging through organs and flesh before tearing free in a sound not unlike an explosion. The creature didn't get to vocalize its reaction, flying back thirty feet in a flailing spin as its gore splattered all over the second-floor railing, the pillars, and the smooth marble floor, blood dripping down the metal flowers.

Its mangled corpse rolled to a stop and did not rise again. He lowered his leg from the odd crane-like position, his arms still behind his back, and waited, watching. Two more like the one he'd just killed were bounding up from the dungeons, each accompanied by three things that looked like a mixture between a rat and an oversized monkey-dog, clambering all over the bat creatures as if they were riding it.

Then the person he came here to see teleported on the high point of the stairs opposite him.

Wreathed in a dozen different spells and effects, a scaled tail, and two massive curling horns of obsidian-colored bone curled over her head like a crown while a skintight halter top dress barely contained her curves, leaving little to nothing to the imagination, cutting off mid-thigh.

Her lips curled into an annoyed sneer. Had he caught her while she was at a social event?

"Elizabeth," he said in greeting, and her tail lashed behind her, as immaculate as the rest of her. The monsters below halted and immediately reversed direction, as did the hundred or so rushing thralls behind him, all of them turning around to calmly walk back to their stations.

"Ghoul," she said back, annoyance fading into a searching look, her slitted amber eyes scrutinizing him. The lack of violence between them likely confused her. Good. He wanted her unbalanced, off her tempo.

An eye not unlike a black pearl peered into her surface thoughts. She had assumed he was here to try and kill her because of her betrayal. She was correct on about half of that, but she didn't need to know that yet. Above him, on the third floor's balcony, he saw a gargantuan spider leg slowly curl over the railing.

"Arach. Did you receive my message?" he asked, and the leg stiffened before retreating over the railing and reappearing on the opposite end of the third floor, behind Elizabeth.

Then the leg was followed by seven more, each several feet long and pointy as spears, revealing a woman seemingly fused with a giant black widow spider, her body sunken into the spider to the waist in the middle of its back.

She was as pitch black as the spider half, her skin looking only a little softer than the spider's chitin. Eight beady red eyes covered her head, and her hair was pulled back in a ponytail as a black corset and the conservative top half of a dress covered her supposed modesty.

Neither of her two sets of eyes swayed from their dead stare on the floor as they slowly slid down, but he knew that that was simply because her little children were tucked into every nook and cranny of the manor, watching him with a hundred little eyes.

The spider gently touched down on the left side of the stairs leading to the first floor, a few feet behind Elizabeth, the joints of its legs reaching six feet tall on their own, and the woman on top of it almost ten. The string detached. Then she hurriedly skittered behind

Elizabeth as if trying to hide her massive form behind her mother, her hands clasped over her stomach as she hunched forward.

She was scared.

Elizabeth stiffened a little, eyes narrowing. Her finger twitched. It seemed like her other children were coming as well, barring Miaro.

"She received your 'message.' Are you here to collect?" she asked with a lidded look of warning.

"Yes. But not in the way you're probably thinking. I'm here to talk about your betrayal, and the problems it has caused us, then negotiate. Also, unless you want them to die, wrangle your children when they get here. I won't let them attack me just because they can't hurt me," he warned, and her eyes chilled as her bronze-scaled tail went very, very still.

He gestured to her office, on the third floor opposite the door. "Shall we?"

She took a deep breath. Then visibly relaxed, even as she kept weaving a dozen different new spells to hold at her fingertips.

"We shall. Arach, go gather your siblings and children, and stay outside. Just in case," she calmly said, her gaze making it no secret that she was telling him to be careful about trying anything in her office.

Not that he was planning to.

A dragon-blooded vampire was something he wasn't even sure he could beat one on one, even if Elizabeth was young compared to the usual for her kind. They might be equally matched.

But she wasn't sure of that, and he could always slaughter her children if she tried anything. In her mind, they would probably help her should he decide to try and kill her, when in truth, they'd just be a very, very good meal.

A spell activated to Elizabeth's side, a rainbow-rimmed portal that made him wish that at least half of his eyes could squint. A lavish dark-wood office contained within, varnished and polished to perfection by a blank-eyed thrall woman that hurried out of sight.

He wordlessly stepped forward.

* * *

"First. I want to ask why you took such a chance. It seems out of character for you," Ghoul said from atop the side of the wide, wingback chair she had presented him.

A very low one, designed as a small power play by making her guests look up at her. Of course, Ghoul just kicked it onto its side before sitting on its left arm and putting his filthy boots on her desk, legs spread and elbows on his knees, his hands steepled in front of him.

"Sometimes you have to shoot before you see the target," she easily replied.

"And sometimes, you have to finish what you shouldn't have started," Ghoul fired back immediately.

She tensed inwardly just a little before working a long sigh out of her nose as she supported her cheekbone with the back of her hand, doing her best to appear bored.

Which meant that she did look bored. She was quite good at acting in her not-at-all-humble opinion.

"Ghoul, I understand attachment. I understand revenge. But you are not unreasonable, generally speaking. You probably understand that this was . . . an opportunity. The time was ripe, the environment was perfect. You would complete several goals with one lucky swing of circumstance. You knew Holocaust would not care about collateral damage. You knew you could abuse her fear of capture by trying to set her to sleep for maximum results. You knew you could use the distraction to open the way for Ironheart's rats to decipher the portal locks the kingdom uses, at least in the short time they had before the portals started melting and exploding. You knew tensions were just enough to provoke this war you've been after this entire time. You would get your war, you would give Ironheart an opportunity, and claim a favor for yourself."

He tilted his head, then straightened it, whatever he'd heard quickly losing his interest.

"You also knew that me and my own, we had no interest in participating in this war, so you wished to see if you could provoke us into fighting the kingdom by making us public enemy number one. A very smart move all around. But if one single thing went wrong, you would show your hand with little to nothing to show for it. I suppose I respect that gamble of fate." Ghoul was calm as always, sounding more like he was talking about the weather than a potential war between themselves.

She nodded with a bored look on her face, not showing her alarm at just how much the bastard knew.

How? Did he have a genuine [Clairvoyant] in his pocket? The kingdom had one on commission terms, and even they could barely afford her services for all but the most important of things.

None of what he knew was ever mentioned besides face-to-face and mana-channel communication crystals. Which were secure enough to make even herself struggle a little in intercepting messages.

"I am indeed not. And I know you care not for pleasantries, so I'll be blunt," she said. "Why did you come here, knowing all this? I was expecting you to try and kill us. Judging by the fact my boy is still alive, albeit barely, you're more amicable to diplomacy than you usually are with those you might see as enemies." She languidly uncrossed her legs and crossed them once more in the opposite direction, leaning back in her chair and puffing her chest out a little.

Force of habit, really. She knew he wouldn't look. She was never sure where his gaze was directed, and trying to use her magical senses to figure out just gave her a headache, but she knew it wasn't on her figure.

"Salvaging this is possible, despite my desire to be . . . rash," he said, not moving an inch as he spoke.

"I'll be blunt too, I suppose. I don't particularly want to fight you, not until Tillenhall and everything that house owns is ashes and dust. And your stunt has cost us a lot. So you will repay us. Unless you'd rather we focus on you first. I have three simple demands in exchange," he started, and she raised a single eyebrow at him, curled like a cat's back before a strike. "Before that, explain your end goal to me. Your condition for all this to have been worth it, a victory."

Her second eyebrow joined the first.

"That's an awful lot to ask for with nothing but vague platitudes to offer me in return," she hummed, glancing down to observe her nails.

"I will offer you nothing but a guarantee that you will not find your children hanging by their entrails from a white-feathered banner," he dryly shot back, and she slowly turned, her serpentine eyes boring into the numbers scrawled onto metal, where eyes should be, slowly narrowing.

Threatening to drag the Dove down here was unwise for even him, but he could evade them much more easily than she and her own could. Somehow.

"Bold threat to make in my own home, corpse," she icily intoned.

"It is," he simply stated, and she settled her unamused, slit-eyed glare onto his faceplate.

She might be able to take him in a fight. But it would never be a certainty which of them would win. It would never be a certainty how many of her children and creations he'd kill before dying either, so even if she won, there was a good chance she might not have really won.

And she knew full well he meant every word.

"The goal is to install House Kervile on the throne and become one of their keys to power. The spear, shield, and cloak and dagger so to speak. The second key, on the religious front, is Fata Morgana and his Crow's Church, and the third would be the East Xhilatni Interseas Trade Company, which would take over as the main trading force. That would be a 'victory,'" she admitted, feeling like she'd just been forced to swallow something sour.

He tilted his head a bit, then nodded.

"House Kervile is beloved by the common people, especially with the Crow's Church's backing. But I don't believe you. You don't settle for seconds. You would either be using House Kervile as a proxy to lead the country from the shadows or hold something over them to make sure they only do as you say. Free of the Six-Winged Dove's pressure and free to access all you could need to strengthen your covenant, without being in public scrutiny or bound to much duty beyond replacing the Guard, essentially. A good plan. One I'm not even disapproving of. I'd like the Dove to have its wings clipped as much as anyone else. Assuming you achieve your goals, somehow. And your other . . . 'allies'?" he asked, in a tone that made it abundantly clear he knew they were no such thing, not really.

"We'd get rid of them, of course," she replied with an easy shrug. "Every crime lord, gang, and general undesirable. The Syndicate the dungeon barons have formed is a shoddy council formed by necessity and haste. It'll crumble into infighting the moment we win, and I'll just mop them up one by one before they realize they're a dying breed." She hid how much she wished to remove Ghoul's head from his shoulders.

She didn't like being questioned like this. But she had betrayed him by making Arach trail Holocaust and prodding her into kicking down the first domino, and judging from his decades-long crusade to destroy Tillenhall, he was unlikely to ever forget it, so she could do the minimum and try to smooth things over a little. He didn't seem inclined to be her mortal enemy, but this was a game of interests. She couldn't be sure.

"I see. My demands are simple, and we'll seal them in a magical contract, of course. First, unless you want me and whoever follows me to be your enemies until the end of time, you will give us every tiny shred of information you have on House Tillenhall, and you will not ever, for any reason, interfere with what we do with that information. And if we fight alongside you against the upper city, you will even actively assist us in destroying Tillenhall, completely and utterly. And nothing, absolutely nothing that they have worked on, researched, or accomplished will ever see the light of day. They will be scrubbed off the history books."

She hummed, staring into space as she considered it. She was planning on getting rid of House Tillenhall anyway. They were too prideful, too secretive, and too powerful for her or any of her genuine allies to be comfortable with the idea of their prolonged existence. Sure, she would lose something of great value, especially considering the possibilities of House Tillenhall's magitech bioengineering and her own monsters created from witchcraft, but was it worth it to keep a viper around just because one wished to milk its venom?

In her mind she'd plotted for it to be a fast, decisive strike that would ruin them before they could get their bearings, but she'd take what she could get. Then she could use her considerably more weighty resources to get rid of Seven-Six-Two, should it be needed.

Because she had the feeling Ghoul would actively work against her until the end of time the moment Tillenhall was done for. The man's entire drive and purpose seemed laser-focused on vengeance, and she'd slighted him quite heavily by double-crossing him.

It was necessary, and she'd do it again if it meant getting the same wonderful results it had reaped for her, but that was the obvious negative to it all. And if Ghoul and his team did get involved, having the chance to essentially buy Ghoul's combat power, even if only once, all in exchange for something that aligned with her goals regardless, like helping them mop up every last Tillenhall associate?

It wasn't a steal of a deal, due to all the trouble it would cause her, but it was surprisingly even-handed.

After another short moment of thinking, she nodded. "Accepted."

"Good. Second demand. I want your arm, and I want Arach's legs. Four of them. If not, four pints of blood would work. I won't reveal details, but your opportunistic backstabbing did a number on Holocaust.

So I have to pick up the slack a little. I'm sure you understand," he said mildly.

She paused, her eyes slowly narrowing as she tapped her nails on the desk.

The way he worded it made it sound like it would be quite a power-up to consume parts of her. And he would be right, if what little she understood of his absurd nature was right.

Additionally, she was not an idiot. She was a vampire, they made blood magic, and they were thus equally capable of making sure it couldn't be used against them. She also knew that they were magical creatures, so any attempt at biochemistry would be quite wasted on them, and nobody capable of it existed outside House Tillenhall.

People that Ghoul would rather skin alive than talk to.

So there was little to no risk to give in to this demand.

The thought of her child hobbling around the manor with half her legs made her inwardly seethe with fury, but she could accept it. They'd grow back in a few days, and amputations were painless with Percilicus around, bless his blood-encrusted leaves.

"Would this demand satisfy that promise of 'drinking her blood' that you made?" she asked, and he nodded.

"Water under the bridge, so on and so forth."

"Accepted."

"Good. Third demand. There will be some people and a beast that will likely come to your attention soon for various reasons. I'll be helping them along, but they must be independent of us. Me, and you. You will help them from the shadows as well, however. Try to curry favor, communicate with them if you please, but do not try to ingratiate them to you, nor try to bring them into your fold, and of course, if they ask, do not let them into your fold. In less formal words, keep your claws off of them but help them along. All within reason, of course. I do not expect you to show yourself to the world just to keep strangers alive. But a nudge and a prod in the right places can make a lot of difference. Resources and connections, especially." And as if sensing her apprehension somehow, he shrugged and continued.

"This might sound vague, but the contract demon will deal with any details and technicalities, of course. On both ends, until—"

"I know how a contract demon works, corpse," she said, her voice terse, and he conceded the point with a tilt of his head.

"One change. You will help us deal with the kingdom and whoever else it might drag down here as muscle, within reason that will be specified, in exchange for our help in extinguishing Tillenhall. No ifs about it. Your wording there seemed rather evasive."

"Not good enough. I'll happily lend you Holocaust for a few fights if you please, proportional to how much you help us, but I and my other members have too much on our plates that is too important. I'm only ever going to come fight the kingdom if you personally come down and help me eviscerate Tillenhall. Tit for tat. As for Holocaust, if you do take her for a couple fights, you will give us notice beforehand to see if she can make it."

He shifted a little, as if stiff, making her wonder if he was acting more human on purpose for some reason.

"I will not send her into a desperate fight without intel or anything like that. I trust you understand that she'll be retreating the moment things start looking bad, and that she is very hard to boss around. And if you try anything on her, no matter what it is or how you do it, I'll make sure to give Tillenhall a break as I make sure everything and everyone you know dies screaming before coming for you." He finished, his voice still as average and calm as ever.

Her lips curled into a mocking sneer as her brows raised.

"Do not presume you can do that much. But," she emphasized as she dragged her spells back under her skin and let her mana thicken that paper-thin barrier that stopped them from exploding, "that is fair enough. Are we in agreement?"

"We are."

He took a little box out of his pocket, and with a brief press of a button and a tilt of his head, a rectangular metal chest appeared over her desk and dropped on it with a heavy thud.

Trusting him not to be so stupid as to attack her immediately after hashing out a deal, and recognizing some of those runes on the box, she stayed her hand despite the lack of consent from her end.

A mechanism unlatched, and the chest opened and unfolded like a mechanical jewelry box with a hundred tiny little cabinets, each unfolding to show something different.

She could guess the nature of the objects, considering what he was here to do. The dry eye of a man who died screaming, a lock of children's hair, broken bottle pieces with flecks of blood on them, a roll of rusted chains, two hearts, each belonging to souls once bound by oaths, and a dozen more things as odd as the rest.

She scoffed as she leaned back in her chair.

"You want to summon the contract demon here? Now?" she asked, and he nodded as he twisted to the side and finally took his boots off the edge of her desk before standing upright, surveying the floor for a good open spot.

"I'm a busy man, Lisa. More so since you pulled your stunt."

She felt her eye twitch. "Do not. Call me that," she carefully intoned as she got up, inwardly seething over that stupid nickname.

"Our friendship ended when you decided that chasing revenge was more important than helping me as I lay dying on the floor with a sword in my chest," she forced out, and he turned his head toward her, just an inch, only to say the absolute last thing she ever expected him to say.

"I am sorry about that. Just as I know that inwardly, you are sorry about what you pulled on me and Holocaust. But we both know that were we to go back, we would do the exact same thing again. What we did, what we must do, and what we will do will not change. So let's not get into that discussion, and just get this over with."

She just stood there for a moment, blankly staring at him. How certainly he said that, that she was sorry about what she had done, that took her entirely by surprise.

How did he know that?

Was he a psychic? She was warded against that, everything within a thousand feet of her dungeons was. He didn't even have mana, he had no soul.

She narrowed her eyes in suspicion.

"Why do you think I'm sorry?" she asked, her impression of incredulity flawless.

And just like usual, it felt like he saw right through it. Somehow.

Fucking bastard.

He didn't smile so much as bare his shark-teeth at her, a sight that made her horns itch to ram into his face.

"I know you and yours, Lisa. Now, if you could get a thrall you don't mind losing?" he said, and pulled his lips back down, reaching for the hearts, before turning around and kicking aside a Peranian rug that she quite liked.

Cleaning her office after this entire debacle was done would take her thralls ages . . .

She sent an order to a few of them, as well as a short list of items they'd need that Ghoul hadn't brought. Then she mutely picked up every single ingredient with her mana, floating them around and skillfully setting them into a perfect four-tiered circle on the floor beside her desk.

Ghoul stared for a second, before mutely offering the hearts to her, which she spitefully took last.

Then they waited.

CHAPTER 2

Aitra stared at her new bronze-acarite wand beside her new shield, bright and waxed on the floor between her and Silthen's beds, gleaming iridescent silver as the enchantment did its work.

Were its price not the lives of half her team, she would have been ecstatic.

In hindsight, her frustration at not being allowed to find that Awakened dog she tried to control next to the Bone Pits with her skill was probably ridiculous. If she had managed to have it as her companion, it would have only added more grief to the whole situation. There was no mere animal that could have survived that.

Her spirit summons had gotten shredded, over and over again until they were wrung dry along with her mana. A flesh-and-bone dog? It would have had no chance. She felt stupid now for having been angry about it.

Her bright blue hair blocked the windows along the top of the room from sight, and that was fine, because it felt like the cheery golden light outside the Adventurer Guild's rooms was mocking her.

Silthen had a similar empty sort of look on his face, his brown hair as unkempt as the stubble on his jaw, staring down at his mismatched, gore-covered greataxe. The bladed end was a buzzsaw glowing orange with heat as it lay idle, red lightning arcing out of the weapon's shaft and blade. Torn right out of an abomination's arm, quite literally.

It looked so small on that horrific pile of flesh and screaming metal joints, yet it was almost as tall as Silthen himself as it lay on the floorboards.

Normally, he would have a large, proud smile on his face. A Factory artifact, on their third tour of the dungeon? A great achievement. But just like her, he did not think the price was worth it. No words were spoken between them, the two empty beds in their room almost accusing in their grim silence.

She wondered if when Ankhan had begun trying to convince them to move a bit farther down, she should have been more adamant in her refusal. More vocal with the fact just because they only made enough money to finish the month and do their maintenance didn't mean they gained nothing.

In the end, everyone but her agreed to go a little deeper.

It wasn't like they went down for miles, or anywhere close to entering a different floor than the fifth. Not even a tenth of the way to another floor. But just three hours away from the portals, they were forced to run back, forced to change their objective from "fight and gather golem corpses" to "survive."

Nakim's fading screams as she got dragged away into the rumbling darkness played in her ears at night like a cackling, mocking melody.

She didn't get to see what happened to her. She was glad. She did see what happened to Ankhan. She wished she hadn't. Just thinking of the sight, that helplessness as she pounded at the glass, not even scratching it, the sound . . . It made her eyes tear up and her stomach clench in preparation to heave.

A few more minutes passed in silence before Silthen shifted. His eyes met hers as she glanced up at him, equally bloodshot, but not nearly as lost, not nearly as doubtful as her own likely seemed.

"It's not your fault, you know?" he quietly offered, and she couldn't help but let her face drop into her palm.

"I know that. You're projecting. It's not your fault either, you know . . ." she muttered, and after a few moments of silence, Silthen made an acknowledging noise, not exactly agreement.

As their leader, he was likely not of the same opinion.

"Ankhan would have called us a bunch of Debbie Downer schmucks for moping around," Silthen mumbled.

She felt a tiny smile curl her lips.

"Then he would have told us to stop grieving a loss and celebrate that we had something to lose in the first place," she muttered, thinking fondly of the man she had thought of as vain and materialistic, only to learn of his past and worldview and gain a sense of understanding of his flamboyant, overspending ways.

"Nakim would have told us to bleed the grief out on the training yard and hold our tears for someone less bitchy . . ." Silthen said.

She snorted, her shoulders shaking in mirth and sadness, tiny sobs mixing with small chuckles as she covered her face with both gauntlets, her shoulders quivering as she hid her tears from the world, palms pressed against her eyes as she fought to stamp down on her emotions with deep, stuttered breaths.

"Yeah. Sounds like her," she eked out, her voice breaking twice in the process.

She felt bad for crying so much. Silthen had known them for years. She knew them for six months. It felt like she didn't have the right to be crying and mourning more than he was, that she was somehow undercutting something she barely got to know before it was gone.

She knew them for six months, and they were still the only real family she'd ever had.

"We've got enough to take a small break, you know? Regroup, reevaluate. Then, we can get to finding new members for Silk Kin. If you still want to be an adventurer, of course. Or a part of this team at all," Silthen softly offered, and for a moment, she really began to wonder.

Was it even worth it, being an adventurer? Were the levels and money worth the risk of losing a friend every time they donned their gear?

"It doesn't matter. I don't have enough money to afford the next trip out of here. It's too late to back out now. And I don't want to live in this shithole if I do. I want to get enough money to where the option of leaving for back home is available. I'll decide then," she quietly said.

Silthen shifted. "Of course. And . . . maybe by then, we'll have a decent enough team to leave together, go back to the Labyrinth. Well, not the Labyrinth, exactly, just, any dungeon that's less . . . less than the Factory," he mumbled, and she mutely nodded.

Going from killing stone constructs and living armors to this factory of horrors was like going from swimming in hot water to swimming in magma.

"Let's go get that drink that Ankhan would have bugged us about. I think he deserves it. Then we can check their storage boxes and see what his will said. Nakim refused to write one," he muttered with a pained smile.

"Okay," she replied quietly.

She had forgotten about that last part entirely. How long had it been since Silthen had put down a legal will in front of her and asked her to write what she left and to whom, in case she died? It must have been one or two months ago at most, but it felt like years.

As she got up and wiped her tears off to follow him, she idly wondered what Ankhan's will might say. Some heartfelt message, some letter to be delivered to a loved one or a past lover?

Two and a half hours later, she could only stare uncomprehendingly at the paper in her hands, the phrase "too handsome to die, baby" being the only thing written on the empty space, in familiar chicken-scratch letters. It didn't even follow the ink lines, written diagonally, half covering the stamp that assured it was genuine.

Silthen peeked over her shoulder.

Then he started laughing, a slowly increasing, ramping thing, starting from a mild chuckle that upgraded to full-blown laughter over the course of a few seconds.

A long time ago, before he was capable of referring to himself as anything more than "Warden," without a pronoun or a mind capable of disobeying, he used to know what to do.

A trap snapped shut in the distance, accompanied by the short cry of its prey.

The prisoners needed to remember that he was around. To remember that Compound Four's warden was ready for them. To hear his chains rattle and scrape against the floor, hear the sound echo across the hallways so they knew to cower in their corners as he continued his eternal march in endless circles.

Another trap snapped shut, followed closely by a second, a third, each with their own sound of something fleshy snapping or tearing.

Trapper shifted, leaning the torso of his armor forward stiffly, his magitech core flexing with his will to move the wooden gears inside his body, which in turn moved his limbs.

Another snap. A tiny spark of satisfaction.

It was the closest he could get to that engineered euphoria he once felt whenever his traps would catch an escaping prisoner. He watched the level he just gained without an ounce of emotion.

The desire to be part of something bigger again was a permanent fixture of his existence by now. Part of something deeper, something more than whatever he had going on, working with people he didn't know or remember the names of, following the orders of a weak-eyed man who paid him with coins he did not know nor care about the value of.

An administrator to a prison and its warden can be many things. Weak and indecisive was not on that list.

So why did he follow?

A pair of golden orbs came to mind, full of steel unyielding, of potential infinite, fearless and savage and wild, gazing at him as if he was but an annoyance, yanking his trap off its arm with enough force to shatter it with a look of contempt that asked, *Is that it?*

There was a certain air about that creature, an air of importance and destiny that he knew he'd never find again.

An idea formed, a slow desire building within him.

He rose with a cacophony of rattling chains and bear traps. He turned. He walked away from the landfill, leaving a dozen different types of traps behind for the scavengers to find and provide him with some level of progress, uncaring of their fate, whether man or beast.

They never gave levels like manually fighting and killing did, not even close, and he didn't know why, but he didn't much care either. He just liked the satisfaction that even without his eye on them, there were prisoners being caught and killed by his traps, in whatever place he decided his prison would be that night.

Some idle part of Katherine thought that maybe with a bit of time, she could get used to peeking over fur and seeing nothing but bottomless abyss after bottomless abyss, that the sudden lurch in her stomach and that mental gasp of mortal fear would stop happening.

By the time their trip had gone on for an hour and the . . . the creature had started to pant and struggle with scraping down anything and everything it saw and could reach, its arms starting to shake a little, she realized that fear probably wouldn't fade anytime soon. If anything, the more tired the monster got, the more the fear grew that it would slip and send them all falling to their deaths.

She hated every second of their descent.

Every time the thing leapt across a gap, or simply swung to the side to grab onto a piece of metal more flat, it made her choke on air and let out sounds she didn't even know she could make, her bladder feeling increasingly loose.

She knew there was a tentacle around her waist that had proven it could lift her with relative ease, so if she somehow slipped her grip, it would probably not let her fall, but there was *a spiked fucking tentacle* around her waist, and that *didn't help.*

Fear of the unknown was a powerful thing.

But seeing the unknown up close and personal was honestly worse.

It gave her time to note all the absurd things covering the beast, how its forearm was almost as thick as Emhreeil's thigh and with enough definition to notice through its thick fur, how there were spikes on its arms and shoulders that would jerk away every time she'd accidentally brush against them like they had a mind of their own, how there were two very human arms on it and the one on the right wasn't holding Scruffy, so it was free to grab stuff and make their descent smoother, which made it impossible to forget that it was there because she kept seeing the damn thing creeping into her field of vision when she least expected it.

Then after a particularly rough landing on a hanging carpet of decorative chain never meant to hold the equivalent of three people made her let out another mortifying sound, Emhreeil reached forward with a hiss of pain to comfortingly pat her back, rub her shoulder.

"Just trust him, all right? He knows his limits. I think. He wouldn't be doing this if he didn't think he could do it without killing all three of us."

As if in agreement to a statement she honestly hoped the creature couldn't understand, the beast let out a strange chuff filled with a sense of . . . "trying-to-comfort," of sorts, a bizarre inflection to it that couldn't be natural. It leaned its head back as far as it could to rub the top of its head against the top of hers as she tried to cringe away, feeling the dried blood on its fur scratch a bit of the skin on her forehead.

It was actually . . . oddly comforting. Some of the fear she had of the monster left her.

Then as its head straightened again and a fourth arm crept into sight so it could shimmy down the length of the chain, she noticed a horrifyingly familiar golden ring suddenly open on the base of its neck. She stared at it uncomprehendingly.

The ring blinked, before glancing down past her head to stare at Emhreeil. The fear that left her quickly returned tenfold, mixed with a healthy dose of disturbed anxiety. She felt a little sick.

"Hey, buddy." Emhreeil reached past her shoulder to rub at the fur beneath the eye, as if this was perfectly normal and expected, and some of her earlier words began making sense.

Why she was so hesitant to speak details of the beast, why she was warning her that she might realize some things about it that would alarm her.

And she was right, it all alarmed her, every inch of the strange creature.

Yet none of it made her mouth dry and forced shivers to crawl up her spine as much as the bizarre, unfathomable ease with which she watched those bloodless claws sink into solid steel like it was literally not even there, over and over and over and over again, leaving behind thin slits inches deep.

She was literally riding on the back of some magical Tillenhall monster that Emhreeil had somehow tamed—or not, actually.

Not tamed. This thing was not fucking tame. If anything it looked more like it was bossing Emhreeil around instead. That realization made everything worse.

Their descent continued, until eventually, while sliding down the smooth backside of a spire, it spotted a thick pillar of steel that led down to a steel bridge connecting two cliffs made of buildings and houses on two opposite dungeon plates, and after another heart-stopping leap, began to slide down, fast and quick.

A second after the smog revealed rough outlines and shapes, she couldn't help but have a moment of panic as she saw the dozens of people on that gargantuan bridge, mere specks of moving black among steel plates almost two hundred feet wide.

Wouldn't they see them?

Then their descent slowed to a stop, and the creature shimmied around the metal pole, opening the eye on its neck again and turning its head to stare behind her.

She turned, seeing nothing but the large, flat arches that followed along atop the bridge, extending several hundred feet off safe ground, giant Π-shaped towers of black-brown steel that extended wires as thick as people down to the bridge below.

It wiggled its legs and butt as it placed itself at an odd tilt, bracing in a way she had grown horribly familiar with as it took a bizarrely deep breath, and she felt her eyes bug out in panic as she realized what this psychotic murder banshee dog was about to do.

The top of the closest tower was at least sixty feet away and half that distance down, there was *no way*—

Coiling black smoke oozed out of the creature's fur and consumed her, devouring all her senses but touch and smell. She stiffened in panic.

Something slammed into her with the force of an iron wall, impact transferred through the creature's back into her front, and she felt air yank at her clothes as her sense of balance began to spin and flip, her blood and organs yanking at her insides as she soundlessly expelled air out of her lungs in a dark, soundless void.

Another impact from behind her, a duller one, and then a third, both enough to take her breath away but not enough to hurt.

A final bone-rattling impact that rolled with the one who tanked it, who seemed to be the monster, and the mixture of that impact slamming into her stomach, the involuntary clench of the tentacle around her stomach, the hours of gut-clenching fear and tension, and the spinning world around her forced her to punch down and writhe to escape as she felt her stomach heave, legs kicking.

She wasn't sure what she punched, but the monster jerked in surprise, the tentacle around her stomach pulling her aside—

And out into the world again, away from that endless void, tossing her away with a lagging flick, the tail unwinding and making her spin as acid filled her mouth, the backpack full of their supplies finally detaching from her shoulder.

She barely managed to roll with the impact of her side hitting the ground. She pushed herself up on her hands and began vomiting on what she assumed was the floor, no matter how much it rocked and spun and wriggled.

A few seconds passed where all she could do was gasp and retch, exhausted, furious and scared and confused and overwhelmed and a dozen other things that all added up to making her feel like she was losing her fucking mind.

Rushed footsteps neared, and a hand tried to clumsily gather her hair, before two smaller ones joined in to keep her black locks away from yesterday's dinner. Heavier, clicking thuds neared too, irregular to the point of being rhythmless, and she flinched away as a snout prodded her head, the smell of blood and filthy wet dog filling her senses.

A soft whine that somehow sounded like a question, followed by a lick to her forehead that had her cringing away even more as the last remnants of spit and acid trickled out of her mouth. Her arms were trembling.

"She's nauseous. So am I, honestly. Just because you don't get dizzy somehow, you cheating fleabag, doesn't mean we don't," Em mumbled tiredly, as if it could understand her, and at this point, who fucking knows, maybe it did. Maybe it could teach Katherine how to count properly, because why the fuck not? It wasn't like this whole situation could get any more absurd than it already was.

Emhreeil's hand abruptly retreated.

Then, a horrid, scratching, scraping noise entered her ears, like a growling, rasping smoker trying to whistle while taking a deep breath as he talked.

As it talked.

"Eeehmreeeeeeiiiiill."

Her head snapped up, wide-eyed, ignoring the fact that Em was wearing a mask with claw marks at the eyes from wherever she got it from, to focus on the beast a little too large to be called a dog, more of a small bear. A lithe, snake-centipede-like bear that was holding Emhreeil's wrist with one of its human arms.

The furry arm then dragged Emhreeil's hand back on Katherine's head as she gaped, and the thing let out a questioning chuff as it tilted its head, eyes on her friend as Emhreeil made a sound she usually did when she was cringing particularly hard or grimacing in guilt.

"Uh, that's, Katherine."

"Uuuhthhaaa—"

"Katherine," Emhreeil repeated, lifting her hand and patting her on the head.

"She—"

"Wh—"

She faintly smelled toast as she blinked rapidly at the sight of her friend kneeling by her side, patting her head like a dog as the mutant creature held it by the wrist while she repeated Katherine's name so the monster could struggle to learn how to say it.

It was fucking talking.

Or . . . learning to. Trying to?

She lurched away from them, stumbling to her feet and swaying backward.

"Fushin . . . fhuwat 'he am—Ijustwhabugfhiun?" she mumbled, not knowing what she was saying herself, just pure gibberish, and despite knowing how it was likely not a good idea to be drunkenly stumbling away from her only allies on top of a giant superstructure hundreds of feet away from safe ground, she turned around, spat the taste of stomach acid out of her mouth, and tried not to sprawl herself out on the metal under their feet while she fought with her trench coat, not bothering to understand what the sounds behind her meant.

After a few seconds of struggling to remember how sleeves and button clips worked, she tripped over her own feet and found herself saved from meeting the floor by two giant tails.

She almost rolled away and kicked them before thinking better of it and aborting the motion before it began, worried she'd roll right off the fucking tower, and after Em shooed her monster friend away, she was left chest down on the floor, watching lights and distant life thrum in the distance over the edge of the tower's flat roof, breathing slow and heavy.

"Kat? Kat, are you okay?" Em whispered gingerly, a supportive hand on her shoulder.

She grimaced at the burn in her throat, and said the truth.

"No," she rasped, and was met with silence as the hand tightened and began to rub at her arm, letting her regain a piece of her senses. "I'm . . . I need to sleep the shock off. And water. I need water," she mumbled, and Emhreeil let out an "okay" before getting up and rushing off to their supplies to get some.

The monster thing then padded closer, sensing its opportunity, nosing at the back of her head and ruffling her hair as she grimaced.

It let out a small, short, concerned whine that was more doglike than anything else she'd heard so far, then immediately ruined it by trying to say her name questioningly in that bone-scrapingly horrendous mockery of speech that made her skin try to detach and squirm away from her flesh, making her feel faintly sick again.

Then, just because it seemed like it was not done, making her equal parts thankful and terrified and immensely uncomfortable, it plopped down next to her, throwing two arms and tails over her back, its snout over her neck.

A snout she had watched literally tear people apart limb from limb. Good riddance to those guys, of course, but it was just . . .

Were she not freezing, and were it less warm than what felt like a radiator on full blast, she would have immediately struggled out of its grip.

As it was, she just gave up.

She couldn't deal with this, she just gave up. It wasn't going to eat her, it was warm, and no matter how many nightmares it would give her, she was probably safer near it than away from it right now. Em certainly trusted it. She'd told her how it had saved her a half dozen times for no discernible reason, so maybe she had a good reason to do so as well.

Emhreeil rushed back and quickly gave her a small cup of water.

"Just rinse your mouth out on this. I'm going to throw away most of our small cutlery stuff, they're taking too much space, so don't worry about this getting dirty, we're leaving it up here."

She drank, swished the water around her mouth, finding it odd while lying sideways, and spat it back out into the cup, then set it down on the floor. The cup was emptied quickly on the metal roof, the water thrown away from them, then washed with a small bit of water, refilled, and given to her to drink, Emhreeil's motions surprisingly swift and sure as she did all that.

She felt like she was back to being sick in Irythiel's mansion, Em fussing over her as she fought through a sickness.

Except she wasn't sick. She was lying on cold metal rather than a bed, and her blanket was made of fur and caked in dried blood and gore.

At least it was exceedingly warm.

It got warmer when Em lay down on the other side of her. Then Scruffy wriggled into place between them.

Then the monster decided to act as a literal blanket on their shitty cuddle pile, carefully wriggling into place to place its upper body on Emhreeil's stomach, its flanks on their legs, and its massive tails curled over Katherine's upper body, curling over her head, its numerous arms mostly dedicated to curling over them to keep them in place and warm them.

She was so absurdly exhausted, yet she couldn't properly sleep for the first hour or so, so high up from safe ground, in such a strange place, covered by a monster that was currently vastly contributing to both her physical comfort and her mental discomfort until the oddity of the mixed feeling was what kept her worried.

But as their breaths all slowly synchronized for some reason, the metal beneath them warmed, and her nostrils got used to the stench of wet dog and blood, she eventually became too physically comfortable and much too tired to resist the allure of sleep.

CHAPTER 3

The new human, the one with the black hair, was still scared of it.

Which was actually good to some extent, it meant she knew who was in charge, but it was also a bit annoying, having her flinch even in her sleep whenever it shifted.

Fortunately, the wolf also did not need as much sleep as its humans.

It wasn't sure how it felt about having an extra two humans in its pack. Honestly, it was *quite* annoyed, even if the sensation of sleeping in a pile was incredibly nostalgic and calming to the more primal parts of its brain.

Dealing with one human was all right; it could handle that. Three was just *too much*.

Still, it was a bit late by now to reject the new humans, especially now that it had very thoroughly marked them with its scent during their shared nap, so it decided to spend some of its time checking on its symbols while it rested.

You have progressed on your Path.
[Hound of the Keeper] Level 29 → Level 32
Base Attributes:
Strength (+3)

Speed (+7)
Dexterity (+2)
Endurance (+12)
Perception (+7)
Resolve (+3)
Intelligence (+8)
Soul (+3)
Available: 3

. . . What?

It *did not* have that many attribute points. When did it put two in Dexterity, and why?

Deciding quickly that its Intelligence would have to wait a bit, despite its large benefits, it quickly put its points in and let the other level-ups flit by its sight, hoping for an explanation, because something about its attribute point distribution was suddenly confusing.

It wasn't good at math, but did the numbers the squiggly symbols represented even add up to thirty-two levels?

Speed (+8)
Endurance (+14)
-[Mana Perception] has Leveled Up. Level 15 → Level 16
-[Mana Manipulation] has Leveled Up. Level 17 → Level 18
-[Echoes of Oblivion] has Leveled Up. Level 22 → Level 23
-[Bloodrush] has Leveled Up. Level 18 → Level 19
-[Logotexnia] has Leveled Up. Level 17 → Level 18
-[Sonic Blast] has Leveled Up. Level 8 → Level 10
-[Danger Sense] has Leveled Up. Level 4 → Level 5
Acquired Skill(s):
[Unearthly Howl] - Level 1
[Spike Shot] - Level 1

It paused, and after a bit of mental squinting, the symbols provided it more information.

[Unearthly Howl]. A skill with a range that had no limit besides how loud it could go, which was a *lot* if it used [Logotexnia]. Every level-up would make the emotions invoked more potent, with the baseline being the howl it made when going down to pick up its human.

It idly wondered if it could level this high enough to make humans drop dead out of sheer terror. That would be pretty funny, actually, if the skill wasn't completely indiscriminate. But best of all, it didn't have to be near the edge of its mind with fury and panic to make that sound again.

[Spike Shot] was much simpler.

It added a bit of force and accuracy to its shots with its spikes with each level. Nice, but nothing as immensely useful as the first.

Acquired Title:
Unseemly Horror: You are known to thousands and feared by just as many, however distorted or obscured your visage in their minds. Gain +2 to all attributes.

Known to thousands . . .

That was probably not great, even if it was expecting it with how much it abused its lungs and mana reserves that fight to make enough noise to buy time.

It also explained the sudden increase in attributes when it was *certain* it had not put that many points into.

That . . .

That was an *absurd* improvement. It *had* been wondering while falling down, what exactly had just given it that sensation of invincibility, that sudden rush. It was this title.

Incredible . . . Then again, how many creatures could do what it did down here? It could think of none. It felt like preening with pride.

With nothing else to do, it turned its mind toward more wide-reaching problems. It needed to find something unique, it needed to hunt something. It couldn't grow complacent.

First, it spent a solid hour trying to come up with any kind of significant improvement beyond small touches, until it eventually remembered the roof-tumor insect.

More specifically, its hydraulic-powered body, a way of movement that could provide incredible power and speed for little cost, but one that utterly crumbled and became useless at even the smallest leak of inner fluid.

Using the same insect's expanding slime veins, however, it theorized that it could make some kind of inner layer of that special fat which it could use nerves to shock into expanding and contracting. If it lined the inside of a chitinous limb with that, blocking any cracks and leaks that might occur to the appendages would not be terribly difficult.

Less abstractly, it wanted that roof tumor's legs. Or at least two of them on each side.

Not only were they nice for climbing purposes, they were also very pointy, which opened the potential for them being used as *weapons* as well as climbing aids, which it certainly would not complain about. Its arms and tentacles were only usable right now because the templates had been on constant healing duty during its climb, which had been severely draining on its essence.

It needed to find food. It had yet to make any substantial stockpile, and after making these new limbs, it would be practically dry.

Its current idea came to life just two hours later, a record time for any change it could remember, fast enough for it to be genuinely baffled.

Maybe it had something to do with the fact it upgraded from rats to humans as its main diet? [Devourer] seemed like the type of skill to care about that, so it could theorize that that was likely the case.

Regardless, as it carefully got off the pile and stealthily hopped away to test its new additions, it quickly stretched and yawned before clacking its teeth shut in satisfaction.

Then it tried to get a hang of its new limbs. It had already formed muscle memory by tugging them around as it slept, so it could at least move them.

On either side of its lower waist, no longer thin with its new additions around it, sheaths were forced to bulge as hydraulic fluids worked with complicated pressure systems to move the limbs inside, anchored to its inner abdominal and back muscles.

Just underneath the secondary pair of latissimus muscles it had made for its human arms, they came out into the open air, just a few inches above its back legs.

The eyes on its hips and lower chest opened to observe, and it noticed a slight problem.

The middle set of eyes on its body, located just under its rib cage, had a bit of a rough time seeing things when the new limbs were out and above, acting like umbrellas that blocked half their upper sight.

It would move them up a bit later.

Its eyes carefully examined the limbs, two coming out of either side of its waist for a total of four, leaving it with five limbs on either side of its body.

Impressively enough, though it had ten limbs plus tails, the tentacle *still* didn't make it feel like it was about to trip over any one of them by accident. It could probably operate a hundred limbs without issue, though it was not expecting to ever need or have that many.

The ability to do this was odd and out of place from what it knew of biology and mind-to-muscle connections.

Maybe an effect of the symbols . . . ?

Now that it moved around a bit with them, it realized they also helped with its balance somewhat, as its upper body had a chronic issue of being far heavier than its lower. The limbs helped.

Focusing back on their appearance, it even tilted its head toward them, wiggling them back and forth, up and down.

Three jointed instead of four, unlike the roof tumor. The roof tumor used its legs to move as well as trap its prey, but the wolf did not want a joint so close to the end of its leg, lest it bend when it was trying to stab something, so it removed a joint for stabbing and slashing stability.

They were also larger, thinner, and much sharper—meant to be used as surprise weapons. The first two joints were pitch-black chitin, but the third was more like a cutting scythe in its shape, similar to the sword the humans sometimes carried. Their cutting edges and tips were an organic mix between hardened chitin and bone, giving them a sickly gray look, while the main body of the scythe-like blade limb was a smooth, solid black.

And just to complement the hydraulics, it had shoved a complex network of several thick tendons along the insides of the limbs, which would allow it to exert far more power than such limbs already had.

Experimentally, it tried to test their range of movement.

It had tried to give them as much as it could, but the system was somewhat rigid out of necessity. When dealing with rigid materials and liquids, it was impressively difficult for it to come up with a way to make things flexible. It had done its best by adding a rotating, locking cylinder on the insectoid base of the limbs made of a combination of interlocking bones like a spine and some organic hinges, and it was time to test it.

So it moved the limbs back and as wide as it could, until the only obstacle to moving them farther back were its own hips, and felt no strain.

Then it moved them in a slow clockwise circle, scraping them against the floor as they moved toward its shoulders from below, then straining a little as they moved past and over its head, until they refused to go further toward its spine, simply moving clockwise, locked in a sixty degree angle from its back. Then, they were back to its hips, a full, uninterrupted rotation.

Their reach was not great, unfortunately, barely able to reach a foot away from its snout from their positions, because no matter how much space it gave the sheath that hid their immense bulk around its waist and stomach, there just wasn't enough room to make them bigger without making them a detriment.

Then it tried to mimic combat movements.

They were *easy.*

Backhanded slashes audibly whistled and cracked through the air with explosive power, and when it would bunch the limbs up along its waist and stab forward with them, they had enough power in the movement that when they reached their max range, it felt its whole body move a little as the limbs tugged its waist forward.

Climbing . . .

Well, it didn't have anything to climb up right now, and it was going to slide down using its claws, so it left that for later. They were flexible enough to help; it didn't need to test that.

Satisfied, it went to put them back into their sheaths.

It was surprisingly infuriating.

The sheath had no muscle, just being a pocket of lubricants and shock-absorbing scar tissue from the spearhead shark, and so while the legs folded effortlessly into a compact shape, wiggling them back into the pouch-like sheath on its stomach was difficult.

Not because it was cautious of poking a hole into its pouch or stomach or anything, it was way too tough to be able to hurt itself like that without its [Devourer]-empowered teeth, even if it tried. It just couldn't quite wiggle them back into the very specific position it had grown them into, which was the only way to make them fit.

It took *ten minutes* to finally get it right, and by then, it was barely containing its snarls of frustration.

It mentally noted to move the eyes under its ribs up a little and make the pouch a little stretchier, then turned around.

The black-haired human, "Katherine," was staring at it, wide-eyed.

It chuffed in acknowledgment. "Katherine" slumped back down on the floor with a strange wheeze and curled back into a ball, the scent of her fear still present in the breeze.

She'd grow out of it like "Emhreeil" did, it wasn't terribly concerned. Now, to hunt.

It wasn't going to sit around and guard its pack all the time. It had goals, and it was smart enough to realize that they would only slow it down in many environments and the like, slow its growth sometimes. So it wasn't going to play guard dog. If they couldn't handle themselves, they'd just have to learn how to do it, and if they got in trouble, the wolf would just run to help them.

It was dangerous, yes, and they could die in the future from this, which it did *not* want to happen, but that was just life. It could take the risk of losing them if it meant they would grow enough to where it didn't have to worry about it, and its own growth wouldn't be stunted by their presence.

It wasn't quite what it was hoping for, but being practical about it, there was no way it could *both* traverse the human nest and hunt prey with humans on its back. It would make it too heavy, make it tire much faster, and would just be overall useless, because it didn't *need* its pack to hunt for food. So it could leave them somewhere, hunt, and go back real quick. It was a good way to operate until it found a place to use as its *own* nest.

Preferably somewhere close to the burning rivers, away from the humans.

It moved to the edge, hooked its nails to it as it swung its body over the side, and carefully slid down the massive tower's darkest wall.

It was so incredibly hungry, it had no idea how it hadn't noticed until now. Perhaps too busy changing itself.

It killed so many humans and didn't even get to eat a *single one*, because it wanted to rush away before more humans arrived to make everything more difficult, like how it ended up being captured by the burning rivers the last time it made such a racket.

It was a little frustrated about letting so much meat go to waste.

It spotted a working human lift beside the bridge, heading straight down, which meant it could go as deep down as that thing went, and have an easy way of getting back up when it decided to roll up the other way.

So, despite its trepidation, it slid down to the bridge's railing, then slunk over it, careful not to let any human see it, crept down a complex, multilayered cage of metal rods on the outer part of the bridge, and slid down the giant pillars of metal supporting the ridiculously oversized structure.

It was glad it did so, because it ended up seeing something it hadn't seen much of before now.

Water.

Not clear water, and it was still tainted by a few creatures it could recognize from down by the burning rivers, but it was currently looking down at a stream of water several feet deep, and surprisingly *not* hissing with toxic chemicals.

It took a moment to consider something as it hung from the metal pillar supporting the bridge above, one that cut the river in two before it joined back together. It tilted its head, glanced to either side of the gaping V-shaped chasm that this hundred-foot-wide river of sorts was within.

A lot of windows, too many to count. An almost equal number of short walkways welded onto buildings that seemed to barely manage to hang over the river too, and it wondered if it could make them all tumble down to their death with a few select snips of its claws.

It didn't have any particular reason to ponder the thought besides amusement, really. If killing thirty attacking humans hadn't given it more than one levels, it wasn't sure it would ever be worth it to kill hundreds of random ones in their sleep just for a couple of levels, either.

It eyed the water again, eyed the jumpy green creature that was usually found by the burning rivers, a weird croaky ball of flesh. It idly watched the bits of glowing moss, the small dark shapes beneath the water as they followed the calm, barely moving stream, the uneven rock and metal plates around the river eventually cutting off about two hundred feet away to plummet onto a lower level, the water following in a lazy drop as it overflowed from the artificial dam trying to keep it in place.

It was likely that these were the waters that got mixed in with the trash later on to fill the burning rivers.

It stared at a dark shape near the bottom of the slowly moving river, small enough to be trivial, and after one final glance at the surrounding windows and walkways on either side, made its claws cut at full capacity, kicking off the pillar and using its human arms to push itself off, diving headfirst into the waters as it closed its ears with the inner cartilage block it had made a long time ago.

It wasn't sure what it was expecting when it dove in headfirst, but enjoyment was not exactly in the list of options.

The sudden silence, both from closing its ears and the water muffling the usual clamor of the human nest, was very calming. The water was rather freezing, but considering how used to overheating it was, it would take this any day.

It took a moment to just let itself go with the river's flow and sink down, only kicking and paddling with its arms enough to not get swept away by it, its eyes all wide open and passively scanning the river's insides.

It had never swam for leisure before, usually just racing across a burning river as something giant and green chased it, or back when it lost its human and had to fight the giant spearhead thing.

And the water was . . . surprisingly clean. It could see stuff for almost twenty feet before the muck and dirt began obscuring things.

When a few drops got through its tightly clenched jaws, it realized another bizarre thing.

The water was absurdly salty.

Were its eyes not protected by those dense protective membranes, it would likely sting a lot.

This was really nice.

And with its Endurance and hyper-oxygenated blood, it could probably stay under the water for something like ten or fifteen minutes before needing to breathe.

So that was what it did, even daring to close its eyes in short bursts, feeling weightless, worriless, at peace. It used its tails and tentacles to scrub all of the matted blood off as well, oddly enjoying the feeling of being clean.

It was still hungry, but the rest of the soothing emotions helped numb that, or at least postpone its urgent tugs.

When its chest began to feel tight, it prepared to go above the water, before remembering the shapes it had seen below the water.

It could still catch glimpses of them, but they seemed to be actively avoiding it.

It wanted to take things from them, see what they might have to offer, but it wasn't exactly a perfect swimmer, it couldn't light them on fire, it couldn't sneak or feel them in the water beyond vague impressions, and they were not sluggish either, bursting into motion randomly with jerky, undulating motions that had them speeding through the water like it wasn't even there.

The oddest thing was that from the glimpses of them it caught, they looked like . . . giant oddly shaped worms with fins, while some others looked like a giant worm with a dozen faintly luminescent blue tentacles coming out of their back. The latter seemed much more interesting.

Still, this situation made the wolf realize that underwater, it was at its weakest. It really had to hunt some water creatures down.

So it decided to try something.

It couldn't inhale air down here, but it rose as close to the surface as it could, and gathered the air it had in its lungs, before mentally straining with the command to hold, to remain cohesive, trying to somehow push that into its skill.

Then it waited until it caught a glimpse of one of the glowy seaworms lazily drifting about, and before the thing could suddenly burst into motion and vanish back into the murk, it pushed out.

The semi-vacuum left behind by the air exiting its lungs was filled by water before it could actually snap its jaws shut, and it hurriedly burst out of the surface, hacking and coughing water out of its lungs, the salt highly unpleasant, almost drying its insides.

It tasted terrible too. Like salt and brine and smoke and a bit of chemical aftertaste.

Still, through the coughing fit, one so intense it felt its eyes water with actual tears, it forced itself to keep the eyes on its lower body open, giving it a stable visual of both below and above water, so it got a good look at how the air bubble exploded far before it was intending it to, almost ten feet short of the seaworm.

Despite that, it could see the worm's limp body float up to the surface through the small cloud of dust the explosion kicked up, slowly, its blue-tinted tentacles glowing as they limply twitched.

It had no idea why. Was it stunned? Did debris smack it on the head? Did the wolf rupture its eardrums?

Not willing to let the prey escape because of a mild annoyance, it continued coughing its throat raw as it used its tails and four arms to paddle like an arrow toward it, and in mere seconds, it could see it through the top of the water, still twitching, now much more lively.

The tentacle in its back came out, and speared through it with its bony tip.

Its prey jerked, and the wolf suddenly choked as electricity raced through the seaworm's corpse, racing up its tentacle and down into its back, a bizarre, horrible sensation, not quite pain but just a constant stream of unpredictable muscle spasms that had it moving normally one moment then randomly swinging its tentacle and twisting its back in strange ways.

Seeing the thing begin to slip from the blade, it waited until a spasm passed, and flicked it onto one of the stone walkways lining the river, then went back to coughing the remnants of salty water out of its lungs.

It clawed its way up the stone flanking it and spent another five or so minutes coughing and chuffing water out of its lungs as it observed the bizarre creature, limp on the ground.

There wasn't much light down here, and it was also not clear light, so it couldn't tell if the thing was some kind of odd brown color or just pink mixing with the yellow light glinting off its strange skin.

It was vaguely shaped like a teardrop with a fin at the end of its tail, with an actual mouth and four beady eyes of varying sizes on its head. The most interesting part, of course, was the few dozen squishy tentacles coming out of its back like branches, still glowing a soft blue in their middles and writhing under the force of their own electricity, tiny arcing sparks appearing between the branches with a faint buzzing sound.

If this thing had electricity, then it also had some way of being immune to electricity.

It inwardly felt a tad annoyed for its [Electricity Resistance] likely becoming redundant after it was done incorporating whatever things this bizarre thing had in its body, but it was a fairly unreasonable emotion that it wasn't exactly sure why it felt.

And just to be sure it could get this thing's biology properly even after the slight intelligence loss that came with getting rid of that symbol on its skull, it waited until it could stop coughing enough to swallow, ate the whole thing in two spasming swallows that were actually surprisingly tasty and savory, and then it dove back into the river to grab a couple more.

Hunting for essence could wait a little, even if it felt like human brains were getting increasingly easier to understand.

Besides, it wasn't like its pack could get down from there on their own. They wouldn't be going anywhere.

"Wake up," a voice called, accompanied by a none-too-gentle shove against her ribs with what felt like the toe of a boot.

She was jerking awake and rolling onto her back in an instant, never relaxed enough to sink into deep sleep.

The golem eye flicked to life, mana gathering at her fingertips.

A man was looming over her wearing a buttoned leather coat and black pants, his head nothing but a metal plate with three numbers on it with three half-melted metal protrusions not unlike horns framing his head.

Before she could even process his presence or how the fuck he seemed to know where they were and where they would be, the man spoke again.

"You said you wanted to turn, right? I've got everything you need, and far more besides. I believe it's time we had a normal conversation. You have questions, I've got answers. Wake your friend up, gather your wits. The wolf is coming up. I'll wait for him to start." He backed up a dozen steps, still staring right at them, arms limp at his sides.

She hissed out a sigh as she flicked the golem eye off and rolled over onto her front, clumsily pushing herself upright with her left hand. Then she shook Katherine vigorously.

Much like her, Katherine startled up, awake and alert, pushing herself up and hurriedly glancing around. Her eyes stuck to the man, wide-eyed, before flicking to her with a questioning look.

"Sewer guy," she explained, lips pursed, and Kat's eyes widened as she hurriedly scrambled upright, keeping a wary eye on the man as Scruffy croaked awake.

Ten minutes of awkward silence passed until said man tilted his head, before abruptly walking to the edge and leaning over to look down.

The wolf's presence lit up in her mind, a mere couple dozen feet between them, exactly where the creepy bastard was looking, tense and caught off guard.

The man turned to her before backing away from the lip of the tower.

Through the colorless lens of the golem eye, she watched her friend's furry head peek over the top, brows furrowed and ears pulled back, staring at them and the man in what she could guess was a look of confusion.

She gave him a half-hearted wave.

He tilted his head at the gesture, then like a snake, crept up the edge, paws wreathed in smoky darkness and chest touching the floor, ready to bolt or fight at a moment's notice.

Her eye moved back to the man, and for the first time, she actually read the numbers on his faceplate.

Kat's explanations of how the civil war started rushed back to her mind, and she gasped in realization. The man's head turned to her, just an inch, not close enough to be looking at her but enough to know she had his attention.

"You're from that, that team. Seven-Six-Two. You're an . . . *adventurer terrorist?*" she blurted out in disbelief and genuine confusion, before inwardly cringing at her almost accusatory wording.

She had thought he might have been an adventurer back then, but by now, she was expecting him to be some secretive assassin crime lord or something.

"Yes. My name is Ghoul. Both adventurer name and real name. Though my team in the guild has been little more than a way to taunt our enemies and gather funds back when we needed them. I wouldn't say our calling is . . . *adventuring*," he calmly said with carefully placed disdain for the notion.

Before she could mouth off another question, the man gave off the impression that he was suddenly completely ignoring them, and fully turned toward the wolf's tense form, one that grew even tenser.

She could see his skin bulge and crawl as things shifted beneath the fur, lumps and edges, spikes softly scraping against each other as they moved.

"Your friend is far smarter than he should be, but to his core, he's still a beast. Don't interfere with the peace offering," the man softly said, before casually crouching and reaching into his coat. The wolf's nostrils flared.

He took out a strange cube with a button that he pressed, and then, a gigantic spider's limb, taller than a human by a good margin, appeared in the air and dropped to the floor with a metallic clang-thud so loud that it was abundantly clear the limb was much heavier than a person.

She gaped at the sheer fucking *size* of the thing, dreading to imagine how large whatever monster he'd torn that out of must have been.

Then with a casual flick of his finger, Ghoul sent the whole thing sliding across the flat top of the tower, until it slid to a halt right in front of the wolf.

Yellow eyes flicked down to the limb, then up to the man. Narrowed.

Then slowly, he began to sniff the limb, clear distaste appearing in the way his nose scrunched, yet regardless, he bit down and began crunching through the chitin, eyes still nailed to the man, but significantly more relaxed in its posture.

Ghoul rose up again and put his arms behind his back.

She was kind of surprised that that worked, and she wasn't sure why, either.

"Why the . . . peace offering?" she asked tentatively.

"Curiosity and practicality. I want to see if a wolf can glean anything out of a vampire's leg, and he was still scared of me due to our first meeting." He talked as if he was about to continue, but then he snapped his jaw shut, and his head jerked to Katherine.

The wolf paused too, raising his head to stare at Katherine as well.

It took her a moment to brush past the shock of hearing that that giant spider leg belonged to a *vampire* to realize what Ghoul had just said, and she couldn't help the sharp, involuntary inhale that it triggered as she turned to her right.

Katherine was still as a statue, not even breathing, eyes wide and slowly trailing over every inch of the wolf that stared back at her with a tilted head and a confused squint.

Kat's eyes slowly slid to the floor, staring through it with a thousand-yard stare. She could almost *hear* the puzzle pieces clicking together in her friend's mind, and all she could do was rush to think of a way to salvage this.

"You . . . realization. You said a . . . realization would come. Tha-that thing is a wolf?" Katherine breathed out, before something like a wheeze left her. "That's a wolf. That it had spider legs this morning. It doesn't now. It-it's a wolf. How— Wh-where, what—?" Katherine fumbled, her gauntlets rising to her clutch at her hair.

With a grimace, she stepped to her side, choosing to ignore Ghoul for the moment, and with her one arm, she grabbed Kat's left forearm and tugged it down, finally getting her eyes to focus and turn to her.

"Kat. Yes. He's a wolf. I was hoping to tell you once you got a bit more used to what he's like. He's a wolf, and I don't know if history is wrong or if it's all bullshit, I don't know if they really turned Crimen into a desert, I don't know if they can birth another wolf every day, I don't know where the fuck he came from or what he's doing here with us and why he's not a psychotic red-eyed monster or whatever, but he is not what those old mythology and ancient history books say, and he sure as hell isn't a mindless killing machine. *Think*. He saved me, like fifteen times by now. He saved *us*. He fucking slept on us like a blanket, and he was concerned for you being all weird and sick. So *calm down*. Okay? Please?" she asked, and despite the faint embarrassment she felt at having to do this in front of an audience, the faint worry that she might have come off as too rough, she felt like she had to do it *now*.

Kat gaped at her for a moment before her brows furrowed.

"Em, it's a *wolf*, he— It might like you, or, or whatever, but it's a-a fucking *wolf.* The longer you keep him around like it's some pet, the more likely it is it's going to snap at you and shred you to the bone—"

"Well, *good thing* he's not my pet and that I'm very firmly trying my best to not even try to control him in any manner *specifically to avoid that outcome*." She raised her voice to not quite yelling, and Kat just opened and closed her mouth for a moment, before glancing at the wolf then back to her.

"It's still a wolf, Em! It's already killed like sixty people. People are going to notice, and then we're going to get caught and burned in a pyre—"

She grabbed her by the collar and yanked her forward, her lips pulled into a determined frown.

"*Let them notice*, then! I don't *care* if the kingdom and the dungeon itself decides we need to fucking die, Kat, I'm not running away from this. I owe him my life twenty times over, and I owe him even more because even if I'd never gone on that fucking cleanup quest, I'd probably have tried to run from my *masters* and gotten my leg tendons snipped so I couldn't try again, and then I'd have blown my fucking brains out with my own spell!" she yelled, chest heaving.

"So what if it's us against the world, then?! Fine, fuck it, whatever! We either fight or die. It's not like it's any different, just harder! And I'd . . . do the same for you in a heartbeat if you were the monster," she finished, voice lowering with every word, energy leaving her as suddenly as it came to her.

Kat stared at her, eyes going from her face to her eye, full of turmoil. Then she closed them and heaved out a soul-deep sigh.

"I—I can't even get mad because you warned me like *fifty times* about what I was getting into, in the *vaguest* way possible . . ." Kat whispered, voice choked with frustration, then grabbed her wrist, ripped it off her chest without an ounce of effort, and tugged her forward into a brief hug.

They separated, and she took a deep breath as she turned, feeling more than a little embarrassed over Ghoul's presence during a moment that felt like it should have been private.

"Okay, fine. Fine. Just . . . okay. I'll just suck it up. I'll get used to it," Katherine mumbled, and Emhreeil smiled at her under the metal mask covering her face.

"Thank you," she warmly whispered.

"Good speech," Ghoul cut in. "Your dedication and loyalty to a monster is actually what made me decide to suggest what I am about to. But to move this forward, come here, elf." The cube clicked again in his hand, his other hand extending forward.

A thick leather-bound book dropped into his hand, and she approached with a frown, feeling the wolf's gaze bore into her back as it tensed, the faint feeling of threat making [Pack Hunter] feed her information.

"It's Emhreeil," she said as she reached forward and took the book, finding it to be far lighter than it should be. No markings, no descriptions.

She wiggled her thumb under the front cover, and swung it open. The first page was covered in glowing runic markings within a small circle. Below the circle, on the bottom of the page, the words *PLACE HAND ON RUNE FOCUS* flashed with red light, and above the circle at the top of the page, the book's name glowed faint purple.

Telepathic Bond Soul Magic, Memory-Shift Spellbook: Verified By Archmage Teineal Arienmi.

She read it once, twice, thrice.

Her jaw slackened as she slowly shifted the eye to gaze up at Ghoul.

"It is hard to properly communicate with the wolf when it can't understand me, or its own pack, for that matter. In exchange for this spellbook, that I trust you know the function of, you will make telepathic bonds for everyone present here. Then, I'll tell you in detail why I'm bothering with your group, and why I am being so exceedingly generous."

She moved her jaw, nothing came out.

She tried again.

"Th-this . . . books like this are-are worth more than a manor," she croaked out, staggering back a step, and hurriedly snapping the book into her storage ring.

"Pocket change," Ghoul responded, and she could only let out a disbelieving laugh-wheeze.

"Holy shit. What the *fuck* do you want us for that's worth this much?" she asked, wondering what insanity he wanted to propose.

"I don't like repeating myself, and we'll have to explain this to the wolf too. But fine. To give you the bare bones of it, I want you to be our peers. Our allies, but not our subordinates. We need equals. Not for fighting the war, or whatever else you're thinking, but for two goals: destroying the Tillenhall family, and their allies. We can handle the main event ourselves, if barely. But I do not have anyone to trust the second to, and judging by the fact the ones hunting you four are the same Tillenhall allies that have to be destroyed, at least on the third floor, our interests align.

"There is more, of course, but I cannot share that. Technically, all I need you to do, is exactly what you've been doing, but more. Keep living, keep fighting, keep growing, until you can stand by our side. The only difference is that I want you to be our closest ally, in the near and far future, instead of nameless nobodies prowling the darkness. You probably have wondered why I am helping you all so much.

It's because loyalty to people and creatures like us"—Ghoul gestured to the wolf with his chin—"as thick as steel and twice as unbending like yours, is nigh impossible to find, and so is a wolf. Especially one that is sane, smart, and able to be reasoned with." He took a step back and gestured to the ring with one of his hands.

"So put your hand on that rune and make us a bond so we can include your . . . team leader, I suppose, in this discussion. Do note that beasts do not think with spoken words, though, and try to get used to thinking like a monster or an animal, or else the bond will be useless and incomprehensible," Ghoul said without an ounce of deceit, in a near-perfect monotone.

She took a minute to digest everything, in disbelief over it all, but with everything that had happened recently, the mere month or two that had passed, which felt like *years*, it was not the biggest surprise, neither the most impossible thing she'd had to accept.

And the chance to be able to get out of this odd limbo of theirs, with the wolf leading but being unable to actually communicate to them and vice versa, they had a chance of fixing that here, even if it would take a bit of getting used to, if Ghoul was to be believed.

She squared her shoulders.

The book flashed back into her hand, still open.

A repulsion field came to life beneath it, holding it in place as she put her hand on the rune circle, sending a small pulse of mana through it. The paper withered under her burned skin.

Her mind cracked open like an egg, and through the cracks of its shell, a thousand pages of information rushed in, her world melting into symbols and the faint taste of purple as hands clamped down on her shoulders to stabilize her.

CHAPTER 4

It didn't like this.

The strong dead human didn't seem like he wished to harm them, but his mere presence was unnerving, unnatural, and hit one of its few sore spots.

Namely, enemies it could not defeat *or* run away from. Or so it assumed, from how fast he moved back when they first met.

It did not like relying on the docile nature or benevolence of someone or something, trusting that they just *wouldn't* strike out, despite the fact they *could* do so, and easily kill the wolf and its pack.

Its human did something with the paper binder and almost fell on the floor, and the scared one was there to keep her in place as the wolf tensed, the insectoid leg forgotten on the floor beneath it.

The dead human was not aiming his faceplate in its direction, staring at "Emhreeil" instead, but still, it did not feel comfortable in his presence.

Its human took a deep, sudden gasp and stiffened, straightening with the "Katherine" human's help.

Then "Emhreeil" made some kind of joyous yipping, high pitched and careless, and it mildly relaxed at the sound, tilting its head in puzzlement as it glanced from her to the dead human and the strange paper binder he'd given her.

She made a bunch of . . . bizarre hand gestures with her hand in front of her own face, staggered a little, then straightened again, before ripping the metal mask off and letting it drop to the floor.

She turned to the wolf and walked to it as quickly as she could, a brisk walk. It let out a low grumble full of confusion, sitting back on its hind legs.

Then she crouched down to its height and began making the same bizarre sequence of hand signals in front of its head, her fingers exuding mana and leaving lines behind, floating in the air in shapes that twisted like writhing worms and felt like they were making it dizzy just to feel.

It stared at her in confusion, tense.

It felt the familiar sensation of something prodding at its mind, not trying to break through, but asking.

A choice was once more presented to it, one without information or anything more than a vague notion of yes or no, and it stiffened.

Was this control? A choice? A choice that had to do with control, maybe?

Suspicion and anger rose within it.

However, two thoughts made it calm down. One, this was not a choice born out of the ether; this was something the human had presented. Its human that had also just done . . . whatever the air symbols were, to herself. And two, the last time it accepted, it got one of its most useful tools.

So after a few seconds of Emhreeil sitting in front of it and patiently waiting as it glared at her in suspicion, it accepted.

It felt a bizarre sensation, like a hollow tunnel made of mental energy and thought, suddenly forming in its mind, linking them together.

Emhreeil's lips spread wide, baring her teeth at it, and it tensed further, suspicion rising.

Too many mixed signals. Humans turned their lips up when happy, but baring their teeth while their lips curled up didn't make sense. Was she just . . . happily threatening it? That didn't make sense.

Baring her teeth without snarling . . . while staring at its eyes so intently with the big yellow one she had, its mechanical, jerky motions a tad too organic to not be disturbing . . .

Was she trying to tell it to back off, despite approaching it first? What? Or maybe she was . . . why was she baring her teeth? It was simultaneously confused at this sudden turn of events and more than a little annoyed.

Maybe she had no idea what she was doing? Humans were terrible at body language, after all. From a more charitable point of view, this could be some bizarre mix of signals that only another human would understand, and the thought made it fractionally relax.

Something was sent through the link and harmlessly bounced off its mental walls, making any such relaxation flee instantly.

It backed up and growled lowly in warning as it puffed up, its mind wandering back to the tight cage in that room full of animals, to the sensation of slowly turning into a puppet in its own body down by the tunnels, wondering if there was something she was trying to do here.

It ignored the way Katherine tensed, her hand going to her "sword" as her fear rose enough for the wolf to smell it in the air, despite her actions making its hair fractionally spike across its back in caution and warning, the starting eddies of suspicion taking root in its heart.

It felt like its very soul *seethed in fury* at the idea of chains, and though it was not that emotionally unstable itself, it could admit to feeling very tense right now, suspicion dragging faint anger to the foreground.

This whole . . . thing, whatever it was, it was making its hackles rise. It just wanted to grab its pack and get going, and now it was here, trying to figure out some bizarre . . . authority challenge? Human ritual? Whatever Emhreeil was currently trying to do.

Additionally, something about how she was acting and poking at its head while not showing an ounce of deference was just *grating* and making all sorts of alarms blare in its head.

The human's teeth-bearing faded, her lips turning back to normal as she tilted her head in confusion, her hand slowly dropping.

"You're still thinking like a human. You see a grin, and it sees bared teeth. You see earnestness in eye contact, it sees challenge. You see convenience in your stance, it sees a shady request without the proper submission. You see confidence in your squared shoulders, it sees readiness. Were this a normal wolf that didn't like you for some reason or another, you'd be dead. Stop thinking like a human. You are only making this more difficult. What would a wolf do? What would a dog do?" the dead human droned on strangely, and Emhreeil startled, her head rising.

"Oh. *Oh.* That . . . makes sense, actually. Shit, okay. Uhm . . ." she said, and it glared, confused, and very much not enjoying how it was the only one here out of the communication loop. It had no idea what they were communicating and their body language never made any sense because humans didn't rely on it.

Stupid humans and their stupid gibbering. Should just leave that to the feathered winged things.

Its human suddenly bent forward, showing her nape in the clearest gesture of submission it had ever learned through distant observation, and it relaxed significantly, now just confused.

So it was not an authority dispute, and she was not trying to threaten it into some kind of mental control submission of sorts . . .

Which left . . . what? Was she trying to make some kind of gift, like the dark giant?

Was that a normal thing that human-shaped things could do? The giant was human shaped before it changed to resemble the wolf.

Whatever gift its human might have wanted to give, it doubted it would be anything close to the one from the dark giant, on *any* level, but it was just curious now.

It stepped forward.

She sent something again, and it washed over its mind like a drop of water on steel. It let out a short whuff and bent down to lick her scalp, nosing her head to encourage her to try again as it lowered its [Mental Resistance]. It could provide her with this much trust, at least, especially considering how human body language made it confused at the best of times. She likely wasn't trying what it thought she had been.

Still, it felt like it had no skin without the skill ramped up to its maximum. Like it was exposed in the worst way.

Resisting the urge to slam the skill back to full power, another something was sent, and it stuck there in the forefront of its mind, like an object or a sound it could not remember but was on the verge of recalling.

It lowered the skill further, and it finally pushed through. A sound echoed in its mind, more like a strange imaginative thought that ran on a separate track to its own mind, but parallel.

"Hello?"

It startled, backing up a step and staring down at the human, wide-eyed.

Emhreeil rose, her lips pulled up in a way that indicated she was vaguely pleased, with no teeth showing this time.

Personally, it was just confused.

She could send sounds to its head. Which . . . would have been useful if they were growls or chuffs or whines or anything like that, anything except the usual human *gibberish*. Much like when it was trying to learn her human sounds, it chuffed a question, tilted its head.

"This is going to take ages if you keep going like this. Make a link with all of us, make yourself the nexus, and you three keep silent and observe while me and the wolf communicate. This is also the best way to learn how a beast thinks and talks, though I'm mostly doing this to save us time."

"Oh. Okay," its human said, then rose.

It watched with its head tilted as she waved her hand in front of each of them in turn, even the dead human, the process taking little more than a couple seconds, before she gestured with her hand toward the wolf, then the dead man.

Something like a faint connection came to life between them, not a tunnel, nor something that could send information, just a presence.

The dead man turned his focus to it, and the wolf stiffened, feeling like it was under a thousand intently staring eyes, uncomfortable.

The fact its vibrational senses couldn't sense much, if anything, about the dead human's head beyond some muddled sense of liquid full of solids, only added to how unnatural his presence was.

Unless his brain was that slushy liquid full of small . . . somethings, he didn't have a brain.

Yet he spoke and moved and *thought*.

As if on cue, a soundless thought made of concepts came from Emhreeil, one that wasn't hers, tainted by the dead man's mental presence, and it discarded its idle thoughts to focus on him.

The dead man lowered himself, his calves to his butt and his elbows on his knees, just about head-level with the wolf. His thoughts echoed on that strange parallel tract to its own thought process, a sense of him trying to say hello in a calm, non-confrontational manner.

It tilted its head.

It sent back a confused greeting.

The man clicked his tongue.

A complicated bundle of ideas came over the connection it had to Emhreeil, the dead-but-alive human sending ideas of his own pack, his own group. A human made of chitin, a raging, screaming inferno in the form of a fragile human with a veneer of calmness.

It was followed by a request of an alliance of sorts, mutual cooperation between their two packs. He sent ideas of protection, distant and from shadows, and thoughts of the wolf's pack killing people in return for it. He specified people that were already hunting it, then for the first time, mentioned the cause of all this, the one thing it had yet to figure out.

Why it was being hunted in the first place. Or rather, by who.

The dead man sent him a crisp mental image of a man with a long face, black-brown hair peppered with white streaks, his face aged but not frail or meek. He was attached to the idea of authority and the wolf's pursuers, their master.

It sent back a simple question, attached to the image of this man.

Why was he hunting it?

The dead man sent him back a rough thought of ignorance.

He didn't know why, but he did know *who*.

The wolf took a moment to think.

So the dead human was offering protection in exchange for them killing the people hunting them?

That wasn't even a question; it was taking that deal. It was planning on getting rid of all of them the moment it could take a moment to breathe and recoup, the problem was *getting* that moment. It was nigh impossible, not until it reached the burning rivers.

It carefully bundled those thoughts into a small mental ball and pushed it through the connection to Emhreeil, who would then send it to everyone else in a bizarre network that it wasn't sure it entirely appreciated, even if the only permanent connection was with her and not the rest of them.

It was still hesitant about the two new humans seeing its thoughts when it sent something over.

Regardless, the dead man's jaw shifted, black fingernails rising to scratch his chin.

An image of metal and glass face masks for its humans. The idea of metamorphosis, of a butterfly breaking through its cocoon, attached to Emhreeil and to the sheer *power* it would bring to her. Then, another image of some kind of bundle of golden metal circles with engravings on their center, attached to the power of value, followed by the concept of trade and various bundles of information, animals and biology, things so foreign and wide-reaching they made it salivate in pure *need*.

Humans would trade shiny stuff for a nigh limitless amount of options, creatures.

Food, things it could incorporate into itself.

The human answered its following question before it could actually pose it.

And he did not leave out details.

It was an awkward few minutes as the man slowly sent information to it, and the wolf simply digested it.

It learned of more "floors" to the human nest, beneath the burning rivers, inhabited by golems like the one it had fought, but limitless, endless. It saw abominations and vague images of machinery, of crystals, crystals that could be exchanged for shining pieces of metal that the humans for some . . . utterly incomprehensible reason, valued highly.

Highly enough to trade the metal pieces for animals, things like the spiked lizard roughly shaped like a dog, like things with wings and feathers and magical crystals growing out of their backs, and a dozen other examples the dead man provided.

Then he offered even more.

Magic enhancers, items of convenience, odd rituals of power.

It took something like ten silent minutes to fully grasp everything the dead man had shared, ten minutes to fully understand its position and plot some kind of path or course of action.

During the entire duration, not once did Witness of Divinity pop up and tell the wolf that he was lying, which made it a lot easier to trust him.

It accepted his deal.

The dead man rose, nodded, and turned to Emhreeil.

Now the wolf was the spectator, and Emhreeil was the one conversing with him.

Still, she took care to send their conversation over as it happened.

The rough understanding the wolf got was that her metamorphosis, or cocoon, was ready, and the dead man wanted to take them to it. It would have understood far more had Emhreeil not been cluttering half her thoughts with the mental equivalent of human sounds.

But if it would make her stronger, it had no reason to disagree, so it went back to crunching through the leg the dead man had given it as a peace offering.

Whatever this was from, it doubted it would give the wolf much. Insects had many legs, and this huge one was a bit too similar to the roof tumor's to expect anything good out of it.

Still, it was free essence as it idly listened in on the mental conversation between its own human and the dead one.

Eventually, the dead man turned and took out a strange metal stick from his coat.

The stick unfolded, gears and wires extending from it to be just a little wider than the wolf's shoulders, one side flat and the other with a half-exposed line of crystals.

He put it on the floor and clicked a button on the right side, stepping back.

A strange sound rose, like the hum of electricity gradually building up to a whine, until eventually, it audibly popped like a bubble, leaving behind a perfectly rectangular . . .

Cut in space, was the best way it could describe it. It stared curiously and moved to observe it from the side. It was like a mirror that reflected back a completely different environment, its edge a swirling rainbow, and the reflection within far too stable.

It was so *unnatural*.

Like it was just a doorway to another place, completely two-dimensional.

The place it led to was another factor to add to its confusion. It leaned closer and turned to the front, head tilted and ears peeled back.

Its vibrational senses weren't working in there. In fact, they didn't pick up anything at all unusual.

It leaned forward a bit more to see the full structure of the room, one of dark-gray stone and blood from what little it could gleam from candlelight and scent, with six giant metal poles arranged in a wide circle, slightly curved in toward the center, where a circle of bizarre symbols drawn in blood lay.

Its eyes moved up the poles, and it grew a little more confused than before.

Twelve humans hung suspended in a tight circle above the center of the circle by their feet, gagged and blindfolded and most definitely alive, lightly swinging from their squirming.

The dead human gestured forward, and after a brief flare of Emhreeil sending apprehension and a request of support, to which it sent back affirmation, she walked in.

It sent a glance behind to make sure the small human and the black-haired one were behind it, and then it turned around and walked in, wondering where on earth the cocoon was and what all this strangeness was for.

The golem eye couldn't see much in this kind of heavy darkness, and she only had one boot left, so the moment her bare right foot met dry stone, she sent out a pulse of mana.

And froze, idly feeling the wolf's fur brush her legs as it trotted up past her and began to sniff the bloody runes drawn on the floor, the swirling furrows scraped through them.

Ghoul sent a message, intended for everyone, and she sluggishly pushed it to the others as she stood there, stiff.

Symbols and runes with a sense of untouchableness, the ritual circle meant only for her, the fresh blood of the wolf mixing with Emhreeil's, and above . . .

The sacrifices.

She felt with phantom fingers a dozen people above her, all hung in the air like pigs in a slaughterhouse in a tight grouping barely six feet wide, crammed into the center of the twenty-foot-wide ritual circle, held up by the rope that bound their feet and hands.

Blindfolded, ears filled with wax, gagged. Dehumanized.

She felt the metal collars they all wore, their purpose obvious by the way they still had flecks of dried blood on them, staining the runes carved into the metal.

She swallowed, took a deep breath.

The scent of blood was as sickly sweet and metallic as ever.

Another message from Ghoul.

A warning, really.

Emhreeil's presence attached to pain and struggle, to a monumental shift. To power.

Katherine put a hand on her shoulder, squeezed briefly. Then she retreated to the side.

The golem eye flicked on, and with it, she could almost pretend the people up there didn't exist, because the light did not reach them, leaving them shrouded in darkness.

Maybe that was the intention Ghoul had when designing this ritual circle. Or maybe he did that to save Scruffy and Katherine the full knowledge of what she would do to change.

The man in question barely shifted, didn't breathe or look around, hands by his sides.

Ghoul sent a question, tied to her, her mental image and idea, and readiness.

"I'm . . ." she started, hesitated, her attention returning to the people above.

A dozen. Men, women. All young but not children.

One a guard, the others . . . who knew, really. Maybe bakers, maybe gangsters. Bad people, good people, she did not know. She sent Ghoul a question, and just like she expected, his reply was simple.

It did not matter who they were, what they had done, what they could have done were they not here at this moment.

To him and the wolf, they were strangers. Strangers were just meat. And to reach their heights, to survive what would likely come, Ghoul believed she had to think the same.

She did not think so, at least not to the extent he did, but she understood what he meant. She couldn't afford to be compassionate anymore. Had the wolf not reached her in time, saving that one girl would have gotten her, Scruffy, and Kat killed, or worse.

So even if it stung and raked at whatever remained of her morals, she did, to some extent, agree with what he was saying.

Katherine let out a shaky sigh as the thoughts reached her and she realized what the strange sounds from above were, what their source was. She shifted her gaze away from the circle. But she did not move away or accuse her. She did not leave or try to convince her to seek another path.

Ghoul sent a message to Katherine and Scruffy specifically, one bereft of compassion but with a sense of bridging a large gap of power, of his assistance to help Katherine keep up with Emhreeil and the wolf, and an offer to teach things to Scruffy, beside an idea of a genius woman covered in chitin.

It was not intended for her, but she still dwelled on it for a moment more to stall for time, at least until she realized she wasn't sure why she was stalling in the first place.

Would her answer really change the more she tormented herself with moral questions? Would it change the fact that try as she might, she couldn't really find it in herself to give away the chance to be whole again, to be *more* than whole, just to save a dozen strangers?

She was struck by how quickly this had all happened, how quickly she'd changed under pressure. And how there was no one definitive moment she could say made her change, not by its lonesome.

Not one circumstance or person she could really pin the blame to. Only a long line of them, paired with actions and decisions that slowly drove her to this point.

The years of suppressed anger under her mother's thumb, anger which slowly taught her how to *hate*, a thing so much more drawn out and caustic than mere anger.

The two years of constantly seeing her image of the world and the people inhabiting it slowly cracking and splitting into fragments that dug into her and scraped away the bright-eyed girl that wanted to be free, leaving this jaded, cynical cripple with only a vague sense of morals left, clinging unhealthily to a genocidal monster because it had treated her better than anyone else in this dungeon ever had.

That hopeless aching chasm in her chest when she laid on wet stone, melting alive, and had her hopes crushed for the millionth time when faced with complete indifference and contempt, left to die were it not for a strange little goblin girl.

The realization she had as she panted on top of a corpse, feeling better than she'd felt in years, feeling powerful and victorious, tasting triumph that was solely hers for the first time, the rush of being the predator for once, and not the prey.

The two rodents she'd boiled alive that taught her how good revenge and sadism felt.

The gangsters she killed, that same feeling of being superior, of being the victor as she once again gasped for air on top of a dead body, just as sweet the second time as it was the first.

Stones that paved her path to here.

Ghoul sent a thought, iron-clad and filled with importance, telling her to strip naked, take nothing with her, and to toss the device he would give her out of the circle the moment she pressed the button.

She did not hesitate to do as he said, not now.

Help? she asked in Katherine's mind, and her friend nodded as she slowly stepped closer.

Her cloak went, followed by her shirt.

Each piece of cloth and leather left her bare, reminding her starkly of all the things she hid away, from both herself and the world.

Her upper body was bare. It forced her to feel and acknowledge properly for the first time how the way the skin around her chest and breasts was but a twisted mess like strips of burned wax all the way down to her navel, the way not an inch of her damaged skin could properly pick up the temperature because the air going into her nostrils felt a dozen times warmer than the ever-present chill she felt on her skin.

Her pants and undergarments were next, and they forced her to recognize the way her right foot twinged along her shin when she'd try to raise it too high, the way her hip bones and ribs jutted out starkly like a starving mutt in the street, a sight she'd seen too many times to count.

With her clothes in a pile around her, Katherine squeezed her shoulder, more insistently this time.

"I . . . Good luck. I'm sorry," Katherine whispered, breathed out, her expression conflicted and lost in a way that showed she did not know what else to say despite wanting to say so much more.

"Thank you," she whispered back, not sure what she was apologizing about, and then turned toward Ghoul.

"I'm ready," she said, her voice steady, firm, only a little heavy with the weight of her choice and nothing more.

Ghoul extended a hand to her, a device with a single button on it. He sent a single thought to her, the controller attached to the collars she'd felt above her, a collection of bizarre emotions and ideas that told her quite clearly that *she* had to be the one to press that button, to kill them.

Her mangled hand reached for the device, the branch-like fingers, burned and abused, wrapping around it.

She felt the lines before her, carved into the smooth stone, thick with dried blood, runic symbols and bones arranged in artful tiered circles.

She stepped past the point of no return with her back straight and her gait steady, into the circle, the swirling lines and furrows in the stone caressing her feet as if in welcome. She felt doors close behind her, and wasn't sure if that was a thing of her imagination and disturbed mind or the ritual telling her that to leave was not possible now.

The wolf sent a pulse of excitement to her, and the way his tails idly wagged behind him helped take the edge off the splinter digging into her chest as she finally made it to the center of the circle.

It was rather ironic, all they risked to save that one girl, only to now do this. To kill a dozen strangers, which no doubt had innocents mixed in with the guards and the gangsters, and if she paid enough attention to them, she might even be able to point them out from how they were reacting up above. She did not try to. She didn't want to know.

The hypocrisy, the nonsensical nature of her own actions, it was almost ridiculous enough to make her amused in a dark, ironic manner. But they couldn't take any of it back. She wasn't sure she would, regardless.

And she'd come too far to back out now. Too close to finally being whole again. It hurt, what she was about to do, but the notion of not doing it hurt even more.

Ghoul shifted, a device in his hand again, his other hand open before him to catch whatever it was he was about to summon.

"Click it," he calmly ordered.

With a deep shuddering breath and with a chest tight with guilt, her thumb clicked the button before she could second-guess herself further.

* * *

The first thing she heard was a strange sound, like someone sharpening a knife mixed with the whistle of wind passing through the shutters of a broken window.

Then, shuffling, choking, gurgling.

Despite her better judgment, she sent out small, quick pulses of mana, enough to not feel so hopelessly blind but not strong enough to give her details of what was happening above.

Even if she knew, she didn't want to feel it. She was a coward that way.

The symbols at her feet seemed to grip at her flesh, keeping her pinned in place, her awareness expanding to match the circle's influence, the ritual circle becoming her and her becoming the ritual circle, a fixture.

The first drops of blood rained down on her, the liquid seeming to pulse and curve midair to land on the upturned crown of her head, trickling down her face, her cheeks, her chest, every scar and injury, pooling in her sockets, before overflowing, tears of blood twisting on her rib cage into bizarre shapes like living snakes as they continued downward.

Each string of slime, a dizzying caress, the brush of a warm living blanket being pulled over her squirming skin, come to chase away that ever-present chill.

She felt those above weaken in their struggles, their lifeblood forming soft fingers that felt at her flesh, broken hands clasping over every inch of her.

She tried to breathe slowly, calmly, but she felt her thoughts fuzzing, context and presence slipping, her soul grasping for something old and twisted as the first whispers of starved ecstasy began to dig into her, making her back arch, her mouth open in a gasp. Flashes of light and sound danced around the edges of her mind, and she stiffened, trembling in place.

"The blood of a vampire and a shadow."

Someone spoke, and she felt their offering, a small trickle of brackish blood along the outer circle, sinking into the symbols carved in space, into her veins, melting into a phantom presence of age and ceaseless struggle that loomed over her, intertwining with her. A creeping shadow, a misbegotten lonely wretch, splitting itself into a million so it would never be alone. A dozen flashing, fleeting memories of darkness and a locked metal door.

A message prodded at her mind, a warning of power and pain.

She knew. He warned her already.

The blood of the sacrifices reached her feet, spreading over the inner circle, the symbols and runes flaring and melting into the floor, the cold stone beneath her warming, breathing with her.

"The blood of a wolf."

Another offering, a steady trickle of blood, bringing with it the scent of death and carnage, of ceaseless, tireless change, of freedom.

It was fresh, so fresh.

It tried to sink into her runes, the fractal spires, and they snapped under its weight. The circles twisted, snapping and squelching like broken bodies as they began to spin across the cold stone beyond her, the sound mixing with reality's harsh, rasping gasps as the ritual pulsed with power.

The blood of ceaseless hunger crawled, raced across the runes, reached her feet, pooling into the grooves in the center, swirling around her, before finally, it began to intertwine with the wretched being's, consuming it, wrapping around her ankles.

Threads of memory and shimmering mirrors reflecting mirrors and mountains made of bones flashed across her mind. The flashes of light at the edge of her mind glimmered and twisted, forming a world wreathed in red, expanding, taking her away into somewhere she should never be.

The skies, a million shades of crimson. The clouds, a miasma of death.

She watched the stars shiver in the distance as nothing but an empty skull, one amongst a million, a billion, rolling and tumbling endlessly in an endless ocean of them, each a soul without a mouth with which to scream, a cacophony of cracking and clacking as they tumbled in a broken pocket of reality, in a prison.

A howling shriek from a thousand maws broke the silence, and the stars wailed for mercy, winking out, one by one.

Nothing but the silent darkness remained, cold and desolate as they waited, rolling and tumbling, a world of the dead and the devoured.

In an instant and an eternity, the silence and darkness receded with a slow scream, the blurry image of a thousand straining chains filling the sky, bending and snapping as something monstrous and divine howled above, straining, thrashing, faster and faster, red whips and coronas flashing through the gaps.

It howled, a shrieking, broken noise, a familiar sound, and the chains rattled, cracking, reforming, straining inch by inch as something made of twisting flesh thrashed and jerked for freedom.

Each howl was filled with the essence of inevitability, of futility. It filled her soul with knowledge so ancient it eclipsed her, an ancient piece of the world.

It would one day break free, to devour all who had restrained it, and all their measly pawns.

Her stomach withered like drying branches as she jerked back to reality with a harsh gasp. She felt her ribs crack, bend backward like spindly fingers, cracking branches, her chest snapping open. Agony choked her scream into a gargling groan as her knees hit the blood-covered stone.

Something split inside her, like the flesh of her soul parting before a scalpel. The blood rushed into the gaping chasm of her chest, covering her like a second skin, more than there should possibly be, more than twelve people could ever provide. The runes began to bleed, the bones turned to ashes.

Crimson pooled around her, softening the stone, breathing and shuddering, racing up from the ground, falling from above, covering every inch of her, twisting like fabric being pulled, a curtain of warmth twisting around her.

Every ragged gasp brought in another rush of ecstasy and agony, of power and the sense of being filled to the brim, and even further. She smelled iron, she tasted starlight.

She felt herself stretch, blood forcing itself into her veins like tendrils. Her flesh stretched, her skin pulsing and splitting, her blood mixing with the rest, and she choked on a word, she didn't know which.

Someone was talking, two voices, one worried, another calm, sending messages she couldn't parse, just shoving them away, unable to comprehend words or meanings. Her ears were ringing, an insistent whine.

On the outer circle, another steady trickle of blood, thick like honey and shimmering, melting into the red, rushing through the ritual's channels, through the pool of blood that slowly rose around her. It joined the tide flooding her chest.

She choked and gagged, spasming, her arm and stump jerking together, her spine bending, in and out. Her lips tasted ash and a new taste that didn't exist. The hunger stole her breath, her mind, her control. She felt her knees quake as she began to gasp and jerk, the flashes of light forming shapes, teeth, and scales, all brushing past her mind, and she felt herself lurch as her eyes opened.

She saw an endless field as far as the eye could see stretched before her, a golden dawn framing a million bodies impaled upon aging, rusting spears. A scene frozen in time formed, like fragments of glass sliding together, and a man she knew, a man she could recognize, lay at the forefront, imperious, shoulders square and the weight of his glare so utterly crushing.

An arrow jutted out of his right eye. A dozen more out of his back, his arms, his legs. A spear had impaled him through the stomach, the man who'd done it dead on the ground, still gripping the shaft. His red cape was tattered, his armor shredded, his body destroyed, his right arm gone, not an inch of him not red in blood, both his and foreign. And yet he still stood, the blood of millions forming rivers behind him, rushing to fill his wounds, an endless tide.

He stared down at a man wreathed in holy light with a glare full of hatred, his boot buried in their chest, his left arm raising another spear above him, hues of gold and red glinting in the waking yawns of dawn that rose behind him.

She felt the damp scrape of wet stone on her half-formed scales. She inhaled the sky and drank in the world's essence as if from a chalice.

She watched a strange human cradle her in her arms. She lay on a crumbling temple's altar, dying, her wings broken, and the woman drank from her, drank her rotting, dying blood, and carved symbols on her own flesh.

A tinkling chime, a flickering mass of existence wreathing Ergos like a veil.

The frozen images winked out, and she was back, her mind pulled between ecstasy and agony. Her skin tore, her fingers snapped backward, and the sensation combined with the pain of her torn-open chest. She shrieked as she collapsed further, her open chest cavity hitting the squishy floor, fire and jagged glass and stabbing electricity racing through her nerves.

Another mental message, one she sent back to all of them without the ability to parse the information, too confused, consumed. Words devolved into incomprehensible sounds.

Something dropped into the slowly sinking pool of blood, a spider leg, another, another.

The blood rose, rushing into her, through every open stretch there was. Through her eyes, her burns and scrapes. The blood pulled, filled her. Her flesh ballooned, tore through her own skin, then turned to goop, her body fading, her mind lost, panicking.

She raised her arm above the blood slowly consuming her, and it bent, squelched. Her wrist and all after it detached with a disgusting gloop sound, like a half-melted slab of butter, and she realized that she was melting alive for the second time.

It didn't hurt nearly enough to make her believe it.

She tried to get up.

Her vision snapped back, and she could see again, feeling eight legs move at her command, spiked and black as she skittered through a tunnel made of webs, a million beady red eyes staring at her through every gap in the silken strands. Then she could not see anything, trying to get up with a hand that only melted into the inch-deep pool of blood around her with every push.

She felt her flesh drip off in wet, goopy chunks, felt her limbs spasm, felt foreign strings inside her yank her in ways she wasn't meant to bend. Her knee snapped backward as she tried to rise, and she tried to shuffle upright, or even just away from this place, only to feel a wet, sticky tide of crimson broil and froth out of her mouth.

Sounds faded in.

"Is she really okay?! This looks like it's killing her!"

"She is not okay at the moment. I told you, it hurts. But she will not die. And for the last piece, the eye of a contract demon," a voice spoke.

Something dropped into the edge of the pool, and she felt it as acutely as if it had dropped onto her head.

Sounds faded out as her skull hollowed.

The eye melted into the bottomless roiling pool that filled her, into her.

A broken, stuttering series of whispers, overlapping each other, a thousand images flashing past her eyes, each a memory with weight yet fleeting, gone before she could even process more than a still, vague impression. A bloodied grate, the inside of a box covered in scratches, her nails bloody and broken, a tongue dripping crimson writing letters on a scroll, a twisted effigy wrapped in her embrace, nails and stakes keeping her pinned around it, pain, betrayal, betrayal, betrayal, betrayal—

A black pool of sludge with a crying old woman slowly wading into its depths—

A humming buzz of ecstasy scattered her thoughts, racing up and down her very soul, her very mind. Despair and careless euphoria, intertwined, sensations never meant to mix filling her, overwhelming her. Heart-rending agony, soul-filling pleasure, the highest of highs and the lowest of lows, despair and hope.

Someone was yelling, something was snarling.

Something was whispering, a susurrus hum at the edge of her hearing.

The circles flared with a shrill grating sound like a despairing wail, and contracted, spasmed. She tried to scream again as she felt her tongue and throat drip down her gaping chest, through where organs should be but weren't, her arm bone struggling to find purchase against the breathing bottom of the pool, moving softly up and down beneath her.

She couldn't breathe, too much blood rushing into her, through her nostrils, her eyes, breaking through the cracks of her bones, into everything she was.

What was she?

The second, third, and fourth circle activated below her, the spider legs finally sinking down into the depths.

The blood rushing around her, inside her, twisted, trying to curl into a ball. Her spine snapped as her torso spun into a spiral, her legs crumpling like paper, breaking, twisting. Her neck was wrenched backward as tendrils of blood coiled around her, tighter, tighter, into a ball, a cocoon, each contortion and tear making equal ecstasy and agony overwhelm her.

Nothingness consumed her.

Katherine's fists shook as she stared at what little she could see, the overwhelming cocktail of emotions leaving her with a strange, panicking numbness.

She couldn't see clearly, none of it, but she could see enough to be disturbed, to wonder if her friend was ever shaped like that.

Her breaths came hard and fast, and her eyes flitted to the left, to the half dozen glowing eyes illuminating Ghoul's silhouette in the pitch-black darkness.

The wolf, the wretched beast, snarled and shuddered, a mass of glaring eyes and tense limbs, glowering at Ghoul and barely restraining itself from jumping into the circle.

She just tried to focus on breathing right, on the simple, logical facts of all of this, even as what little she could see from within the circle and its glowing runes looked like Emhreeil was writhing and twisting horrifically.

That shriek echoed in her head.

Ghoul would not have gone through all this trouble just to kill Emhreeil by fucking up his ritual. He had warned them of this. Pain and power.

Then the sphere of roiling blood that had encased Emhreeil began to sink into the puddle of blood on the floor, a puddle that couldn't possibly be as deep as the bloody sphere was tall, yet it still continued to submerge. She took two hurried steps forward without realizing.

A hand of steel clamped down on her arm and yanked her back a little.

Her head whipped to the side, staring up at the faint reflection of gold on the edge of Ghoul's metal headplate. Her eyes flicked to the wolf, half its eyes on Ghoul, the others on the ritual.

It wasn't moving or attacking. Not running either.

Emhreeil . . .

Her head jerked to the right to look at the tranquil ring of blood, empty. No monstrous spider limbs, no bizarre eyes with six pupils in one iris. No strange wolf blood glowing across the runes and creeping forth like the trail of a snake.

Nothing.

"Where is she?" she demanded, teeth gritted, forgetting for a moment that there was a wolf that was scared of this man, or at least wary enough of him to cower at first sight.

"Being reborn. In a sense. All part of the ritual. Just wait."

She clenched her jaw and nodded, eyes glued to the perfect still circle.

It felt like there should be something to disturb it. Some breeze, some stray drop of blood from the people above, a tremor through the floor to send ripples across the tranquil surface.

For a minute, however, there was nothing.

Then she felt it. Felt her.

She was so happy about [Pack Hunter] including her in its bizarre sensory ability that she was tempted to try and forget what the curious-looking ball of limbs and eyes in the corner of her vision was.

She could feel Emhreeil in the center of the bloody puddle, but deeper.

Not in the floor, either, just . . . somehow deeper than the ring was thick.

And she felt different. It was strange and distorted and too new a sense to be sure, but something about her felt off.

Did that mean it worked or not?

Regardless, she neared the circle, mirroring the wolf by accident, both of them staring into the tranquil, inch-deep puddle that somehow held their . . . mutual friend within, only fifteen feet across.

She could feel Emhreeil twisting and bucking and moving . . . upward? Swiping down? No, just . . . undulating like a ribbon. Or maybe flapping like fabric? It was making her dizzy trying to figure out how she was moving and what she was doing.

"Come on," she muttered softly, trying to encourage her even if she didn't really know how to, regardless of if she could even hear her.

"I would suggest you back away," Ghoul droned, and it took her a moment to remember why his instructions to the wolf before Emhreeil stopped relaying the messages.

Emhreeil would be hungry.

With a deep breath and a nod, she stepped back, not stopping until she was several feet away.

The first sign of life brought with it elation, and she slumped a little with a sigh of relief.

Fingers triumphantly jutted out of the puddle for a moment, before jerking, twisting, as if they were moving through quicksand. They disappeared again, leaving the ripples of the pond behind, before the hand they were attached to speared forward, up to the thumb.

That was where elation began to mix with apprehension, as she began to notice the details, how the fingers were a little too bulky and ended in sharp tips like the clawed gauntlets Katherine herself was wearing. The wrist began to tilt, and another note of apprehension rose as she saw how far back and forward the hand could bend.

Said wrist was almost as thick as the wolf's. She said she would accept Emhreeil regardless. She meant it. Still, she fervently wished that what came out of that puddle was not a monster. Not another one.

As if peripherally thinking of the beast had summoned it, the wolf excitedly began to circle around, keeping its head pointed at the middle, damn near prancing around, tongue lolling out of its mouth like a common stupid dog.

If it wasn't for the uncanny, unnaturally human anatomy of its upper body, she might have found the sight a little cute. As it was, it was uncomfortable enough to turn her eyes back to Emhreeil, jerking and bucking to free her forearm, like she was stuck in wet mud.

"Does she need help? Can we help?" she asked, and Ghoul scoffed through his mouth.

"I told you this already when the elf could still relay my messages. Stop worrying."

"That's not a no."

Ghoul somehow managed to portray a sense of annoyance without shifting an inch or changing anything about the way he talked.

"No, you cannot help her. Struggle is the essence of all life and creation. The chick that cannot break through its own shell will not be strong enough to survive what lies outside it. To help her would change her and weaken her. It would violate the spirit of the ritual, even if not in its rules."

She turned back to the puddle, the wolf now bouncing around as it ran circles around it, its cheery demeanor contrasting terribly with the slaughterhouse aesthetic of the entire thing.

She was never one to understand magics and rituals and the arcane by any measure. She just didn't really get it. What spirit? Was the ritual done by a spirit? The blood had looked to be alive, from what little she could glimpse from the candlelight.

Or did he mean the spirit in a more general fashion, the idea of it? That didn't seem right either.

Would it really weaken her physically and magically, or did he mean it mentally? Or spiritually? She was really starting to hate this man, even if she wouldn't dare say it out loud.

She stopped thinking about it.

Emhreeil's hand was out, up to the elbow now, and she grimaced at what she could see. The blood made it difficult to be sure, but the smooth bumps, the curving, dripping spikes that randomly dotted her forearm that looked suspiciously like clumps of wet fur?

Whatever Emhreeil looked like now, that arm was not human. The wolf seemed to understand Ghoul's idea more than she did, because even when it began to slow and tilt its head, pretty much bouncing in place in anticipation, it didn't take one step inside the ritual circle. The elbow was freed, and she flinched as she watched those clawed fingers slam into the puddle, sending a wild spray with enough force for a few drops to pepper her face as far away as she was.

No sound of breaking stone, somehow. Was there even stone under the blood anymore? She pursed her lips, annoyance and concern battling for space in her head. She wanted to help, but she couldn't.

She wasn't much stronger than the average street thug, even if she had much better training due to House Kervile's generous employment, but she wasn't delusional. Emhreeil was, bizarrely enough, stronger than her ever since they'd reunited. And that was before she turned into whatever she just turned into.

So she just observed, even if it grated on her. Emhreeil's hand looked . . . more like a thick paw covered in harsh edges and plates, with small lines and patches of other textures she couldn't see from afar.

The final joint of each finger was just one long line on the lower side, barely curving downwards into a sharp point. After the sharp point, it was a backward line all the way up to the upper side, giving a sort of slanted axe head look to each finger. It looked vicious. More for grabbing and grappling and crushing than actually cutting.

It wasn't what she was expecting on someone like Emhreeil, who fought like a snake from what she had seen. Emhreeil would wait, make or see an opening, and strike it hard and fast with everything she had, like a nigh-suicidal assassin. That arm looked like it belonged on the wolf.

Did the ritual put no thought toward what she was like?

The shoulder finally emerged, and it was the wolf's intense gaze that lit up what she had been squinting at all this time, gold and orange light mixing to provide her with an image.

The entire arm from the wrist up was a twisting vortex of soaked fur, scales, and some kind of smooth, segmented plating. Chitin, she could guess, from those huge spider legs. The muscles were off too, like someone who didn't know anatomy tried to draw them, strange bumps and misplaced or duplicated muscles covering the entire arm.

The shoulder slowly turned into something like gnarled leather as it neared her collarbone, the texture slowly turning to smooth skin near her neck, the delt covered in small cone-shaped spikes. Then the right side of the head began to peel off of the puddle, and she groaned, a sharp, deep sound of relief, slumping forward to support herself on her knees.

That was a human head. No ears on the sides, but that was a human head. She'd half expected some six-armed monstrosity to crawl out of that puddle and start talking to her like the wolf did, and then she'd probably just give up on life making sense forever.

"Oh, thank gods," she breathed out, breathing low and deep.

So it was just the right arm. That was completely fine by her. Em deserved to be mobile and able again. It even looked strong as hell. That was good.

An excited yip-whine followed by a strangely low-pitched snarl made her raise her head, and she paid more attention.

Emhreeil . . .

Didn't look the same, snarling and straining to pull her hair out of the pit.

Her eye shape was more hawkish, her brows more angular. There were spots on her face that had scales or randomly shaped plates, even a bit of fur coming out beside her right eye, just around her cheekbone. They'd almost look like highlights if they were a little more symmetrical and orderly, but now, they just straddled the line between looking like an unfortunate defensive mutation and a cosmetic highlight.

Her facial structure had also changed. Cheekbones were a bit higher, her jaw was a little more angular, her eyes somehow even bigger than they had been before, to the point it looked a little eerie, even when they stayed firmly shut.

But besides her appearance, what made her heart drop was that Emhreeil wasn't *acting* like Emhreeil. Emhreeil wouldn't be thrashing and pulling like an animal in a pit of quicksand, wouldn't be snarling with a vocal range human throats just didn't have.

Her eyes moved to the nape of her neck, where her spine jutted out in strange, blocky ridges, nothing like a human spine, and much too thick to be.

The neck muscles were wrong too. The front two tendons to pull the head down were there, but they were also on every other side of her neck, standing out against her skin as she tried to remove her hair from the puddle.

Another minute later of awkward silence broken only by Emhreeil and the wolf, she finally yanked her hair out and shook her head like a dog, spraying blood everywhere for a moment before she began twisting at the waist, hunching over and pushing down, slowly managing to dig her left shoulder out, then her left arm.

Her entire musculature had changed in ways that didn't seem to make sense. Why did her forearm have two of those tubes of muscle curling over the top, and why did one go under the other and around to her tricep? So she could snap her elbow backward at will?

There were small bunches of other odd muscles at her shoulders and around her deltoids that also didn't make sense. Lady Anna had taught her anatomy fairly well. What she was watching made no sense.

The wolf didn't seem to care much, its massive tails sweeping the floor in quick, wide wags as it hopped back and forth, its front half always pointed to Emhreeil.

She wished she could ask it what on earth was going through its head right now. Was it happy Em might match it, in some way?

Emhreeil's chest slowly dug out of the mire, significantly faster with the help of both arms, and as her utterly soaked hair settled, she spotted movement in said hair, fast twitches, before something triangular dug itself out. The ears weren't exactly like the wolf's. They were furred, but much thinner and more maneuverable, judging by the way they erratically spasmed to free themselves of her hair. They were also a fair bit longer.

Her chest had a modest bulge where breasts might once have been, but it was just a flat plane now, half covered by a crooked V-shape of scales on one side and a bunch of segmented chitin plates on the other.

The puddle quickly reached Emhreeil's stomach, which presented more inhuman musculature that made her so utterly confused. The muscle definition, born more out of a lack of fat than exercise, helped her see it all.

Her abdominals weren't the classic, blocky pairs, instead being pairs of downward-tilting rectangles forming rough chevron shapes, almost a dozen of them. The muscles on her waist and sides looked like ropes with skin over them, more than obliques. The addition of half-random-seeming patches of scales, plates, and fur did not help with the aesthetic. She didn't look monstrous, not really. The sight wasn't nearly as horrifying as the wolf when he wasn't hiding everything. She just looked . . . inhuman. Strangely twisted.

A particularly violent, snarling twist made her realize she may have spoken too soon about Em not being a six-armed monstrosity.

She wasn't sure what she saw, but she saw something behind Emhreeil's back twist, watched some of her frontal chest muscles contract as if pulling something around her.

Ghoul had said something about a dragon vampire or something as he emptied a large jar of blood into the circle, so she assumed it was wings.

When Emhreeil had dug herself out enough to reach her hips, her snakelike middle shifting to free the hip bones as she flattened herself forward, Katherine assumed she was right, to some extent. It looked like bulky, muscled wings mixed with a spider's leg, without the membrane or the little bones in the interim, just one large mass that seemed to dig itself out from beneath her shoulder blades and fold its tips near the base of her back.

They were huge.

Maybe it was morbid curiosity or just impatience, but nevertheless, she began to circle opposite the wolf, trying to get a better image.

With most of herself out of the muddy floor, Emhreeil's body language had more room to unnerve her. There was more room for the inhuman musculature to contract and pull things in just the right way to make something instinctive in herself a little squeamish, nothing like watching the wolf move but enough to make her uneasy.

With a struggling groan and a pull full of quivering tension, the tips of the spiderlike wings freed themselves, snapping up into the air with a spray of blood, into the darkness where she couldn't catch many details.

She did catch the glint of the light reflecting off something that moved where it shouldn't, and only when the wings slammed down into the puddle to help Emhreeil dig her thighs and legs out did she realize what she was looking at.

Hands at the tip of the wings, where nothing but a thin bone should be.

The palms alone were larger than Katherine's head, each finger almost two feet long, the last joints nothing but bleached blades of bone that seemed to refuse to let blood cling to them.

She gulped, suddenly worried that they had been lied to by Ghoul. That maybe this was all some ploy to turn Emhreeil into a monster. It wouldn't be out of character with how terribly their lives had gone up to this point, but she still held out hope. Ghoul had told them how this would go. Emhreeil would be . . . feral for a little bit. Hungry, rabid.

That was the wolf's job to deal with.

Still, as long legs covered by patchwork biological armor rose, segmented plates and coarse fur and large scales, she felt somehow responsible. Complicit, in a sense.

She didn't have much time to ruminate or stew in her guilt before another monstrous detail came into sight as she circled behind Em. A tail, rigidly stuck behind her leg as it stretched down to the floor with tension, barely squirming.

Her eyes followed the appendage, noting that it looked more like Emhreeil's spine decided to continue far past where it should have stopped, something like a blocky whip just barely covered with everything except human skin.

Her eyes roamed up to the bizarre, twisting muscles on Emhreeil's back, only a pair of bat-wing-shaped muscles on her upper back looking even vaguely familiar.

Emhreeil suddenly threw herself backward, back flat to the floor as all four arms scraped for purchase in the blood, slowly working her knees out of it, panting, eyes still closed.

After digging her shins halfway out, Emhreeil tensed her legs and arms, throwing herself upright with a frustrated cry, quickly pushing down with her hands and twisting.

Then she was free.

Or so Katherine thought, until Em twisted around to grab her squirming tail in all four hands, plant her feet down, and pull.

The way those bony knife fingers jutted out where they clenched like gigantic urchins clamped onto the tail made it easy to remind herself this might not be Emhreeil at all, even if only for a bit.

It looked painful, but only a familiar, determined sneer lay on Emhreeil's face. The tail came out, and out, and out, until it was almost seven or something feet long, and finally, Emhreeil lurched back with a barely audible pop, her tail in her hands.

The wing arms snapped backward to catch her before she could hit the floor, and Katherine felt faintly sick at the sight. Arms, three jointed and not bending right, like someone took a wing, stripped it, covered it in a wild mash of armor and fur, and added two gigantic hands at the tips. But . . . no, they didn't look like wings, they didn't look like spider legs, and they didn't move like arms, despite looking like they were some kind of hybrid of all three.

It just looked wrong in that sickening way that was hard to look away from.

Emhreeil straightened, slumped forward, staggered in place, the ears on her head twitching manically as she panted.

A humanoid arm, the only one that Emhreeil had, the left, extended down to the pool.

The blood suddenly began to whirl and rise, wavering in the air as it retreated from the edges of the ritual circle to carefully and slowly begin to rise toward Emhreeil's head. Her mouth opened, the faint glint of fangs making Katherine wince in the middle of her pacing. Then the mouth opened even wider, muscles on her face she hadn't seen before pulling the cheeks back like stretching rubber, and it opened even wider like her face was degloving—

She looked away, closed her eyes, and tried to swallow down the bile that rose into her mouth.

"It is still her. Give it some time. The wolf will deal with her until she's past the initial frenzy. I'll step in if needed," Ghoul said blankly.

Was it still her?

It wasn't like she could do something here. Best she could do was take his word for it and hope.

Worst-case scenario, she'd follow the wolf until it took revenge. It looked like the spiteful type, at least. No wonder he and Em seemed to resonate so much together, much as she didn't want to see or admit it out loud.

She took a deep breath and glanced back.

The blood on the floor was gathering into a swirling spire that fed straight into Emhreeil's mouth. A mouth wide with perfect teeth and eight thin, needlelike fangs on the front, wide enough to make her feel like it could clamp around the lower half of her own face without much issue, the gums exposed as the skin and patches of other materials gathered around the base of her jaw and behind her cheekbones. It looked like the grin of a madman turned beast.

Her stomach roiled with unease.

Ghoul said it was still her. She just had to believe that.

It was a little difficult.

Emhreeil looked like something out of a nightmare as she stood there, hunched over, arms and shoulders limp, her hair a wet, crusting curtain. Even the blood that covered her seemed to gather into streams and crawl forward to feed into her gaping maw, her winglike arms barely moving, their bladelike tips softly feeling the floor's markings as if tapping a rhythm.

She watched the last of the crimson ichor gather off the floor and float into Emhreeil's mouth, watched Em stand there for a moment, not even breathing. Did she need to anymore?

It was silent enough to hear a pin drop.

Instead, it was the sound of a single drop hitting stone, and Katherine's eyes jerked to the right, where the wolf had dug into its own wrist with its claws. It put its paws down and unfurled its limbs, crouching in preparation, tails wagging despite its battle-ready stance.

Emhreeil's eyes opened.

Two orbs of pure golden light, with no white sclera in sight, the pupil just a giant slit like a cat's eyes.

A very, very thin slit.

Emhreeil took a deep breath through her nose, turned her head to stare with unseeing eyes at the wolf. Her ears twisted to the side, then pressed back and flat against her own head.

One moment she was there.

The next, she'd practically teleported to the wolf with a jerky blur of motion, and all Katherine saw was a tangled yarn of snarling limbs tumbling off into the darkness as they collided.

Her jaw dropped.

"Did you expect the wolf to give its blood without struggle?" Ghoul asked, something that might have sounded amused if he didn't sound so bored.

"Yes," she numbly breathed out, watching the flashes of golden light tumbling and striking at each other, snarls and thudding impacts making her flinch.

"Shouldn't we . . ."

"They're not in danger. The wolf is in the mood for some play-fighting before it gives up its blood. There's no point to a game if one capitulates immediately, there has to be some illusion of struggle," Ghoul explained, watching alongside her.

She watched the jumble of golden eyes slam into the floor, a blur of teeth and jerky motions following the meaty thuds of flesh striking flesh. A roll of some kind, Emhreeil's body tumbling for a moment before she hit the floor, and immediately charged the wolf again.

"That's not play-fighting," she said, fists clenched.

She hated how little control and impact she had in this. All of this.

An intrusive thought rose, and she discarded it for the moment. Maybe later. Maybe when she got a little more used to this insanity.

As if to accentuate her doubts of this being some kind of casual fight, the wolf lurched, dragged, then a moment later, was thrown into the metal poles around the ritual, bowling them over, the aftershock of its impact snuffing out the candles entirely.

Something tapped her shoulder, and a small, thin pipe was pressed into her hand before she could react.

"Flashlight. Shame to miss such a show," Ghoul casually explained without sounding like he cared at all or felt any such shame about missing the fucking "show," and she backed away in caution before she found the button and clicked it. Pale, weak light shone in a wide cone, barely enough to see.

The wolf was . . .

Getting destroyed.

Emhreeil was keeping it off the ground, battering it around then stabbing at it with those bladed fingers, trying to latch on to its bleeding wrist, only for the wolf to constantly twist it out of the way, throw her off, and then just charge into her like a mindless brute, only using its limbs to grapple and smack Emhreeil away.

But it was getting hit more and more, getting more and more careless.

As the seconds turned to a solid minute, and Emhreeil's snarls began to sound more enraged and more savage than even the wolf's, she quickly realized that while Emhreeil was flagging, the wolf barely seemed to notice anything. It wasn't dodging anything except the right arm by now, as if it had tested how hard Em could hit and wasn't worried. And even though it barely dodged anymore, she could still only barely follow them with the light, they moved so damn fast.

She watched Emhreeil slam her wing's claws into its unprotected throat, and the sudden stop made her feel like she just watched Em try to punch through solid steel.

It wasn't even feeling the strikes. She just wasn't doing any damage to it. The wolf was letting her tire herself out, wagging its tails between whips and flashing a wolfish grin between snarls.

She could see it now. Ghoul was right. It was playing.

Until it wasn't.

Emhreeil charged in again, and for once, the wolf didn't let her.

A ball of air exploded on Emhreeil's left foot mid-charge, a tail slamming into her shoulder. Her wings tried to scrabble onto the floor to prevent her suddenly spinning fall, and the tentacle on the wolf's back whipped out to ensnare them in a tight grip against each other as it let their bodies collide. The tails tightly wrapped around the right arm, twisting it around her back.

A dizzying twist and shuffle of a dozen limbs, and Emhreeil's panting, snarling form was on the floor, wings wrenched painfully to the side, arms pinned by the wolf's. The right one seemed to be giving it a lot more trouble than it was expecting, making it growl in frustration and use both tails and its main left arm to keep it pinned, writhing to shift its weight onto it.

Then it jammed its bleeding wrist into Emhreeil's mouth and settled down on top of her as she struggled to free herself, biting down on the arm and futilely punching its ribs with the other arm.

Each impact sounded like it should have turned bone to splinters, but other than grunts and annoyed flicks of its ear, the wolf barely seemed to care. Emhreeil slowly calmed, then just stopped struggling entirely. Then she began shuddering and writhing and making sounds that were almost scandalous, if it weren't for the fact the scene was disturbing and horrifying enough to make any such insinuation downright sickening.

The wolf tried to peel its wrist back after releasing her limbs, and Em's head rose with it, clamped.

It gave her an unamused look that was bizarrely legible and expressive for a wolfish face, its brows flattening into a line.

Emhreeil's left hand rose to flick its ear.

The wolf growled, and then they started grappling on the floor again, Emhreeil laughing through its fur, still latched on, letting out muffled squeals and woops of joy as they rolled on the cold stone.

Em twisted to her, and their eyes met.

Her eyes were so large, practically twinkling with pure joy, happiness.

She couldn't help but beam back at her, tension leaving her, feeling like she'd just turned weightless after carrying the entire world on her back.

That was Emhreeil. Her friend was still here. Even if she was now . . . six and a half feet tall or so, and built like a disfigured beastkin with too much mixed blood to have a category.

The wolf's jaws clamped over Emhreeil's head, damn near swallowing the whole thing in its massive jaws, and Em made a disgusted sound, a muffled protest that sounded like "my hair!" leaving her mouth as she twisted out of its grip. Still refusing to let go of its wrist.

Everything had worked out. Miraculously. Emhreeil was fine, the wolf was fine, they were all alive and nothing had gone horrifically wrong and turned her friend into a gibberish hellspawn like she had been afraid of.

The light was shaking.

She looked down.

Her hand was shaking.

"I feel lightheaded," she mumbled, suddenly feeling oddly numb about the whole situation.

Was she in shock? Or just so relieved she couldn't process it?

A hand clamped down over her nape, bunching her clothes up in its fist, and her feet left the ground.

She turned the light to the side, staring at Ghoul as he held her up in the air like a disobedient kitten.

"You can faint if you wish."

She couldn't tell if he was joking, but it didn't sound like it. And that only made it more absurd, so she couldn't stop the hysterical, slightly manic giggle that left her, dropping the flashlight to cover her face with her hands, unsure if she was sobbing in disbelief, relief, or laughing, or just making weird coughs.

Scruffy at least tried to pull her down, bless her little heart.

It was almost a full minute later that Ghoul let go of her, only for her to be picked up by something else distinctly humanoid.

She knew these arms, even if they were built wrong and there was way too much fur and chitin and scales to make it work. She hugged back.

"You okay?" Emhreeil whispered, her voice shivery and jerky, but also a little too deep to feel like it was actually Emhreeil talking to her.

She took a moment to think about it.

"Yeah. Going to need some time to get used to you again. Make my . . . mental image match you again. Right now you feel like a little like a stranger with Em's memories. But I'm all right," she mumbled.

Emhreeil grimaced with a slight sound of understanding.

"I'm a bit offended, but fair enough. I know that feeling more than well enough. Wolf as a friend and all that. He changes a lot." Emhreeil hummed, then hugged her tighter, her mouth on her shoulder making it all too easy to know that she was beaming, even as she shivered with worrying intensity.

The hug was making her ribs creak, but she didn't have the heart to tell her to let up, seeing as it didn't hurt yet.

"I can *see again*. I can move again, I can feel heat and cold, and nothing . . . nothing hurts at all, I can fucking wrestle with him, and my right arm feels like it's made of fucking granite. I have *wing arms!*" Emhreeil rambled with a light laugh, then twisted. "Ghoul. Thank you."

"You're welcome. I'll drop you off nearby, somewhere with more than enough morally acceptable targets for all three of you to rack up a kill count without it being a complete slaughter. Somewhere close to the middle of the third floor. Can't go farther. I'll give you a couple things for communication and such, and occasionally feed you information."

Before Ghoul and Em could start going back and forth with details, she cleared her throat, blinking the remnants of tears out of her eyes, whatever emotion caused them gone by now.

"Can you put me down first?" she asked.

There was no reply for a moment.

"I'm tall as hell. Taller than Ghoul. I . . . wow." Emhreeil breathed out with an air of awe.

She pinched Emhreeil's side in reply, getting mildly annoyed with being manhandled. Especially after hours of enduring such things from the wolf yesterday.

All it did was make her gauntlets slide over skin that felt like porcelain.

"Put me down."

"Right, right."

Her feet touched the floor, and she took a step back, trying to reorganize, her head feeling swamped and overwhelmed.

"Ghoul, do you want to come with us? Eating in a group is good for bonding and all that, and I assume at least three of us eat people now, since your name is Ghoul, and . . . This sounded a lot better in my head," Emhreeil muttered, then shifted. "Wait, I'm naked?" she half asked, patting her chest as if checking for where her breasts were.

"Strange invitation. No. Maybe when I have time. If it makes you feel better about being naked, the goblin and the human cannot see in the dark," Ghoul said.

"It doesn't. I won't even fit in my old clothes anymore . . . Do you . . . have a tailor? You seem much better dressed than last time."

"Yes. I'll leave some of my contacts with the rest of the items."

Some walking, some shuffling. She couldn't see who, not really, despite the soft glow of her friend's and the wolf's eyes. She picked up the flashlight and looked around for a moment.

Emhreeil gasped.

"Wait, do our eyes match?" Emhreeil asked, sounding oddly excited, staring right at the wolf. Then she shifted and squinted.

Another familiar prod at Katherine's mind, which she accepted.

The wolf stared back, then a moment later, it accepted too, as did Scruffy, and Emhreeil sent them all her question after a dozen seconds of sitting there with her brows furrowed in concentration. The same question. Did their eyes match?

The wolf replied with a blatant sense of confirmation before any of them could, and Katherine got to watch the uniquely disturbing sight of Emhreeil throwing her hands up in triumph, only for her massive wings to follow, flaring up and to the side in a twisted imitation of a human gesture, her tail, seven feet of bony leather and scale, whipping and wagging.

She tried to bundle that feeling of unease, and sent it through.

Emhreeil blinked, before turning to her.

"Oh."

A few seconds of awkward silence reigned before a bundle of apology and a begrudging sense that she'd just have to get used to it was sent by Em. The wolf was just confused about what made her uneasy about their forms. Typical.

She sent back agreement to Em after a few lagging seconds of trying to get a hang of the strangeness of not thinking with sounds and words in her own head.

She would just have to get used to that too.

If only she could get more than a single damn day between disturbing developments and spine-curling changes.

"Not to ruin your conversation, but I have places to be," Ghoul said dryly, and Emhreeil nodded, suddenly all business. Then she turned to her, owl-wide eyes staring at her in the darkness.

She raised the light to be able to see her rather than pointing it at the floor.

Emhreeil was a lot paler than she remembered.

"Hey, uhm . . . could you help me dress a little? It's . . . going to be a little awkward to see what might fit or not with three . . . or four new limbs," Em said with a guilty grimace.

Katherine shook her head.

"No, it's fine. Have to get used to it. Yes, I'll help," she said, a little more hesitantly than she would have liked, then sent a message through the link.

Scruffy, hold the flashlight on us?

The wolf sent annoyance at the human sounds, but she didn't care at the moment.

Scruffy sent back agreement as she stepped forward, and after the flashlight swapped hands, she joined Em in seeing which of her clothes could still be worn.

She tripped on something that moved and pushed her foot to the side, likely Emhreeil's new tail, and a giant, twisted palm slapped itself down on her chest to stop her fall, one she instinctively grabbed onto before freezing up, staring at the foot-something-long blades just an inch or two away from her neck.

"Sorry, sorry!" Em rushed, pushing her back and upright a bit. "Not used to having a tail yet. It just . . . moves on its own." She shrugged, and her wings moved with the motion. "So do these," she added, clicking the claws on her other wing together to emphasize.

Katherine stiffly nodded as she pushed off of the limb, finding it as unbending as iron, and swallowed, emptying whatever feelings were still inside her.

She cleared her throat, and without another word, sidestepped the new appendages a little, not wishing to get any closer to them than she had to, and bent down to rifle through the heap with Em.

The cloak and underwear might be serviceable. Dart launcher and mask too, maybe. It would be a bit hard without ears on the side to catch the fabric strips . . .

Emhreeil's left hand, the human one, reached for her wrist, then took her hand.

It helped.

"You're squeezing way too tight," she complained as she unfolded the cloak with one arm, well-practiced.

The wolf was off to the side, enjoying pets and scratches from Scruffy, who somehow didn't seem to give one single damn about any of this, her free hand pointing the flashlight at them.

Was she more of a coward than a literal *goblin*?

The notion was offensive enough to force her to push through any disgust or unease, and keep them aside, shoved into a corner, still present, still there, but no longer as overwhelming.

"Sorry. Stronger now," Em said, and relaxed, a hint of worry in her voice. A familiar flavor of worry, in fact.

"Stop thinking I'm about to leave and never come back every time I feel weird or disturbed. It's *seriously annoying*. I'm staying," she said, her voice full of steel, almost spitting the words out.

Emhreeil smiled widely at the corner of her sight, her mouth normal, not that stretching grin from before, and averted her gaze before nodding.

Her eyes flicked up to the ears as they bobbed with the motion.

"And I want to pet them," she blurted out. She wasn't sure why, but she just didn't like the quiet, or maybe her brain was too frazzled to filter her thoughts properly.

Em turned to blink at her with those too-big eyes, ears twitching. "I . . . okay? Later."

Katherine turned back to the dart launcher, theorizing if they'd have to change anything to refit it back onto Em's left arm.

She nodded resolutely. "Later."

She wanted to send a smidge of gratitude to Scruffy for making her "man up" a little, but she was a little too embarrassed to use the telepathy channels for it, and speaking of it wouldn't be much better.

A wet snout nosed her hair, and she only minutely flinched this time as it licked her temple once before walking around them both.

She couldn't see much when she turned to see where it was going, the flashlight not pointed up enough, but she caught some glimpses of husk-like figures in the darkness, those tied to the crumpled metal poles and thus significantly lower than the rest were, and watched the wolf shimmy up the poles to get to them.

She just turned back around. She didn't want to see more.

She wasn't sure if it was healthy or if something was bleeding over from the wolf and Em, but she couldn't wait to get to those acceptable targets, if only to use the action to unwind.

She also wasn't sure when the potential threat of injury and death became less overwhelming than dealing with all of this, but it had, and she itched to swing her sword at something squishy.

She watched Ghoul snap out another unfolding stick covered in enchantments, another portal gadget, and hurried along as she heard corpses hit the floor behind her, the wolf presumably gathering them to take with them. Or maybe it had some way of swallowing them whole.

"You should probably tell the wolf that Ghoul is in a hurry," she murmured, and Em took a moment to process that before nodding and closing her eyes to focus. The mental prod was sent.

The sounds from behind them abruptly began to quicken in pace instead of stopping.

"Greedy," Em mumbled, smiling with fond exasperation.

She didn't know how to take that, so she ignored it.

"Give me that enchanted dagger," she requested, and Em grabbed the ring off the floor then let go of her hand to pop the handle into her palm.

She quickly set to making holes and carefully adjusting straps where needed. There wouldn't be much that would fit, but a decent amount would.

Ghoul stood in the corner, somehow projecting an air of impatience without doing anything.

Fuck him. He could wait a minute or two.

CHAPTER 5

She'd have thought that suddenly growing a bit over half a foot would have just made her feel taller, but it actually just made the entire world around her feel discomfortingly *smaller*.

It would take some getting used to.

All of this would, she imagined.

Despite having drunk more than her fair fill just a few minutes ago, she was already starting to feel like she wanted a bit of blood. That would probably get annoying fast.

She lifted her right arm, slowly turning it, flexing her fingers.

It was hideous, bulky, and it looked like it was made to pull people's guts out of their stomachs.

She loved it.

It felt *strong*, and it *was*. Axe-head-shaped talons made of white bone at her fingertips, with the bottom side stretching forward before fading into a plated gauntlet of black chitin past the claws.

Just past the wrist, it shifted into a mess of different materials.

But it wasn't as random as it looked. Patches of fur sat just around her wrist, elbow, and shoulder joints to allow her maximum mobility. Her lower forearm had a slanted triangle of thick scales, but from there, it was a spinning mess of faintly iridescent black scales, chitin, and fur, like someone took strips of each material then twisted them up with a clockwise vortex before gluing them to the muscular limb all the way up to the shoulder. There was not a hint of skin to be seen.

Kat said it would unbalance her with how thick it was, so she'd have to put a bit of weight on her left side, likely some kind of pauldron, but that would be fine.

She shifted her head away and turned to look at her right shoulder. It was not difficult at all. She felt like she was made of rubber and could twist herself into a knot if needed.

Her shoulder had a few patches of short and stubby chitin spikes around the joint, and then the skin turned into something that looked like a mix between bark and leather, slowly turning gray then white as it met her equally white skin.

She lifted her left hand and rubbed the odd leatherlike flesh.

Certainly felt like it.

She turned her head down, absentmindedly listening in on a conversation between Katherine and Scruffy, a stumbling, confused one. The wolf was busy gnawing on the husks he dragged through the portal on the other side of the outcrop they were waiting on.

So greedy. It was funny for some reason.

Her attention turned back to her chest, which . . . well, she was not particularly attached to whatever bust she had, but it was . . . odd to see and feel parts of herself so suddenly different. It was like someone made a breastplate of black scales and chitin and just covered her with it, except it was patchy and the scales sank into her skin along the edges before fading.

And there *was* some padding behind this armor, like . . . scar tissue or fat or something, even if there was nothing salacious behind it. It didn't feel like the humanoid mind was wired well to such things. If she hadn't been wanting this so much, she'd probably feel oddly sick and repulsed by it all.

But in a way, it covered her modesty better than a bra would. Which was good, because her old one didn't fit, and her bottom underwear barely did.

She brought her left hand forward a bit to examine it in the scarce yellow light from the lanterns below.

Her skin was ridiculously pale. Not *corpse pale*, but literally *fresh-fallen snow* pale. Katherine had looked quite shocked when they came out here where there were actual hints of normal light besides the white from the flashlight, and she could guess why now. Kat had likely thought the white skin was just a trick of lighting before they came out here.

There were strange things and people in the dungeon, everywhere, but she likely ranked quite high on the absurdity scale.

She'd have to cover up a lot better soon, but once the wolf was done chewing, they could go kill the people below and she could use whatever clothes survived.

She jutted her hips and stomach out a little, staring at her abdomen.

She never had *visible* abs before.

Certainly not weirdly rectangular ones like this, that were for some reason all leaning downward on the inner side, forming chevrons on her flesh, following the V of her hips.

Huh, no belly button either.

There were segmented plates of chitin on the left side of her abdomen, hiding a portion of the odd chevrons, and there was a large patch of fur on her right hip. Three strips of black scales moved from just above said hip to the bottom of her rib cage on the right side of her abdomen, each a couple inches across, looking almost like claw marks.

For all she remembered of whatever bizarre visions she had during that ritual, they might be.

She twisted her torso to the side to look at the ropelike muscles on her waist and the side of her ribs, which were curiously devoid of rigid materials, only strips and winding patches of fur, then turned even further to look at the base of her back and the seven-foot-long black tail extending out of it.

It was extremely flexible and actually helped with her balance a lot, thankfully, or otherwise it would be nothing but a pain in the ass tipped with a bony spike at the end. Just to get it out of the way, she tightly wrapped the patchy tail around her own neck like a scarf.

Her spine, whatever she could see of it past her waist-length pitch-black hair, looked . . . *solid*. Oddly blocky, but thick and strong.

It took a moment to realize she had essentially twisted her upper body around without moving her lower, and she blinked in surprise for a moment, before experimentally trying to turn even farther, keeping her feet pinned to the ground.

She ended up with her shoulders parallel to her hips on the wrong side, seeing and feeling the muscles on her waist and chest pull and strain to keep her like this as she stared in mute amazement at her waist, which looked like a twisted, narrow stretch of fabric.

That looked disturbing, even to her. How was she even doing this?

Somehow, it didn't hurt. Strained and burned a bit, like keeping a difficult stretch going for too long, but it was as if she didn't have any organs to pull and stretch.

Wait, *did she* have organs? She had lungs, and she had a heart for sure. She couldn't be sure of the rest though.

She also had a nice butt now, and her hips were a bit wider. Which . . . was nice for her self-esteem, she supposed, but it didn't really matter.

She twisted her upper torso to face the right way again, and bent forward to examine her legs.

They were strangely armored, compared to her torso, which was much more important in her opinion. But then again, looking for sense in this kind of thing seemed nonsensical in itself.

Her left outer thigh was covered in large black scales all the way up to her hip bone, while the inner thigh had a few flat plates of chitin, but was mostly just white skin. Her right outer thigh was covered in two half circles of bent, lumpy chitin plates mixed along with fur, up to just below her upper thigh, while her inner thigh was covered in a large patch of black scales, all the way down to her knee.

Both knees were covered in thin, almost skin-conforming plates, not quite as thick or angular as the rest, and her shins were covered in horizontally aligned V-shaped plates, each about two inches thick and curving around to the side.

There were some negligible patches and sprinklings of fur and scales on her calves, again looking more like ribbons or like something monstrous was about to burst out of her skin rather than randomly placed.

She didn't know if that was a good thing or not. It looked almost purposeful, but . . .

Well, if she had some kind of transformation ability, it would show up in her system screen, and she was curious regardless, so she stopped ogling at herself and glanced over the rocky lip of the outcrop they were on to make sure nobody would be coming out of the safehouse anytime soon.

Which, they shouldn't, because according to Ghoul, his associate that they would meet "soon" had killed the gangster's boss a few minutes prior, and they were to wait for him to return, however long it took.

It was a nice opportunity. A bunch of gangsters all conveniently boxed into that creaking shed of a building. Like meat in a can.

. . .

That was a more morbid thought than usual.

She checked her wings again, finding them to be roughly the same thing as her right arm, a spiraling mess of stripes and patches that were either chitin, fur, or scale, the hands themselves being the only parts that had skin.

The skin was pitch black and leathery, of course, but it was still skin.

She folded her wings back a little and glanced at the wolf.

He had a couple dried husks left to go, and she'd rather not think too much about who he was eating, a sentiment Katherine shared judging by how she'd gone in the complete opposite direction to have her *"conversation"* with Scruffy.

She shook her head, and opened her system screen, still unable to keep the smile from her face.

-Species: Humanoid
-Race: Elven Vampire
-Name: Embreeil
-Path: [Augmentor] Level 18

Base Attributes:
Strength (+0)
Speed (+0)
Dexterity (+0)
Endurance (+0)
Perception (+0)
Resolve (+0)
Intelligence (+0)
Soul (+0)
Available: 18

She checked again.

Her brows lowered and lowered as she opened and closed the screen rapidly, seeing the same thing over and over.

That . . . she didn't even know that that could happen beyond some very vague mutterings in the guild, people wishing the system would give them a reset but not knowing how to get one or if it was just some stupid rumor.

Apparently it wasn't.

She might have stopped to wonder if she could replicate such a reset again, but she suspected that she only got one because of the monumental change she'd gone through, or maybe due to her race changing, so she wasn't going to bother. Might trade the information with someone when she got back to another Adventurer's Guild office, though.

She moved on for the moment.

-Racial Skills: [Attuned], [Quick Learner], [Enhanced Senses], [Blood Dominion], [Psychometric Vision], [Arcane Heart], [Dominating Mind], [Form Release], [Bloodlust]

That . . . that was *a lot* of racial skills.

What the hell?

Through fuzzy memories, she could guess where *some* of that might have come from, if that was how the ritual worked at all. [Enhanced Senses] and [Blood Dominion] seemed like vampire skills. [Form Release] sounded . . . concerning, and [Bloodlust] might have come from the wolf's blood? She remembered what he was like when he was furious.

From what little she remembered of mythology, it fit.

She had no idea about the rest.

She squinted at the letters, letting the rest of the world fade into fuzzy shapes and dark impressions, not even paying attention to the messages she was relaying with the telepathic bond at this point.

[Enhanced Senses] was self-explanatory, and she already knew she had those, she'd just assumed it was a part of her changed biology.

She could hear someone slurping soup down in the safehouse, the crunch of bone and tear of dried flesh to her right, and snippets of mixed conversation all around her mixing with the passive ambiance of a commercial spire, or the underside of one, at least.

So it wasn't like she could *not* notice the difference.

She focused on the skill for a moment, understanding filling her.

This skill wasn't just giving her enhanced senses, if anything, it actually didn't give her that big of a boost compared to her biological alterations. Its secondary function was to make her more able to process whatever stimuli she was receiving, which was nice and explained why she wasn't feeling very overwhelmed.

It could have accomplished the same by giving her a Perception boost, but this *was* the System.

Clunky, convoluted, nonsensical piece of shit. She was surprised anyone would ever worship this thing.

[Blood Dominion] was . . . nice, but weak and simple. It was essentially a form of weak hemokinesis. She'd likely never be able to make people explode into a burst of gore or anything, not do anything like make blood whips or something truly incredible, but if her opponents were bleeding, she could yank that blood out, hasten how quick they bled, and she could make it draw itself to her, ready to patch up her wounds and rejuvenate her without chasing a meal in the middle of a fight.

Drawn-out fights were her biggest weakness prior to this. Once she blew her mana, she was done for. With this and her new physical upgrades, she had patched up that weakness quite nicely. The longer a fight went on, the more their enemies would bleed out their strength and the more she'd heal from it.

Probably.

Did vampires heal from drinking blood? She wasn't even sure. It wasn't a well-researched race, if one could call it that, and definitely not something her family would have put in front of her.

[Psychometric Vision] was . . . an activatable skill, which was rather rare for racial skills as far as she knew. Most were passive.

The impressions she got from it were tough to understand, so she tried to push the System to explain it with words, like it normally did, only just now realizing that it seemed to have changed.

It didn't do anything like that. No words, no explanation, no description, not even a mental one.

She turned to [Sparkburst], a skill whose description she had *memorized* because it used to be the only thing she could actually see for a while.

It refused to show.

Her brows lowered with irritation.

"Nonsensical piece of *shit*," she growled quietly, and turned her gaze back to [Psychometric Vision].

She activated it.

Nothing happened.

She turned the System screen off, and immediately, information began to flood her mind, like words that weren't words but not sounds or thoughts either. Blinking rapidly, she turned her gaze to the building.

Old construction. Built anywhere from thirty to forty years ago by amateurs. Doors replaced the past decade, scuff marks and residue insinuate heavy passage and the occasional struggle, paint has faint claw marks along the edges, likely used for human trafficking or prostitution before owners changed its purpose. Leaking roof along the right side, less than an inch thick metal, eaten through with rust, non-treated metal—

She closed her eyes, taking a step back. Then she opened them again and turned to look at the wolf, curious.

Impatient, eager. Wants to kill, will kill regardless of companions' opinions.

Well . . . it was nice to have confirmation on that. The guilt had dulled significantly, but it had been nagging at her in her subconscious, asking if she could have found a way to stop the wolf from doing what it did.

Impatient for something else, unknown what. Posture and motions excited. Wants to kill with his companions. Sees it as a goal, a personal pride. Wants to test something or someone. Way of eating and tearing with extra force suggests frustration at something. Slightly annoyed about sharing prey, isn't aware, subconscious frustration. Wants to drink water, does not enjoy dried flesh, tongue feels dry. Bulges at waist, hidden limbs, dangerous. Tails are prehensile, spikes capable of something more, unknown. Spikes along shoulders and forearms are venomous, likely lethal. Build along the abdomen suggests lack of digestive system. Has eaten more than is physically possible for own size, has nonstandard ways of digestion or possible nonstandard space inside its body. Is a wolf. Extremely dangerous, confident. Proud. Male, used to pain, used to threat of death, fears little. Lacks reproductive system—

Okay, she didn't need to know most of that.

And she knew a lot of what it told her already. Still, the skill was incredible for information gathering.

Some of what it said sounded like simple, logical deductions that she probably wouldn't or couldn't have made, while others sounded almost like mind reading, or like a limited sense of omniscience. The potential was wild.

She wished she'd turned this on before Ghoul had dropped them off here, tossed them a communication crystal and a piece of paper, then did that strange step-teleportation, gone without giving them the chance to ask even a single question.

What could she have learned about him?

Honestly, probably not that much. The guy seemed impervious to everything.

She focused on the next skill.

[Arcane Heart].

It was actually fairly straightforward, but immensely powerful. It gave her an instinctive, deep-rooted connection to magic, more than her [Attuned] skill did.

In combination with [Attuned], however, she might actually be able to learn spells by watching someone use them a few times, or just skimming through a spellbook. Everything about magic and spells should make more sense, more like she was relearning how to write by observation, rather than learning the alphabet from scratch to some-day *get* to the writing part.

As far as she knew, only some phoenixes and dragons had this skill, and . . .

She was a little scared to ask how Ghoul got his hands on dragon blood, if he even did. She vaguely remembered some vision of wings and a woman drinking her blood.

Maybe he got it from a phoenix. She hoped he wasn't strong enough to hurt a dragon, or find one in general, even if he was on their side. She'd be more comfortable if nobody but her and the wolf had such abilities.

[Dominating Mind] was also simple and straightforward, but she couldn't exactly test it here.

It was essentially the ability to dominate lesser minds, even take control or just guide them, see through their lenses, or just feel their individual locations and distances.

Beyond that, it had a number of applications she could come up with, but the disparity between her and the mind she was trying to control had to be quite extreme. She doubted she'd ever be able to use this on anything more than critters and maybe some rats, maybe mice. Bats would be amazing for sense sharing. They had good hearing; she remembered reading that on some monster manual for the mutated ones.

A distant explosion drew her away from her thinking for a moment, and she turned her head fractionally, rotating her ears to catch the sound better, the distant thud-rumble mixing with a dozen other ambient noises.

Assuming they were in the middle of the third floor, and close to the walls . . . that was probably just a chemical plant having its weekly hazardous explosion.

She ignored it, and tried to ignore how much this entire place smelled like burnt paint, the rickety old storage building underneath them nestled into a dead-end corner along a massive spire that people built things on, for some reason. Likely because it was easier to hide.

She flicked the System screen back up.

The [Form Release] skill was a bit concerning but also potentially powerful.

Her suspicions of why she had strips of chitin and fur and scales, almost like a design meant to show there was something under her skin, were correct. She *did* have a transformation, a mix between every creature she'd drunk from, and every type of blood that had gone into the ritual, if the word fit.

It took another mute minute of prodding the skill to figure out the full scope of this.

It was a transformation that had a simple expenditure, a simple cost.

Power in exchange for damage and exhaustion.

Everything about her, from her regeneration to her speed and strength and mana regeneration, everything would balloon and flare for as long as she could keep it up, but there was a backlash afterward, and a significant drain on her energy.

She wondered what that form would look like, really.

She'd drunk from rats, a bunch from people, a little bit from the slaughterhouse animals once or twice when Kat would buy blood bags, a *lot* from the wolf, some from a dragon or a phoenix, judging by both [Arcane Heart] and the bulky winged arms on her back, and she vaguely remembered Ghoul dropping some gigantic spider legs into the edge of her blood. Or the . . . ritual's edge?

He also said something about a demon's eye, if she remembered right, which . . . was likely where [Psychometric Vision] came from. That sounded exactly like what a demon would have.

She tried to mash all the forms she could remember drinking from, or being involved in the ritual, all into some kind of singular body, and grimaced.

It would likely be horrific enough to make Katherine green in the face, and the wolf happy enough to tackle her. She'd keep it for an emergency, or when they had room to experiment.

The last but not least of the racial skills was [Bloodlust], which . . .

Honestly, it seemed like both a curse as a benefit, though the benefit seemed more potent.

She would apparently never be satisfied, not truly, and any satisfaction she could get would only last a moment before she wished for more blood again. In return, the more she drank over time, the stronger everything about her would become.

She couldn't tell if this came from the wolf, or if [Form Release] did. This sounded like a regular vampire skill.

It certainly incentivized overeating which . . .

Honestly, was she even against that anymore? She'd love to clean the third floor up, to slaughter every gangster, drug pusher, slaver and guard, every loan shark and abuser, and eventually, her mother and near-vegetative father.

By the time she'd run out of those to kill in the dungeon of all places, Katherine would be a grandmother.

Another thing she just realized. She didn't age anymore. The wolf didn't either. Katherine did.

She'd have to convince Katherine to go down the same path she did, unless Katherine truly wished to be a normal human, and refused to budge.

If Kat didn't budge, however, how would she keep up? How would Scruffy keep up?

Emhreeil and the wolf were . . . not on the same wavelength yet, not really. He proved he could still scrub the floor with her without much effort, but they could at least keep up with each other.

Much as she wanted to launch herself straight into that safehouse and kill everything, to fight on somewhat equal ground to her monstrous little friend, see what she was capable of, she didn't want to give up on Katherine. She refused.

She'd push and *push* if she had to, but if Katherine didn't give up on her, she wouldn't give up on her.

That meant that the fight they were waiting to get into should . . . probably change directions a little. Be more focused on Katherine.

She had no idea what to do with Scruffy, honestly. Soon, she'd likely die if she stayed with them.

Something Ghoul mentioned came to mind, and she frowned.

She could give Scruffy to him and his team, to learn from the woman of chitin. He had suggested it. It felt too much like getting rid of her, but the way Ghoul had worded it sounded more like a member swap so he could put Scruffy to actual use rather than having her tag along until someone accidentally sneezed the wrong spell in her direction and pasted her.

And from what she had observed, Scruffy was not stupid. She loved to mess with that clock she bought her, and in Katherine's apartment, she'd started poking at the heating box almost immediately. She'd also worked in that waste facility for a decent while, she could guess.

Maybe that "chitin woman" that Ghoul hadn't named could teach Scruffy a way to put that curiosity and interest to use.

She knew that she herself definitely couldn't.

It would be better for Scruffy to go with Ghoul's team, and even though letting her go would hurt a bit, because she honestly really enjoyed having her around, things were just . . . heating up too much, too fast. Scruffy could not tag along with them for long and survive.

Well, she had the dimensional ring, and she had the crystal. She could tell Ghoul anytime. And with her telepathy, Scruffy could probably talk for herself now, finally, or try for an approximation of it.

She let the rest of the symbols fade past her sight, checking for any other significant changes.

-Acquired Skills:
[Magic Resistance - Level 5]

[Mental Resistance - Level 6]
[Poison Resistance - Level 13]
[Pain Resistance - Level 26]
[Illumina - Level 8]
[Sparkburst - Level 21]
[Haste - Level 21]
[Mana Perception - Level 24]
[Mana Manipulation - Level 26]
[Mana Tank - Level 9]
[Mana Conduit - Level 13]
[Mana Touch] - Level 14]
[Tough Skin - Level 9]
[Infection Resistance - Level 4]
[Disease Resistance - Level 2]
[Telemantic Construct - Level 18]
[Telepathic Link - Level 1]
[Telepathic Message - Level 1]
[Telepathic Bond - Level 1]

-Acquired Titles:

Wolf-Blooded: Your hunger will never truly be satisfied, and you are destined for conflict and struggle. You are tougher, and your limits are more malleable than most, should your will be found to match your needs.

Dragon-Blooded: You and your flight are destined to reach for the top where you belong, whether consciously, unconsciously, by circumstance, or by necessity. Your hide is made of iron, and your magic is as pure as pure can be, regardless of yourself.

-Acquired Traits:

Enduring (1 / 5): You have felt the chill of death multiple times and survived. You are slightly tougher.

She lost the Vampiric trait, which made sense.

And she got *two* titles. Sure, they sounded just as much like curses as they did blessings, but the curse-like parts were already things she was probably heading for.

You and your flight caught her eye. A gathering of dragons was called a flight, like how a gathering of crows was called a murder. A flight of dragons, a murder of crows.

Did that mean that this title would only work on any draconic companions she had? She hoped so. She was a bit iffy on having a title that nudged or dictated "destiny" for her entire group.

She wasn't sure what it meant by saying her magic would be pure, but that sounded positive as well. Maybe it meant efficiency? Impurities in the world's mana tended to make things inefficient.

Interesting, but she had more things to check. She brought up the attributes again.

Base Attributes:
Strength (+0)
Speed (+0)
Dexterity (+0)
Endurance (+0)
Perception (+0)
Resolve (+0)
Intelligence (+0)
Soul (+0)
Available: 18

She already felt stronger than ever, and she still had *eighteen* points to put into things. She felt like making excited *squee* sounds, like a ten-year-old.

But she had to put thought into this. She'd likely never again go through another change so monumental that the System would give her a reset. She couldn't believe her luck in getting *this one* in the first place. Resets were so rare they were basically a rumor in the guild, from what she remembered.

She wasn't sure what to go for.

Her magic remained her greatest weapon. She *could* throw herself into a melee now, especially if the Dragon-Blooded title was accurate about her skin being made of iron.

But even if she put half a dozen points into Strength and Speed, she doubted her strikes would do as much damage as a well-charged [Sparkburst] detonated against a weak point. It was one thing to stab straight through someone's torso or punch someone's ribs to splinters, which was arguably survivable if she missed the heart, it was another to make someone's torso explode like a bag of gore.

There was no surviving that, not if something was *alive* in the first place.

And with how the points worked, according to the literature, it was always better to focus on one's natural strongpoints. A flat ten-percent increase to something someone sucked at was a wasted point, whereas if tossed onto something one was good at, it could have much higher yield. She wasn't sure if the ten-percent example was accurate, a rule, or an example, but she agreed with it.

Play to your strengths instead of wasting points trying to circumvent shoring up your weaknesses naturally.

So what *were* her strengths, really? Magic was the biggest one. She could probably detonate someone into little gibbets now by just shoving her hand against their ribs and using [Sparkburst], assuming they didn't have too much Endurance or [Magic Resistance] or some other esoteric effect to protect them.

She was probably about as strong as Katherine right now, physically, and probably a bit faster, without any spells or attributes in the way.

Her soul *felt* vast and powerful, but it wasn't like she had a frame of reference there. She could have a soul weaker than Scruffy's for all she knew. So maybe making it bigger by putting some points into the Soul attribute would be nice, allowing her to regenerate mana even faster.

Speed and Strength were a possibility too, but she could get Speed from [Haste] without huge costs now that she had Augmentor as a Path, and while Strength was useful, she couldn't really come up with too many ways it would benefit her in a fight. She wasn't a brute, she didn't want to be getting into fistfights if she could avoid it, and if she did get into one, her right arm should be enough.

Resolve was . . . not really something she needed. She had plenty by herself.

Dexterity . . .

Dexterity might actually be useful. She was always clumsy. And even though she felt more aware and in control of her body than she had in a long time, it could really help her to be pinpoint accurate with her movements and be able to twist herself around *even more*. If she combined [Haste] with a field of [Mana Touch] and had a bit of Dexterity, she could probably dance circles around most opponents without even trying.

She was no wolf. She couldn't tank the amount of damage he could. She still remembered trying to break his ribs when she was overcome with rabid hunger and madness.

It had felt like punching an iron wall covered by a layer of rubber.

So dodging would be much more efficient than tanking hits.

Perception felt unnecessary because [Haste] could fill that gap exceedingly well, and Intelligence . . . Intelligence helped with pattern recognition, deduction, and memory retention. There were probably other bits she'd forgotten, but it had been a while since she'd last had an actual conversation with someone who knew about any of this stuff.

Intelligence was also something that she couldn't exactly *naturally* increase.

So her focus should be . . . Soul, to generate mana faster, grow her mana core faster, and fill her body up with mana even faster. Maybe a couple points into Dexterity to get rid of any clumsiness left over, and for dodging. A couple points in Endurance so that slipping up once wouldn't kill her, a couple points in Intelligence for overall benefits . . .

And maybe save a couple points for when she had a better, more accurate reading of her situation and newfound fighting "style," if one could call her flailing as such.

She spent a minute rethinking it all, and eventually felt sure enough to commit.

Strength (+0)
Speed (+1)
Dexterity (+2)
Endurance (+3)
Perception (+0)
Resolve (+0)
Intelligence (+2)
Soul (+7)
Available: 3

She almost *physically* felt something in her chest swell like an over-filled balloon, a strangely euphoric feeling. She felt her body harden, her mind get noticeably sharper, her body a tiny bit lighter, her limbs more present and responsive.

With a deep, pleased breath, she closed the screen with a mental flick, focusing back on the bizarre, stilted conversation Scruffy was having with Katherine. Something about Katherine trying to get Scruffy to recite her system screen to her . . . ?

She glanced to the side at the wolf, then at the warehouse below.

She wiggled her toes onto the cold stone, the sensation being oddly pleasant, then bent down to grab her modified clothes off the floor.

They consisted of her cloak shredded into five thick ribbons, so she could be able to extend her wings without throwing the whole thing off, her dart launcher attached to a full left sleeve of armor, significantly loosened, her trophy mask with an extra strap on the top to go between her new ears and keep the thing steady, and her dimensional ring.

That and new panties. The size barely fit, but it was what they had in their backpack.

She wasn't sure if it was confidence or just desensitization, or just her body being weird and inhuman at this point, but she didn't feel all that embarrassed to be naked in the open, even if they were in a dark corner. It was strangely liberating, and nobody here cared.

She shrugged the cloak on, fiddled with the straps of the arm-brace for the dart launcher until she finally managed to squeeze her arm in it without tearing it to pieces with her bulky right arm. Then she picked up her ring and put her mask on.

It took her another three minutes to bundle up the explanation of what she wanted to do as her general plan, and shift it into a sort of mental package, but she eventually managed. With a faint struggle, she pushed it to everyone she'd linked up, right as the wolf finished eating the last scrap of meat off the floor.

He jolted in surprise for a moment, then smacked his jaws shut and stared off into the distance, deciphering her reasoning.

She activated [Psychometric Vision].

Frustrated. Annoyed at the suggestion of being the only combatant denied actual combat. Understands reasoning. Agrees with reasoning. Does not want to agree with reasoning. Hopes that its companions will miss some fleeing humans so it can have some fun too.

She could do that. Leave the cowards for him to toy with while she and Katherine practiced fighting and keeping the fight challenging and dangerous enough to not skimp out on leveling.

Preferably while having him somewhat close by, just in case.

Hungry. Impatient for something else. Curious. Has questions for Emhreeil. Has questions for Scruffy. Finds Scruffy weird. Finds Scruffy endearing, surprised and confused about her lack of fear. Confused on why Katherine's fear won't fade, has questions for Katherine. Wants to toy with prey, wants to drag it out for sadistic pleasure and spiteful satisfaction. Does not want to agree with Emhreeil's plan. Will likely agree with Emhreeil's plan. Does not want Katherine to stay weak. Understands his companions have a bond and history, does not care to get in the way or interfere with it. Is inwardly jealous of the bond, to some extent. Unaware of it, entirely sub-conscious. Perceived cowardice of Katherine and jealousy is slowly budding into gradual distaste. Does not dislike Katherine yet. Will likely not dislike Katherine until a fair period of time has passed without anything changing.

Oh.

That . . . that could be a problem in the future. Maybe.

She turned the skill off to think.

The solutions were to either make Katherine stop being "cowardly," or in her opinion, a perfectly normal and sane response to what is happening around her, really, or to find ways to make everyone in the group feel included.

Likely the telepathic bond, then. She imagined them talking with words rather than the link so the wolf could be included too, then the option available wouldn't feel like a purposeful exclusion to him. She could see that being the case, and how it could build up drops of resentment or annoyance.

The *last* thing they needed was group friction. They couldn't afford it, and she'd never be able to make a choice if it came down to it.

She disliked using this link, truth be told. It felt like learning how to speak again, like she was some stunted toddler trying to figure out how to translate feelings and ideas from words and sounds into bizarre mind-bending concepts so the wolf could understand.

It was a sudden role reversal from the wolf trying to learn human speech to her now trying to learn a wolf's way of thought.

On the upside, the method definitely helped expand her way of thinking in an oddly pleasant way.

Katherine sent uncertainty, a question of confidence directed at her.

That was . . . asking Emhreeil if she was sure of her plan?

She bundled up confirmation, sent it out, then took a few seconds to bundle up a request for the wolf to stick close in case they needed backup in there, and a promise that she'd toss out anyone too strong for them, as well as let any cowards flee so he could take them.

The wolf sent back disagreement, much to her surprise, then sent something different as he turned away from the warehouse, staring at her with a serious, hungry gaze.

She had known he was smart, but she still felt her brows rise at the plan he gave them.

It began with a detailed mental map of the entire *area* around the place, including the underground sections, with mental *buzzing* around where the groups of people were concentrated, and paths of entrance for them to sandwich the people inside, one for her and one for Katherine, while leaving just enough wiggle room for the cowards of the group to flee from the available exits around the back.

The picture, the plan, the layout and ideas, they were so *crisp* and vivid. It was just a mental map and some conceptual ideas attached to it, but it was worth more than a thousand words.

Maybe learning how to think and communicate like this would be better in the long run. It sure felt like it. It had visualization skills *she* didn't.

An idea rose.

She could teach him *so much* magic. He was so talented in visualization that it would be a piece of cake if she could somehow explain the basic principles of magic to him. He even had human hands to do the first couple casts with until he got the skills to do it for him.

A project for later. A *very interesting* project for later.

For now, the wolf's plan was similar to hers, but more thought out, and actually had an interesting, albeit cruel, idea tacked on at the end.

The wolf could crawl along the rafters or prowl around the building, waiting for escapees or survivors, strong or weak, and put a little bit of paralytic in their veins to make them stay down.

Then they could just take the stronger members of the safehouse with them for her and Katherine to train with, by force, in another nearby area. Plenty of abandoned places around the dungeon.

Meanwhile he could play around with the weaker members until they gave up and it killed them for its amusement, providing a fresh snack for both of them.

It was quite horrible, morally.

But these people were a walking cancer upon the dungeon. She remembered hearing what gangs did to people, enemies or just victims, who happened to be in the wrong place at the wrong time.

Children taken from their families at swordpoint for the brothels, led to an early, diseased grave. Men and women senselessly murdered in dark alleys for their organs and a small handful of coppers from the butchers and the witch shops, wives torn from their families for the sadistic pleasures of whoever was willing to pay, endless masses destroying their lives in the clutches of addiction of one drug or another, people trying to provide for their families being beaten and tortured and enslaved.

Ghar had quite liked tormenting her with tales of how nice and *benevolent* they were when they enslaved her, rattling off all the different ways she could have met a horrific end in this place if it weren't for his *kindness*.

This strange little group they had here, the four of them? They could kill a thousand *innocent* people and they'd still not have done as much damage to the people of Carmera than even just one or two gangs.

So why not use them for a bit of light practice before killing them? Why not let the wolf have his fun? It wasn't like he was likely to listen to her unless she managed to make it sound like a logical argument instead of a moral one, and she didn't care enough to argue in the first place. Fuck them.

They had made their choices, just like she and Katherine and the wolf had. Even Scruffy.

Ghoul had phrased it well. They were just acceptable targets.

The main difference between his worldview and the worldview she was just now starting to solidify in her head, was that Ghoul considered *strangers* what she considered her *acceptable targets*.

Meat.

Katherine sent a reluctant acceptance to the wolf's plan, surprisingly.

Em sent a firm acceptance.

He bared his teeth and sent a mental push for movement.

She didn't need her racial skill to see how he was practically vibrating with the need to move and kill something. She felt something similar.

In the dark, as he glued his chest to the stone and began to crawl over the uneven lip of their perch, his bared teeth looked like a fox's grin.

She extended her right hand to gesture Kat forward, and idly wondered what name the wolf might pick when she asked him.

Probably something exceedingly arrogant. Or he would refuse a name.

Katherine gathered herself quickly, letting Scruffy clamber up onto her back, and a brief use of her [Psychometric Vision] had her brows rising.

Her friend was just as eager for a fight as they were. That was a surprise.

Maybe she wouldn't need to do anything about the potential friction in the first place. At this rate, it would sort itself out.

"How many?" Katherine asked as Emhreeil turned around and kneeled, spreading her wing arms to the sides. "And what are you doing?"

"They are enough. And I'm giving you a piggyback ride," she said, and unwound her tail from around her neck, using it to balance. After a moment, she felt Kat's hands on her shoulders before she clumsily wrapped herself around her.

She rose, and . . . it was surprisingly easy to lift them, even if the backpack had been left behind for now.

How strong was she? Enough to tackle the wolf, at least—she remembered doing that. She'd get to test her strength in a minute.

She turned around before creeping down past the edge and on the slanted wall, using her wings' claws to slowly scrape and slide her way down. The movement jolted her passengers a bit, but they could deal with it.

She was surprised to see and feel her wings' claws cut into the rocks, leaving deep marks and furrows or just catching randomly.

After how easily the wolf had shrugged her attacks off, she'd thought they weren't all that sharp or pointy.

"*Enough* is not really an answer, you know," Katherine said absent-mindedly, glancing around above them, and she huffed through her nostrils as she used her left hand to make sure they wouldn't tumble down and break a bone or something. It was hard to balance like this, with so much weight on her back, even if the rock wall was slanted forward.

It felt like gravity was always about to yank her backward and give them a few broken bones.

It took her more mental effort than she was willing to admit, to send a telepathic message to Kat, urging her to just ask the wolf how many there were inside.

She didn't know, but if he could somehow map out the entire building, he could probably figure out specific numbers.

Kat's face twisted in distaste, something she felt with a pulse of mana, but she nodded.

Turns out that he did know, and after another minute of slowly scraping down as the wolf paced around a walkway just next to the warehouse's roof, he sent them the answer as they touched down on the lightly rattling catwalk.

Fourteen people.

Huh.

Something told her that Ghoul knew they would pick this course of action instead of bringing the wolf with them inside to kill everything, because there was no way just *fourteen* people in a random warehouse would be "enough to not be a slaughter" if the wolf was involved.

Either that, or they were fairly strong people and were not random at all.

She wasn't sure she liked either possibility, honestly.

CHAPTER 6

It felt . . .

Jittery and twitchy.

Like there was some electricity inside its muscles buzzing away and not letting it relax.

It hadn't incorporated that weird water worm's biology yet, so it was mostly just a need to move, to do something.

The fact it wouldn't be fighting had a lot to do with that.

It had been very excited to fight side by side with its human for the first time, and judging by their tumbling earlier, she could somewhat keep up now.

But it understood the need for the Katherine human to fight and get her own growth in, and if it involved itself, there wouldn't be a fight, not really.

It wasn't like it would gain anything from fighting these humans. They all *walked* like they were a threat, but it didn't really feel like any of them were, not really. There was none of that measured pace and fluid grace that people who knew how to move possessed, they were all basically stumbling on their feet.

There was no point in fighting them beyond its own entertainment, whereas if Katherine fought them with Emhreeil, they could both get a bit of experience and maybe even some levels.

It was still connected to the strange mental tunnel Emhreeil had made for them, as was the weird little green human walking with it, the "Scruffy" one, but it was tempted to ramp up [Mental Resistance] and be done with it. It felt naked without having it up.

The green human was odd. And fairly refreshing in her lack of fear.

It circled slowly, deciding to leave the decision-making to its humans, content to stew in some faint haze of annoyance bubbling into the back of its mind.

There wasn't too much room for circling, however, and that fed into its inner frustrations.

The odd tower the building was perched on was more akin to a titanic metal screw that had stone and rubble growing out of it like tumors, and the downward metal slide didn't extend much farther past the building before it dropped off into the abyss, the metal warped and melted from some past conflict or accident, hanging above light-speckled mists below.

Off to the side of the wide metal curve supporting all of them was a fairly unreliable-looking walkway that extended off in the far distance to the right, to a messy network of railings and caged stairways, almost like a wall made of iron sticks. Glowing signs covered in symbols peeked through the mess, some leading to a small open window where white light shone from deeper within while along the edges, light crystals fought to keep the dark mists away, and the steps visible.

It took a deep breath, nearly able to taste the undermining tang of rust and iron beneath the scent of burnt rubber and something like rotten smoke and human waste.

It smelled familiar. Comforting, even.

Maybe it wouldn't be so bad to not be involved in a fight. It wouldn't be that exciting anyway, not against weak humans like this. And it would get its pound of flesh regardless. Emhreeil feasted on blood, not flesh.

Besides, their prey was cornered. A few might still try to run out of the side entrances or windows or just jump off the roof hatch because of fear, but they didn't really have anywhere to go. Running up the cork-screwing path would be like running up a steep metal hill, running down would send them to the abyss after a hundred feet, and running to the walkway that ran off to the side over the abyss would be unsafe.

There wouldn't be a chase, even if some of the humans inside ran away.

It let out a long exhale, and felt the green human's hand pat its head, scratch a bit behind its ear.

That felt *bizarrely* nice.

It felt its leg twitch, and that immediately soured the experience, making it move its head out of reach as its ears tugged backward, resuming its half-hearted patrol.

It was a mild thing, but it didn't like not having control of itself or its limbs. Reflex or not, it was uncomfortable and made it . . . *snarly* for a lack of a better expression to the mood it was put in by the brief experience.

It slowed to a stroll, smelling the oddly sweet smoke in the wind, flitting through the spongelike planks boarding up the windows, twitching its ears to catch human sounds it could try to mimic.

The humans inside did not think to put someone outside on lookout, so it passed by its two pack members as they huddled in a dark corner, making their human gibbering as they planned for how to engage the people inside. Emhreeil glanced at it and made some kind of hand-wag. A human greeting, as far as it had observed.

It wagged its tail a bit in acknowledgment as it continued prowling around.

Impatience and restlessness were slowly blooming.

The spiral around the tower they were on was mercifully gigantic, so neither was the slope too steep nor the sides too thin.

Still, it was annoying to not have much space around. Even if a human escaped, they wouldn't get to run. No chase, no action, no fight.

Boring.

It took another lap around the building, watching Emhreeil brace against the front doors in a peculiar stance, Katherine standing behind on the opposite side of the building, far more cautious.

It glanced through the mess of lights and iron sticks and walkways to the distant right, barely paying attention.

A light jerked oddly, unnaturally, merely a blur at the edge of its vision, and it took a moment to process that and whip its head to the side to find it again. Its steps paused, and two more eyes on its flank opened, searching.

It found the odd light a moment later, now still as any other.

It stared at the yellow circle, barely visible underneath three layers of metal bars and grates, in the corner of a staircase. Scarce light and reflections outlined a vaguely humanoid silhouette of tattered fabric.

But the light was perfectly still, and quite far away, to the point it wondered if it was seeing things.

It slowly began to move ahead, turning its head mostly forward, side-eyeing the yellow circle.

The light moved, just a little bit, imperceptible, almost. Like its innards shifted. It was the same structure and jerky way of movement that had alerted it to the light on Emhreeil's sternum being some kind of mechanical eye, back when she needed it. The way there were plates and rings in the light that shifted and moved in a bizarrely organic manner as if to mimic an iris and a pupil.

It stopped moving, four gold eyes staring into a sickly yellow. It wasn't sure why, exactly, but it couldn't help but stare, feeling a ramping tension coil up around it like a physical force. Throwing [Mental Resistance] up as high as it could go, it felt messages prod at its mind feebly and ignored them in favor of trying to decide what to do.

Someone or something was staring at it *very, very intently* from a great distance. That knowledge was obviously quite uncomfortable to think about, and there wasn't exactly much cover around. But there *was* some.

With a haphazard plan, it began to trot along the same line again, changing its trajectory quite a bit so it could move behind a stack of boxes up and to the right of the building, enough to hide from the eye, and then it stopped, turning to the green human.

Big brown eyes stared at it, and it lifted a hand to point at her with a claw.

She tilted her head and pointed at herself.

It let out a positive chuff, then pointed past her, swirling its hand in a circle, before quickly miming a calm walk, trotting in place.

The green human blinked at it before bobbing her head up and down, something it assumed meant agreement by now, and without a second thought, turned around and kept walking along the path they'd made.

More messages and prods hit its mental shield, and it ignored them in favor of covering its paws, palms, and eyes with darkness. Then it let its chest brush the floor as it stalked around the boxes, pressing its ears flat as it took a peek past them at the bridge.

It was a bit hard to see through the murky sight of [Echoes of Oblivion], but after a moment of squinting, it could see that the light had moved, now away from the staircase and closer to the boxlike floors of metal grating lining the rooms they provided access to. The eye's holder was sitting in a corner while curled into a ball, their eye still unerringly focused on the visible section of the path, staring somewhere to the wolf's right.

Chaos erupted behind it, and the wolf ignored it for the most part, too uneasy and curious to move.

It waited, its attention split two ways, eyes focused on the hooded figure and its antenna loosely following the chaos of the melee in the building, writhing softly against the floor like a hundred little tentacles unsheathing out of its forearms.

The hooded figure slowly rose, in a movement too measured and precise to be organic, and began to move forward, closer, almost sliding forward onto the long walkway separating the wolf's spire from the opposite nest structure, steel cable softly groaning on both sides as the bridge ever-so-subtly shifted.

Steel striking steel and shouts rose from behind it, and the figure seemed to speed up, the glowing eye beneath its hood unerringly focused on the same spot, a tattered cloak sliding against gray iron. An errant breeze and a metal bulge parted the cloak, just enough to show something angular, metallic, and vaguely familiar.

It had seen that way of moving before. A smooth, unnaturally even gait that looked less like running and more like a blur of metal stilts pounding the floor.

It had seen a large eye like that before, big, yellow, in the middle of a head that was likely not wreathed by flesh but metal plates.

The realization made it abruptly stiffen and twitch.

It had wanted a fight, but it wasn't sure if it wanted to face anything like that metal human it had run into while deep under the human nests.

Then again, it was *far* stronger now than it had been then.

It wasn't sure what one of these things was doing up here. It had only ever seen one metallic person before, and it had been deep inside the human nest's guts.

Did the tunnels send this one?

It could understand how even to itself, that sounded more than a little dubious, but what else was it supposed to think? It escaped the tunnels once, twice, and now it had what was likely a human that had been consumed by the metal, stalking it.

It tuned in to the fight happening a mere two dozen feet behind it.

From a cursory look, they seemed to be struggling, but winning, which was perfect in its opinion.

It didn't want to interrupt them, it didn't want the green human or Katherine near one of these metal men creatures, and it *certainly* was in the mood for a good fight now.

So it stopped peeking over the edge of the small wall of rotting crates and went to the other side, not bothering to hide as it strolled to the edge, eyes nailed to the puppet-like creature.

The yellow eye jerked to the side a little from where the thing had been looking and focused on the wolf.

It sat on the edge and waited for the metal man to charge forward, gathering air into its throat in preparation, just to see how much damage it could do with one blast.

Unlike what it had been expecting, the hooded figure stopped cold, and without an ounce of hesitation, turned around and tripled its speed, rushing away.

For a moment, it just blinked at the figure's back, bewildered.

Then it growled and strained its will, mentally projecting for the skill it was using to keep the ball together as long as possible.

It spit the ball forward and turned to the right, leaping down onto the metal stairs that led to the bridge with a deafening crash and a precarious wobble, pivoting with its lower body to kick off the railing and down the flight of stairs.

It turned its head right as it slid to a stop in front of the narrow bridge and witnessed [Sonic Blast] detonate above the bridge with a sharp crack of air halfway across the bridge, sending the hooded figure down and back into the bridge's segmented platelike sections, denting them as it bounced and rolled backward, barely managing to stay on the bridge thanks to the mangled railings.

Sharp shrieks and creaks and clunks continued for a moment as the sound traveled back to the wolf, bolts and fragments of chain peppering the mists below as the bridge rocked violently from side to side in front of the wolf, the cables groaning on either side of it.

It wasn't enthused about crossing the threshold from the stable metal platform it was on and onto the rocking bridge, but it didn't feel letting the metal man thing run would be a good choice. Mostly because it couldn't understand *why* it would run just from seeing it. The last of its kind the wolf had fought had been extremely tough and mindless.

It activated [Bloodrush] and lunged forward with a burst of sparks as its claws raked through metal for more traction.

For the second time, not even three bounds onto the bridge, its eyes widened in bewilderment when the cloaked figure stumbled upward jerkily, and without an ounce of hesitation, threw themselves over the wavering railing in a smooth motion, tumbling out of sight.

It slid to a stop and grabbed onto the railing, raising itself over it as if it were a human, and barely caught the metal ball of limbs and yellow circles tumbling through the slowly shifting smog clouds below, its tattered covering trailing after it, slowly enough to seem weightless, detached from its heavy form.

It caught a glimpse of a painted eyeball within a gear, painted in red on the back, before the mists curled around the cloth and that too disappeared.

It spent a few seconds staring into the mists with a sense of dissatisfied confusion.

That was too nonsensical for the wolf to feel like a problem had been solved. It felt more like it just watched a problem *escape*.

The sounds of fighting from above heightened, and its snout curled into an annoyed snarl as it turned back around and rushed up the stairs, seeing snippets of the fight inside, muted by the vibrations moving through so many different materials. It was more than enough to see that one person had run away, stumbling straight toward it, waving its arms oddly.

Its pack was still fighting, but [Pack Hunter] didn't make it seem like they were struggling too much, so it wasn't concerned.

It paused near the top of the stairs and decided to wait for the human to come to it instead, hoping his blood might wash off the taste of failure.

She sent requests to the wolf to get an update on the positions of the people inside, but he was blocking them all, so after a moment of hesitation, she decided to let him be and do whatever it was he was doing. It could wait for later.

Scruffy sent back an image of him staring out into an undefined vast space, which wasn't . . . terribly helpful. Was he sightseeing? *Now?*

She shook her head and braced.

Her left hand was pressed against the shoddy front doors of the building, right where the locks were, gathering a substantial [Sparkburst], and her right was reared back to slam into the first person she saw.

Katherine was waiting on the opposite door for her cue.

She formed another spell on her right hand, charging up an [Illumina] for a short but violent flare. A third prepared itself in the back of her mind, [Haste] charging with a slight boost.

She let go of her first spell, and the doors exploded inward, folding and breaking in half as they showered the inner occupants in dust and splinters.

A brief push of [Telemantic Construct] further propelled the dust and splinters to push forward, blinding her immediate opponents and clearing her own sight to catch an actual glimpse of the inside.

It was a building made of metal sheets, lit by lantern light and with a firepit right in front of the entrance, just ten feet away from her. Four people were around it, their hands occupied with something she couldn't see through the splinters, in the middle of turning around.

The one closest to her, with his back turned to her, would be the first unfortunate she would use to test how strong her right arm was.

She straightened her fingers to the best of her ability and lunged ten feet forward by kicking forth and using her wing arms to propel her, slapping against the patch of cobbles outside.

She felt ribs and organs snap and part before her hand like it was nothing but jelly. Her elbow sank through the man's half-turned torso, her claws slamming into the ribs on the other side and finally stopping as he jerked and went limp.

Distantly, she realized this guy likely had nothing in Endurance. His flesh felt like firm pudding.

Her wing arms had a similar range of movement to actual wings, so she couldn't exactly move them over her shoulders to kill the other three. So she twisted her body to the right, tearing her arm out of the convulsing gangster's body, a mass of gore in her fist, and thrust her left shoulder forward, bending her back so the wing could swing.

Or unfold, rather. It zipped forward like a loaded spring, five thin bladelike claws spearing through a gangster in the middle of yelling as he stumbled backward over his seat, and carrying him for another foot before her wingspan maxed out at twelve feet, momentum pushing the man off her claws and causing him to tumble into a metal table.

Katherine burst through the back door by kicking it open, and immediately, someone whirled on her.

She couldn't afford to pay attention to Katherine too, but [Pack Hunter] made her feel how she moved with that dagger, nothing but efficient strokes and cuts and thrusts.

Two down, two in front of her. Katherine dealing with another, and eight or so people in her peripheral vision scrambling upright or unsheathing weapons.

One thing that she felt quite keenly was the blood. She could *feel it*, smell and taste it. She tugged it with [Blood Dominion]. It felt like stretching a muscle she never knew was so sore. It felt *good*.

She began to exude mana in a steady stream. A sword flashed toward her wing from the left, and she folded it just enough to let it fly back before she grabbed onto the hand holding it, and spun, tossing him to the group coming in from the right.

Something slammed into the fire pit, washing her with fire and ash, and she felt right at home.

She jerked out of the way of a punch, feeling like they were all fighting through molasses while she was as free as the wind, and with a jerk of her right shoulder, a head went flying. A metal arrow cracked through the air and into her wing, sticking into the bone, and she briefly grunted from the pain of it embedding into the bone. It was a nice reminder that she was still fragile, even if she was strong and *fast*.

"Kat!" she barked, mentally pushing [Illumina] through the mental link and then placing the spell between herself and the group of six rushing at her.

Distantly, she noted how the wolf's form flared up somewhere behind her, much farther than he should be.

Katherine jerked around, throwing her hands over her head, and Emhreeil simply looked away, turning around as she hopped back.

Illumina flashed for a fraction of a second, and she heard the shouts turn into screams as retinas burned and reflected light rendered even those who were not looking into stumbling buffoons, at least for a while. Someone rattled the rusted doorknob of a side door, before falling outside in a half run, retreating.

In fact, *everyone* was retreating. Most just couldn't find an exit or weren't trying to.

The main reaction to getting blinded seemed to be roughly flailing in her direction to ward her off as they scrambled away from her.

[Illumina] was such a cheat spell when used right . . .

She spun out of the way of a wide swing from a spear that looked more like a sharpened fire poker.

Katherine fought two people on the corner of her vision, one flailing and the other stumbling with squinting, teary eyes. She could have easily killed them and moved on, but she was just beating on them.

She suppressed the urge to snap at her to *kill them* when the swipe of the spear abruptly changed direction and was thrust at her throat, but it was too slow, and it was so impossible to misjudge distance when she could feel every last inch of space around her as if she was touching it with her fingers.

She ducked her shoulder under it and leaned away, then used her right wing to slap the floor and keep herself upright when she realized she had leaned way too far.

Grabbing the ten-foot-long spear with her right arm, she yanked it past her, its wielder dropping face first into the remnants of the fire pit with a cry. Not knowing how to use a spear whatsoever, she simply spun it and put her whole weight and all her strength into impaling its previous wielder through the back, wincing at his animalistic howl as he began to writhe on the floor, feebly trying to reach the spear as his blood crawled toward her.

Someone in a dark corner shouted something, then they rushed up the stairs to the half floor above.

She caught a glimpse of a metal bow glinting in the lantern light behind the men as she darted forward over the dying man at her feet, placing herself between a gangster and the bow as cover, wing arms wide open in a no-doubt nightmarish sight.

The arrow cracked forward again, this time *through* the gangster she was using as cover, weaving between his ribs with impossible accuracy to shoot straight for her head, and she jerked to the right, lowering her left shoulder, throwing a foot in front of her to slow down.

Even so, she felt its flared edges cut into the corner of her brow as it flew past, and she idly realized that even if these were manageable opponents, she should not be underestimating them so much, or be so arrogant just because she *felt* invincible.

A few inches to the side and a little slower in her reaction, and she would have had an arrow through her eye. Another odd sensation rose from her brow, a sense of control and hyperawareness that surprised her too much to delve into.

Her wing arms had much better reach, so she spun her torso to the left, unfurling her right wing.

Half stumbling and half crouched as the men in front of her were, two of them already dead and four blind and retreating, it wasn't too hard to use her wing as an awkward broom and throw them out of the way of the archer.

He didn't look like much. If anything, he looked like some middle-aged man with a cleft chin.

But his eyes were sharp and severe, locked on to her with unsettling confidence.

How did he not get blinded?

He had notched another arrow already, and aimed it to the side, a little too far to the left to be aiming at her wing. At Katherine.

She jerked her head to the left as she zipped forward, imbuing Katherine with a strong [Haste] buff as she pushed a warning to her. She hooked her right arm to the floor, doing the same with her wings before wrenching all of them down, throwing herself forward like an arrow, preparing a repulsion field next to the standing archer.

Something brushed along her mana field, coming from above and in front of her, the tips of boots breaking through in rapid descent.

The bow was almost in line with her, so she used the repulsion field to throw it to the side and lifted her left arm to launch two darts that punched into the archer's stomach.

The arrow went flying midway through the motion as the archer jerked with a muted cry of pain, and she only had a brief moment to panic for her friend before a shortsword slapped the arrow away in the corner of her vision, shattering into a dozen pieces as Katherine quick-stepped away from the fragments.

The boots lowered, followed by muscular legs, and she threw a large chunk of mana into a stronger [Haste] cast.

The sudden burst of added speed let her dart under her falling assailant, and she brought her arms forward until her wrists were touching, her shoulder blades shifting forward in ways that she felt should be agonizing, all to line her wings up to the archer that had fallen against the wall, struggling to reach for another arrow.

Her wing arms unfolded from her back, ten fingers with bladelike claws ramming through the man's arms and raised leg to spear through his torso and into the metal wall behind him.

With a sound like a whimpered, wheezing snarl, his eyes widened as they met hers.

He went limp, life fleeing his eyes, and she felt another pang of something heavy in her gut, even if she knew from their uniform-like wear that they were part of one gang or another. She ripped her claws out of him, pulling his blood toward her almost subconsciously.

The man that had tried to drop on her made a double under-armpit slash for her tail with his machetes before the body of the archer had even hit the floor. She whipped it out of the way as she turned, only for him to abort the slash for an expert throw.

One of his machetes flew for her chest, and she was about to slap it away with her right arm before she reminded herself *again* how easily she could have died just a little bit ago, how fragile she still actually was. Why take unnecessary risk?

She twisted her waist in that ridiculous way again, letting the weapon fly past her chest as her eyes moved past him to check up on Katherine, who was, surprisingly enough, fighting four people, only one of them half blinded, judging from his pained squint, and not appearing like she was having too hard of a time.

It was her first time actually seeing Katherine fight, and she was genuinely impressed at the skill it took to dual wield a dagger and a pipe against four people and *win*, regardless of boosts.

The machete struck the wall behind her with the handle in the time it took her to make that thought.

He rushed forward with a physics-defying quickstep, his second machete rising in a diagonal uppercut, perfectly dodgeable. His other hand made a pulling motion at empty air, and she faltered mid-dodge as she felt the machete behind her suddenly rush straight for her back, heading exactly where she planned to dodge into.

The other machete was swinging in an arc that denied her other way out.

She realized she was boxed in, despite being significantly faster, and after a moment of freezing, she spun and used her right arm to slap away the machete from the flat side, sending it off to the side.

Seeing his chance, the man shifted his stance to stab forward instead of swiping in an arc, and she darted out of the way, moving her tail to grab his leg.

He yanked his foot out before she could do so, despite being slower than her, and a bubble of frustration mixed with adrenaline to make her brow twitch.

His second machete spun into his hand as he let his knee hit the floor and spun on it, ending up with both his weapons held in a loose X in front of him.

She jumped back, over writhing bodies, and sidestepped stumbling blind people, grabbing them and throwing them over each other to put more distance between her and the bizarre man with the machetes. She unwound one of her wings to slam into someone to her right, who was trying to sneak up on her with a giant axe, cutting a deep, wide furrow through his stomach and up his neck, his choked scream turning into a gurgle as he stumbled back and toppled to the floor. She tried to ignore the feeling of his innards spilling out of his stomach, maintaining her field of mana.

For the first time, she got enough of a gap to catch an actual glimpse of the man wielding the machetes as he followed her, hopping and twisting through the mess of bodies and corpses as if he was making it a dance.

He barely looked like an adult, yet his eyes had less humanity in them than the golem eye she used to wear on her neck. It was how she imagined Ghoul's eyes to look. A dull brown, cold and sharp. His clothes were more put-together than the gangsters' too, a simple brown short sleeve and tight, elastic pants supported by a belt, from which two sheaths hung for his weapons.

That was about as much observation as she could make before he kicked the remnants of the firepit at her, and she blasted a hasty [Sparkburst] at him and the burning coals to force both back, mind reeling.

She wasn't in *severe* danger, but she doubted she could beat him in melee, and she needed just a second or two to *think* about her options instead of flailing.

Katherine was almost done with the rest of the gangsters, impressively enough, but she didn't care about them more than she did the immediate threat in front of her.

She didn't get that second or two she wished, and trying to use [Telemantic Construct] on a moving target was rather futile.

So she laid a trap for where she expected him to be as her wings slammed into the floor and threw her away from another double swipe.

She had twelve feet of reach; he had maybe three and a half.

And there were only two ways for him to reach her.

He went for the second one that she expected, throwing both machetes at her, one center mass and the other to her left as he lowered his center of gravity and zigzagged toward her, his eyes not straying from hers.

She recognized a similar trick to what the archer had done. Pretending to have a bad throw to hit something behind her.

If [Pack Hunter] wasn't including them, she would have dodged both and given Katherine a machete to the back of the neck.

As it was, she dodged out of the way of the one aimed at her center of mass and grabbed the second machete by the blade with her right hand, trusting the thick plates to withstand what looked like an ordinary blade before twisting it and slamming the handle into her knee to break it, something she was surprised actually worked, even if just barely.

Judging by how the faint sense of mana she could feel inside the weapon abruptly vanished, she had been right in her assumption. He could only move the weapons because of some kind of enchantment, otherwise he would be throwing and returning all manner of other weapons and debris strewn about the floor.

He recalled the other one, and lunged low as she tossed the broken blade in her hand aside.

Despite his entrance, he liked having contact with the ground. Everyone did when moving at such speeds. To deny him that, she activated the trap, one repulsion field slamming sheer force into his stomach with just enough power to get his bottom half off the floor, and she whipped her tail at the back of his head, snapping her right arm toward him with her spin.

His right hand got in the way of her tail, breaking the bones within with a series of sharp cracks, and he rolled with the momentum and sudden change with shocking ease, tucking himself into a tight roll that placed nothing vital in her strike path.

She didn't need something vital.

She reached for his foot instead of her intended punch target, which was now awkwardly far, and narrowly avoided a lightning-fast kick to her head. She tried to grab his leg, and he hit the floor with his other foot to spin like a top and flip himself to his feet, dodging her.

She could probably overpower him by just throwing her entire mana pool at him, but something about how he fought *bothered her.*

He wasn't faster than her.

Yet, as she twisted to hit him with her wing and its claws, backing up, he dodged the strike, tilted his body, and managed to narrowly avoid another whip of her tail by twisting his hip out of the way, damn near managing to cut the tip off with a counterstrike.

She thrust an open hand to him, a simple [Sparkburst] at her palm, watching him intently as she cast another [Haste] spell on herself, throwing a monstrous amount of mana into it.

The world slowed to a complete crawl, and her equally monstrous mana regeneration was the only reason she wasn't dry of mana right now.

She could tune her perception, mentally, to speed up, but she didn't want to at this moment.

She *slowly* cast [Sparkburst] and noted how by the time her hand had actually thrust forward, he was *already* dodging out of the way.

What bothered her about how he fought seemed so simple in hindsight.

He seemed to dodge before she even began to move.

She activated [Psychometric Vision], her slowed perception of time allowing her skill to do its work in technical fast-forward.

Tightness around the eyes suggests mild emotional response. Is feeling muted grief. Expects to die by the end of this fight. Accepts death. Injured right hand. Wishes to kill at least one of the assailants before he dies. Had some attachment to the unnamed archer.

She focused more on his movement, squinting.

Eyes very briefly flick to center of mass and points of tension on Emhreeil's torso, is reading the pull of muscle and the shift of Emhreeil's shoulders and feet to anticipate the sort of movement she will make and preemptively dodges, is making up for lack of speed with skill.

She had expected it to be some kind of short-term precognition. Maybe a skill.

But just pure, raw skill?

It felt like both a slap in the face and a reality check.

With time on her side, she slowly dredged up the last bits of mana in her body and some from her core to make a bunch of explosive repulsion fields at key points along his body.

Then she allowed her perception to speed up.

A push to his knee, another at his weapon, and one at the back of his head, all throwing him out of order as he crumpled three different ways.

Yet still, he was already shifting his weight onto his right foot to roll with his momentum off to the side.

She felt a brief sense of shame, not personal, just a sense that it was such a waste that someone this skilled worked for a gang.

Then she hopped back, took a slight running start, and dashed forward to slam her right fist into his downturned face in a vicious uppercut.

She felt bone crack and fold inward from the force, and her lips formed a grim line as she watched the force of her blow distort his flesh in a clear wave, felt one of his eyes pop like a grape against her knuckle.

She let time flow fast enough to almost be normal, just to save herself the slow-motion look, and winced as he folded backward, the two-way momentum making him spin once in place, legs kicking up high into the air before crumpling down with the rest of him, dead.

She shook her right hand free from all the gore that had accumulated along the scales and fur, unconcerned with the single thug Katherine seemed to be beating to a pulp behind her, the high Perception almost enough to allow her to judge distance and *movements* from sheer hearing.

She stood there and stared at the man's corpse, someone who, if they had the same tools she did, would have absolutely *destroyed her* without a shadow of a doubt. Her eyes flicked to the side where a man with a metal bow might have managed to kill her had she not dodged.

Her hand rose to the small cut she remembered being there, and she frowned when she noticed it was already gone.

She watched the blood slowly crawl across the room on the floor, gathering around her feet in a lazy swirl, as easy and natural to control as breathing air.

She'd come in here expecting . . . something different. Something more like one-sided slaughter.

To some extent, it was, but it had the real potential to *not be*, had she been a little more careless and had [Pack Hunter] not helped her save Kat's hide at least *once*.

Part of her felt like this was what Ghoul's intention was with this fight. Something seemingly easy so she could let herself get arrogant and high off her newfound power, only for one or two seemingly random people to put a slight scrape on that image and remind her not to be stupid in the future.

A dash of humility here where she could afford to make some mistakes, rather than a chance to indulge. She wasn't sure if she should be thankful or angry at him.

She was leaning toward being thankful. Had she gone into a *real* tough fight without learning that lesson, *again*, she'd probably have died or gotten really injured.

Though getting injured had a much less potent kick to it now.

She glanced aside to Katherine who was panting and wiping sweat off her brow.

Katherine had dealt with just as many gangsters as she had, though admittedly, she handled the two most dangerous ones.

And Katherine had that . . . that same sense of discipline and stiff efficiency.

Kat glanced at her, saw her examining gaze, and sent a sense of confusion at her, a mental *What?*

"You know how to fight."

Kat's brows furrowed faintly in puzzlement, staring around at the moaning and groaning bodies around them, those that Kat had been too softhearted to kill.

"You did most of the work by blinding them," Katherine said.

She shook her head. "No, I just . . . I mean that the way you move, the way your feet place themselves, it's . . . the way you move, really. It feels like you know what you're doing even if I'm not sure I can point to why, exactly. You know how to fight. And I . . ." She paused, licked her lips.

She thought back to how she fought.

She fought dirty. She fought with tricks, she used people as shields against their allies, she fought for surprise, and she did her damn best to keep any fair fighting to a minimum. She'd stumbled and missed repeatedly, as well as pretty much freezing at least once, even if only for a moment.

Having fought in mostly close range, as a sort of self-test today, she couldn't say she was enthused about her performance, even if the machete-wielding guy was immensely skilled.

Getting into melees felt inevitable. She was suited for close range and supportive mayhem, which was likely why fighting like this felt so off to her, despite how good it felt, how she could still feel some remaining jitters of adrenaline in her limbs.

Brawling like this was *doable*, but she would have felt so much more comfortable fighting behind the wolf, dashing in and out with quick executions and flashing balls of light in people's faces at critical moments to make any cohesion and resistance crumble.

If *Kat* had the same powers and spells she had, what kind of damage could *she* do?

"I don't know how to fight."

Instead of offering some kind of reassurance or denial, Kat nodded, and she blinked in surprise, lifting her gaze off the wall to stare at her.

"It's—well, I saw the punch. You gave me a boost too, remember? Which, I did *not* know you could do with mere line of sight, so that would have been nice to know beforehand. I assumed it was touch only," Kat commented, shaking her wrist a little as if to loosen it, and continued before Emhreeil could sputter out a defense about how she had been kind of *blind* for a while, so she'd just gotten used to tapping things to boost them.

"Anyway, you don't know how to properly drive force into the target, your hips are stiff, and your stance is either too narrow or too wide whenever I could catch a glimpse of you. You had some moments of brilliance where I think I saw you maneuver yourself between people to use them as shields, and you somehow dodged a few attacks I felt like you had no way of knowing were coming, but I'm not sure if that's experience or because you have skills you haven't told me about. You know, we still haven't sat down and discussed what we can each *do*, as a team. Both you and me, and the wolf," Katherine pointed out, and she opened her mouth to object, only to realize that beyond some off-hand remarks while traveling about her spells, she hadn't actually sat down and asked Kat what her path or even her skills were, or told her everything *she* could do.

"Yeah, that's . . . true. Fair. I'll hound the wolf to sit down and explain his skills to us once we get somewhere quiet, we can have a . . . group planning session. Sorry about the . . . boost thing," she said with a mild chuckle, unsure of how to word it. "Say, can you point to a couple people who haven't been blinded entirely that we could take with us and use for practice? I'll kill the rest. Though you should kill someone too, just to desensitize yourself and not freeze up when it becomes necessary to do it," she added with a falsely mild tone, and grimaced at how the whole sentence just sounded off and manipulative.

Katherine shook her head.

"I can kill. I'd just *really* rather not. You and the wolf can deal with that," Katherine said in a tone that made it clear she didn't intend on arguing about it, and she smiled a little at the assertiveness. Good for her.

The Katherine she knew from before the dungeon would not have said that, not in that tone.

"Also, while practicing with weak strangers might get us some level of progression due to their very real desire to kill or hurt us and escape, I think we'd have more luck just having me train you. I know what I'm doing, as you said." Katherine shrugged, her trench coat bobbing up from the motion.

"I'd like that," she said with a genuine smile, and summoned her dagger. "Now, which ones might be able to actually see us? Could you tie them up?" she asked, jutting her chin at the selection of seven living people they had ended up with.

Katherine took a deep breath and moved forward, pointing to one, and then another. Then she shook her head and brushed past her to make some bindings from the clothes of the corpses, whipping out a plain dagger and sawing at wet cloth.

The smell made her feel like there was a black hole in her stomach, and she idly floated up a tendril of blood to slowly push into her half-open mouth in a sedate sip as she moved up to an unconscious man to slit his throat, once again ignoring the tiny pang of nauseated unease it set off in her gut.

A familiar chuff came from where the doors used to stand, and she turned toward him with a smile, sending a mental prod through their private bond as he licked the blood off his own snout in a sight she found to be oddly cute.

Her message didn't . . . *catch*, for a lack of a better word. She tried again, and it did catch this time, whatever he had been doing to block her being momentarily lowered.

So she began to slowly ask some basic things, about how exactly they were going to find some quiet place to cool off in, while he sent back some strange images and events that made her distinctly *uneasy*.

She could have sworn she'd seen that symbol on the cloak somewhere.

And golems did not *run*, ever. Nor commit suicide, assuming it died from that fall, which it *should*.

With a pensive frown, she set off to kill another coughing form on the floor, doing the grisly work her nature now required and making sure to leave no witnesses.

Besides that golem.

How did a *golem* get all the way up to the third floor? In the middle of it?

Another question to save for later, in case Ghoul somehow had a clue.

She watched the wolf stroll to a corpse and begin eating immediately out of the corner of her eye, not bothering to let her bleed it out, and sighed.

By the time he would be done, she'd have the rest nice and dry, hopefully. She wasn't interested in having to contest food against a greedy wolf. Though she could try to convince him . . .

Maybe next time.

CHAPTER 7

In the end, they decided to stay in the building, at least for a day's rest. They were all tired, to varying degrees.

But it wasn't that long ago that its pack was woken up by "Ghoul," followed by a ritual and a fight, all exhausting in their own ways, so its humans were quite content to play with their catch, alternating from one search it didn't understand or care about to another, unearthing things from the floor, the walls, and from just plain old chests strewn about the place.

Then play-fighting amongst themselves and their captures.

As for itself, after an hour or two of vigorously chewing through a dozen corpses while Emhreeil drained their blood by sitting there and calmly sipping at the floating stream, a thing it was quite annoyed about, it was content and eager to get to work with its changes, so it had walked up to the second half floor of the building and flopped down to rest while the small green human climbed up to the roof to act as overwatch.

The thing it had eaten was apparently called a lungburn fish.

Weird, weird names, as usual.

The fish had a small mountain's worth of *potentially* useful things the wolf could add to its arsenal, but the problem was that it couldn't quite understand a whole lot of its biology. It *could* just blindly copy it, but if it wanted to modify it in depth and experiment, it would probably be best to catch a few more, once it found those streams again.

What it did understand and see, however, was both incredible and daunting.

The process of generating and discharging electricity was about as complex as a human brain. Six different types of tissues with dozens of different proteins and enzymes that are all engaged in chemical reactions, three different organs producing three different substances which were all necessary, and that wasn't to mention the genius way the fish could breathe underwater or use electroreceptors and mechanoreceptors to be able to navigate around predator and prey underwater.

It didn't quite understand the concept or put a word to the emotion, but seeing all of its prey's biology felt awe-inspiring in a way it couldn't quite remember feeling before.

While true understanding eluded it, copying and modifying things a bit was still entirely possible.

It looked at its body's insides and frowned.

There wasn't much room to work with.

So the first thing it did was *make* room.

Its liver was the first to go.

The liver was a fairly useful organ, but it was large, bulky, and without the wolf ever having to worry about poisons that wouldn't, at the very least, explode when meeting open air, and its adaptive mana cells working with its immune system to give it immunity to poisons the more it was exposed to them, *as well* as not having *any* need for bile and stomach acids, it just wasn't needed.

It was the largest solid organ in its body as well.

It removed toxins from the body's blood supply, maintained healthy blood sugar levels, regulated blood clotting, and performed something like a dozen other vital but small functions. It was the only reason it hadn't removed it up until now, but more than half those functions were redundant or replaceable.

The essence drain from having those few useful functions regulated by nothing but [Devourer] was also not much more than simply having to fuel the organ itself, so it didn't really lose much.

After removing the organ for room, it moved the teeth it had pocketed within its insides into the bottom of that empty space.

Progress on having its [Devourer]-infused teeth turned to blades or armor plates was coming along nicely, but slowly. Each had elongated to about two inches of awkwardly shaped murder.

It would have time before it would have to move them again, with this glacial growth.

It removed two of the flamethrower systems it had attached to its tails and inspected the new room it had. Combined with its still-growing body and some of the free space it already had, it wasn't an insignificant little pocket.

It would be enough.

Now to think about what it could do with the fish's biology . . .

A mental catalog of the fish's abilities was made, and the wolf pondered what it wanted the most and how it could fit it into itself.

The fish had a lot of things, all useful.

To start with, it had nerves made of some kind of biological *metal* that was more like rubber, but with the conductivity of iron.

It would not have sounded like much if the wolf didn't know better.

There was always a delay between thought, reaction, and action. The electrical signals had to traverse the complex system of nerves, and that took *time*.

It didn't have numbers, but it was a not-insignificant amount of time that was lost, purely because the travel time for commands to go from its brain to its body and vice versa was so inefficient. Nerves were not great at moving electric signals.

The exact mechanics of electricity far eluded it, but it could understand that the fizzy energy would move a lot easier through some materials than some others.

The fish's nerves were *made* to be carriers for this energy. They would send information a dozen times faster than normal ones, as close to instantaneous as one could reasonably get to.

Normally, this would also open up the issue of the nerves getting a light outside shock and having their user spasm uncontrollably.

The fish's immunity to electricity was, thankfully, entirely biological. It came from a super-complex type of cell that was functionally immune to electricity and came in two forms, the dense hardened sleeve that was tightly wrapped around the nerves to ignore outside influence, and the thin, smaller bundles that were produced by one of its organs and then spread out throughout its bloodstream to latch on to blood cells, growing over them like an insulative shield.

Theoretically, some muscle fibers would still spasm when electricity was directly applied to them by outside forces, and it might feel a faint tingle if some electrified spike hit an artery or something, but it wouldn't travel at *all* beyond the exact fibers getting the shock.

So not *complete* immunity, but close enough for the difference to not matter.

It tried to look into these insulative cells, but their complexity was just . . . too much, and it felt like there were small chunks of information just missing. Its auxiliary brains helped it not get a headache just from looking into them, but it just couldn't quite understand it without zoning out.

It was like trying to decipher a spiraling maze with small, but not-insignificant sections blacked out, except the maze was layered.

It could see enough to understand that it wouldn't likely poison itself by incorporating these cells into itself, however, so it set

[Devourer] to the task of replacing all of its nerve systems with these metal ones, all the way up to the base of its brain.

The second interesting part of its prey's biology was the ability to expel electricity.

Of the three main, unnamed organs associated with its electrical nature, the first was dedicated to making the protective cells that would enter the bloodstream, and was independent.

The second and third organ were both dedicated to making two specific unique cocktails, attached together like lungs along its back. The fish would then just squeeze some muscles along the insides of the lunglike organs, which would release the different cocktails into a central chamber to mix with some mild contractions.

This is where the chain reaction from the two substances meeting would create some form of liquid lightning, like electrically supercharged plasma.

Normally, this should flash cook the little creature, but the organs' innards were lined with *another* separate insulative gel that would harden and puff up when faced with heat, and trap all the heat inside.

All along this chamber, nerves were interspersed from top to bottom, leading out of the branch-like stalks coming out of the lower half of the fish's back, surrounded by muscle and fat, to siphon the electricity out into the waters.

Likely to stun aquatic prey, considering that water was pretty good at transferring electricity, or so it could remember from dipping its paws into electrified puddles.

Strictly speaking, it had no reason to add this part to itself. Electricity was an interesting energy and form of attack to consider, but making it work in open air would be far, far more difficult than in water.

That was unless it considered a simpler method of attack, like launching the plasma out as a liquid. It wasn't sure what would happen if it met open air, but it was curious enough to find out.

The problem was how the entire *structure* of the organ made it impossible to launch out of a pouch or using a flamethrower system, not without burning a giant hole in its body every time it used it.

Instead, it decided to try something more and less inventive.

In the upper part of the free space left behind by its liver, well-hidden behind its ribs, it formed an upsized version of the pair of lungs and ran some tight, wirelike bundles of nerves down the inside of its wrist, until it had a small smattering of needlelike protrusions coming out of its wolfen palms.

If it could get its hands on something, it should theoretically have one more way to murder it.

It briefly considered how painful it would be to have exposed nerves on its palms, then realized that it wouldn't feel any of them because they had no receptiveness.

From simple guesswork, it could assume that it would end up feeling a whole lot more numb than before when its changes were done.

Another pause had it considering the fact that without the water around the nerves to cool them down, they would . . . probably liquefy from the heat? Electricity was warm.

And while the film of insulative cells around the nerves would keep them from losing their shape or capabilities, and hopefully from burning through into its flesh, if they were exposed to open air to transfer the electricity, the wolf would surely end up with melted nerves bleeding out of its palms after one or two shocks.

Unless the metal was somehow different, which was entirely possible because the wolf simply didn't *know* what its properties were. It was treating it like a rubbery sort of iron, for the moment.

Still, even if it had melted neural roots on its palms, it was nothing even a few seconds of work wouldn't fix during its sleep, but not great if it had to go without sleeping for an extended period of time.

There was some worry of a shock penetrating the insulative layer and zapping its entire nervous system, but the fish's biology had seemed to account for that as well with multiple stopgap measures in the form of insulative cell bundles sitting near a lot of the roots of the fish's body, ready to form barricades against a returning force that would exceed some kind of capacity.

If it cared to be honest with itself, it had no idea how that worked, or if it did work at all, but it would see how it worked out. This was more of an experiment than anything, to see what this would be like.

Moving on, it added the smaller of the three organs that would flood its organs with insulation cells, low in its gut, using the freed-up space from the flamethrowers it removed.

It moved on to the other things the fish had to offer.

After a brief consideration of gills, it discarded the idea as unnecessary and space-taking, and turned to a final alteration it wished to make.

It wanted to see what it could do with *biological metal.*

The mere notion was so bizarre that it was baffling.

It hadn't tried to eat metal yet, or form it, because not only did it have no idea how—and neither did [Devourer]—it just didn't register as a biological material.

Yet the fish had it.

How did it form?

Best idea it could come up with was a complex mess of iron bacteria in the water, likely from running through a seemingly endless nest utterly *covered* in it, which the fish somehow consumed, absorbed, or had some kind of symbiotic relationship with in the past, interacting with various chemical reactions to turn into *actual* iron as it grew older, and somehow replaced its nerves with that.

It just didn't know how.

But the important thing was that the metal registered as biological in [Devourer], so despite its *absurd* cost, it could make it now, even if it had no idea how it worked.

The problem was that it had no idea what to use it for.

It was too soft and yielding to be armor, too heavy as well, and its properties were not all that similar to actual metal. It didn't hold its position, it wasn't rigid, it wasn't tough.

The spider leg it had consumed didn't give it much of anything. It gave the wolf a possible name for the creature, and a rough idea of how large it was, but its biology was . . . almost blank. Even the chitin seemed like a blank slate that was biological enough to be registered by the skill but not enough for there to be any genetic data in it. It was bizarre, like trying to look into its own teeth.

Without any other ideas forthcoming, it decided to confirm its changes, update its "template" for regeneration purposes, and sleep away the . . .

Singular hour they would take to happen.

Singular hour they would take to happen.

[Devourer] seemed to be speeding up constantly.

It ended up sleeping for six hours and woke up feeling like it should have slept a dozen more, stumbling to its feet and stretching with a yawn.

Its brain slowly came up to speed, and it raised a vaguely humanoid arm, squinting at its palm.

It couldn't actually see the nerves, even if it knew that it had covered its palm in them.

Clenching and unclenching a fist, it tilted its head.

The sensation was strange. It felt like half the feeling in its body, in its body's insides, just vanished.

It could still feel pain, because its body's tissues were still loaded with pain receptors, and the signals would still travel, better than ever now, but it was just . . . like it didn't have insides.

It curled its elbow, twisted its spine, and felt like something was *missing*.

Very odd, but it could get used to it, especially with how much more responsive its body felt. It felt like when Emhreeil would give it a huge boost, body and mind becoming one single thing without intermediary messages to slow things down.

It glanced down at the floor, and after a brief moment of consideration, scratched out a small clump of metal.

One human arm held the nugget up for scrutiny, and its front arms snipped off the jagged edges with phasing claws, rounding it to something that would not tear at its throat as it went down.

A passing consideration to try and sculpt it into some shape or object rose, but it pushed it away.

With a hesitant stare, it opened its jaws and tossed the nugget into its throat.

It swallowed and waited.

After ten seconds, it realized that it didn't actually know if it had vanished into [Devourer] or not. It could use the skill while awake now, but nothing popped up, and its stomach didn't feel any heavier. It could try to dive into its biology and check manually, but it preferred to not have a crippling headache immediately after waking up.

It left that curious interaction for the next time it slept.

It padded over to the edge as it unfurled its antennae, finding Emhreeil to be on guard duty now, lounging on the slanted roof, while Katherine and Scruffy were clanking away in little pots.

It tilted its head down and stared with puzzlement as they slurped an oddly colored liquid.

Oh. Eating.

They were eating.

It forgot they were actually still humans, mentally, for a moment. It had been half expecting them to just be eating raw flesh like normal creatures.

It glanced at the corner, staring curiously at the single dried-out husk of a corpse and the unconscious second captive, annoyed that it had missed a fight. Or a kill.

It really, really, really, *really* wanted to kill something.

There was no real reason it could pinpoint, it just wanted to kill something. Additionally, it still felt hungry, even after eating twelve people, and if it wanted to make more of those braided plant strips for armor, it would have to find more essence.

After another moment of curiously watching its packmates sipping at some watery soup over a makeshift flame, it raised its right hand and curiously flexed that little bundle of muscle near where its liver used to be.

Instantly, searing *heat* bloomed in its chest, and its eyes widened in panic as it jerked its head down, twisting to stare at its rib cage.

The heat quickly retreated as something within shifted, likely the gel hardening, and the boiling heat quickly receded to a pleasant warmth, like a muted furnace in its chest.

There was an indigo glow behind its right-side bottom ribs, vaguely outlining the bones, likely the plasma glowing through the gel.

If it was actually plasma. It couldn't honestly tell, or understand it. Since the organ was going to digest the liquid after it had expended all of its energy, it assumed that it . . . was?

It was times like this that made it wish it hadn't removed the symbol in its skull, or at least that it hadn't been some kind of mental control trigger so that the wolf could have kept it. It would have been quite content to have a library of knowledge occasionally tossing it information when it asked, if it hadn't been for that.

It stared at the odd purple-blue glow, finding it oddly pretty.

The fact it glowed through gel, flesh, plant-armor plate, then its ribs, and finally its fur, did not escape notice. It would likely burn out its retinas in open air if it was *that* bright.

It could feel the buzz, the nerves embedded in the gel and smeared across the entire organ somehow not liquefying from the intense heat.

Like twitching a muscle, it activated the nerves.

With a ridiculously loud *buzzing, crackling,* snarl sort of sound, arcs of blue light danced around its palms, and it stared at them in wide-eyed wonder for a moment before cutting them off, ignoring the cry of surprise from Katherine below.

It sniffed and smelled smoke.

It supported itself on its secondary arms as it lifted its left hand off the ground and stared at the pockmarked slate of steel, burned and still glowing orange in some spots.

Sitting on its haunches, it *pulled* but didn't let the pressure release, slowly draining the liquid, tilting its head down to stare at the dimming orb of light in its chest.

It felt Emhreeil put her head through the roof hatch to stare, but ignored her.

Its ears flattened in irritation when it realized that it didn't have fine enough control to draw energy into only one arm, deciding to rectify that as soon as possible, even if it meant only one arm could use its new trick.

Two weak shocks were not even close to being as useful as one big, strong one.

Finally, it released the buzzing trill it could feel in its arms, ignoring the oddly pleasant sensation of its hairs standing on end, and yipped in surprise when a white arc shot out of its palms with a thunderclap, its aftershocks dancing along the railing and the floor.

Sounds of surprise from Katherine and Scruffy reached its ears a moment later.

Its left paw slipped through said floor, and it hurriedly pulled it up through the molten hole it had made, staring wide-eyed at it, tails rigid and ears straight in surprise.

The liquid in its chest cooled down with absurd speed, barely even warmer than the rest of its insides, and it felt the organ shift back into a less rigid state.

A prod at its mind, and after another moment of pleasantly surprised incredulity, it lowered its mental walls as Emhreeil hung upside down from the roof hatch like one of those weird squeaky flying things that hung around the spires by the burning river, baring her teeth at it.

Weird human.

The next prod took almost half a minute to arrive as Katherine kept grumbling below, slurping at her little pot.

The slowness of communication was *grating*, but it endured because it had no other choice.

When Emhreeil's message did arrive, it immediately disregarded it.

Why would it need a human sound to address itself? It was itself.

After it put that thought forward and experimentally began rolling and slashing at nothing to test how in *tune* and *faster* its body felt, Emhreeil sent a reply another half minute later.

It slowed, tilting its head.

It made sense, in a way. They had to address it somehow, and their whole communication and thought system worked on sounds. Unique sounds, but sounds all the same.

As it thought, Emhreeil experimentally poked the ladder, and after no shock met her, she slowly slithered down the ladder, closing the hatch behind her, ragged cloaks and ill-fitting coverings softly rustling as she moved down to its level.

"Hey, Kat, time to have a chat?" Emhreeil asked over the railing.

"Okay," Katherine replied.

It sent back what it wanted to be called.

Emhreeil turned to it, wide-eyed, before bursting into another happy fit of yipping, stumbling past it.

It tilted its head.

What was so amusing or happiness-inducing about "the hungry wolf that will always hunt"?

Emhreeil clicked her fingers as she drew close, likely to draw attention to her hands, still making odd snickering sounds, and after some pantomiming, it understood her intent and followed her down the stairs.

Then it squeezed past her because something about following rubbed it the wrong way. It would lead.

Scruffy slid aside as it neared and hovered next to the fire, and Emhreeil walked past to sit by the waning little fire of clothes and broken boxes, patting the space next to her.

Not having anything else to do besides kill the man in the corner, which could wait, it trotted up to the fire, and sat on its haunches, pushing the same unique sound for itself back at her with a questioning lilt.

It took a morose two minutes for her to reply, during which it decided to just curl up on the floor and watch the pretty fire.

Her reply was a bit odd.

Humans apparently liked to summarize their unique "name" sounds into a single "word," a small but continuous sound.

Which was true, as far as it could tell. Scruffy, Katherine, Emhreeil.

Plenty of humans had called it a lot of things, all one word. "Mutt," "fleabag," "gutter scum," even "doggie" from some of the nicer ones.

So it began to ask her what those meant, trying to bring back muffled memories of gruff voices, distorted and hazy, and pushing them to her.

"Mutt" was apparently a dog with bad breeding.

Which . . . it could see why they might have made that assumption. It had been an inch away from death back then, for a while.

"Fleabag" was apparently a reference to having insects or ticks in its fur and a generally weak appearance.

Frankly, it liked that one.

Mostly because of how it reminded the wolf of where it had started and where it was now. Every time someone would say it, it could remember where it had been, a bag of bones covered in parasitic insects, dying, and compare it to itself now, several dozen times heavier, bigger than any other dog it had seen so far, and able to slaughter humans by the dozens if it wanted to. An extra bit of push to grow even stronger, and a reminder of how pathetic it once had been.

In the middle of Emhreeil trying to figure out how to word the next human sound and translate it, it pushed back its chosen name sound.

It felt both humans go still and turn to stare at it.

It cracked open an eye on its hip, examining the awed expressions on their faces.

"It—he wants to be called *Fleabag*," Katherine murmured, voice strange. "The wolf wants its name to be *Fleabag*."

"I—I mean i-it's quite—quite fuhahaah!" Emhreeil burst out into uproarious, joyous yipping, collapsing on her back, and it rose back up on its haunches, jutting its chest out in pride with a low, wavering howl, trying to mimic the hiccup-sounding noise.

It didn't succeed, but Katherine started making the yipping sound too, a more subdued version, so they were both very happy with its chosen name as well.

Not that it cared, it would have chosen it even if they found it annoying, but it was an added benefit.

"Fleabag."

It had meaning and depth, and if the humans all understood the sound the same way, it was *incredibly* deceptive. They'd be surprised if they came to kill a fleabag and met the wolf, underprepared and entirely unsure of what it could do. If name sounds were a descriptor for someone, then its deception would be staggeringly effective. Easy pickings.

Emhreeil extended a weird wing arm around it and retracted it, her hand curled around its side as she pulled it in, breaking its pose.

It mock-growled and pounced.

It wanted to kill something right now, but pretending to do so would have to do for a bit.

Emhreeil rolled around the floor with it, her various appendages fighting to keep its jaws and tongue away from her face.

"Em, you're going to ruin your clothes again."

"You tr-ow! You try telling him to stop after laughing at him!" Emhreeil yelped back, and it redoubled its efforts, slithering around her grapples to wrap its arms around her neck and place its fangs on her skull, blunted, tails thwapping the floor.

Emhreeil went limp with a huff.

It won.

It twisted around her again before sprawling out on top of her, four arms widely limp on the floor beside them, content with its victory, yawning widely and ignoring her groan.

A lull came by as it settled on the mildly complaining human, until another message was pushed to its mind, almost a full ten minutes later as Katherine washed out the metal bits she used to cook her food off to the side.

It was . . . complex.

The other two humans turned to look at it as they parsed through the same. Its eyes glazed over as it tried to decipher the messy bundle.

It was a mess of clarifications, requests, and half-muddled explanations. In short, it made no sense. It couldn't even tell if the random segments were connected to each other.

It sent back confusion before deciding to ask its own questions, now that it finally, *finally* had the opportunity to.

Indecision kicked in as it sent the mental equivalent of a reprimanding growl through the bond with a shove for *quiet*, and the humans thankfully obeyed.

It remembered having *hundreds* of questions, with only more growing, but gradually, as it crawled through miles of tunnels and fought day after day to get even a peek of a better life, they just gradually faded, leaving behind a vaguely confused mess.

Five minutes passed before it asked the simplest and most important one.

In a succinct manner, it simply asked what was outside the nest, if there even *was* an outside, if it encompassed the whole world. Then it rolled that question along with a clarification about what the sky was, because from the vague ideas the rune in its skull had given it, it hadn't actually seen it yet.

Katherine's head jerked up to stare at it, wide-eyed, and Emhreeil did the same.

It turned its head and opened an eye on its hip to stare back at both, mildly confused.

When Emhreeil's reply came back, it was laden with pity and sympathy that made its mood sour instantly, but that was quickly forgotten as images came in.

It got off of her, taking a step back and to the side, eyes unfocused, before it closed them entirely, to focus on the images.

The nest had an end and a defined size, which was *monstrously huge* but still quantifiable. Which was interesting and relieving, but the second question's answer moved the wolf far more.

The sky was . . .

Nonsensical.

Beautiful.

It had never seen something so bright in its entire life. It had never seen that much clear, endless *blue*. It was so uniform and perfect and smooth it couldn't help but wonder what it might feel like to rub or lick. Would it feel as smooth as glass?

The fuzzy white banks of mist, clouds, were even more beautiful, the contrast and breaks in the blue somehow making it even more impressive.

It asked where the sky was, where it could find it, if it could touch it, because for a supposed void, the sky looked quite solid.

The muted feelings of pity and some kind of disbelieving realization attached to the following replies once again grew, grating all the same.

Those feelings did not compare to the reply it got from the two big humans, too drowned in another nonsensical explanation to process the mixture, images, and concepts slowly, slowly rolling in.

Scruffy said she'd never seen the sky either, and it felt an even bigger sense of kinship with the odd, useless little human.

A hand landed on its head, and it sat on its haunches, allowing Emhreeil to pet it as it lost itself in images it could hardly believe.

It asked where all the light came from, learned about the sun and the moon, about how both them and the sky they were in were both completely and utterly unreachable, meant to be admired from afar.

It asked how big the outside world was, only to learn that this human nest was little more than a small *pebble* within a nigh-infinite world.

It couldn't even fathom or comprehend that size.

It asked why humans bared their teeth, why their body language made no sense, and found the rough gist of it explained, a backwards thought process with too much nuance for the wolf to ever be able to grasp or truly understand.

It learned the confusing action of "laughing," the happy yipping its pack did. It learned of how humans laughed for a dozen different reasons, all dependent on *tone*, tiny expressions, and a myriad more confusing conditions that it decided were too much trouble to try and interpret.

Eventually, it sat back down and stared at the smoldering embers of the fire, the only faint light left behind, Katherine lying on her side in a similar pose on the opposite end with Emhreeil curled up to its back for warmth.

And it continued asking, receiving endless answers to its endless questions, images, and sensations.

It saw *trees*. It saw flowers and leaves and green grass. A dusty expanse of sand interspersed with mountains, sent from Katherine, tainted with resentment and pain.

It learned what years and hours and months and seasons were, things so irrelevant to the wolf but so *interesting*. It learned about music and why the humans listened to it. It learned what the sea was.

It took three hours for them to ask a simple question that made several dozen things click.

Did it know what it was?

Of course it did, and it said so.

Then they explained why its existence was apparently seen as a scourge upon the world itself by most if not all humans, how some kind of supposedly perfect human they called the Oracle had declared that not a single wolf existed whose heart beat or whose body drew breath, how it was the first in almost a thousand *years* to be heard of.

Emhreeil tried to use that as a springboard to explain why it should stop eating random humans and only target certain groups to avoid drawing more ire, and it half listened, a bit stunned and struggling to comprehend that time frame.

Moreover, it was difficult to comprehend that besides these three humans and Ghoul's pack, the entire world was an enemy to it, and it specifically.

It was difficult to not feel that urgency again, that urge to grow stronger and stronger, because it had once thought that maybe if it grew strong enough, it could live a nice, exciting, fulfilling life.

If things were how its pack had described it, that would never come until it was invincible and undeniable. The world would be its enemy, until either one or the other gave up.

And the one thing the wolf didn't do, ever, was give up.

By the time Emhreeil had gotten to the question she initially wanted to ask—what its skills and abilities were—it was too mentally exhausted to care to answer and so were they, having spent five hours in a constant back-and-forth with its pack, getting to know them by the taint and taste of their thoughts, their experiences.

Eventually, it had enough and simply shoved back the notion of *sleep* to its pack, forcibly dragged Katherine over to join the sleeping pile, then extricated itself and grabbed a hold of their male captive, dragging him out the back of the building as he stirred awake.

A snack to gnaw on while it kept a lookout.

They'd gotten their respite, their day of rest.

Tomorrow, they'd cross the bridge if it could still hold them, and keep descending.

As it snapped the slowly awakening human's neck and pulped his neck in its jaws, using the tentacle in its back to drag the corpse along and mark a circle of blood around the building as it paced and ate, it lost itself in thought, occasionally tilting its head up to stare at the snaking fog.

It wondered how dangerous it would be to try and get to the surface of the human nest and see the sky.

It wondered how plausible it was that it might be able to clear the nest of humans entirely. How strong it might get from that.

Because despite what Emhreeil said, it didn't believe it would be ignored so long as it just targeted the *right* groups of humans, not if what she said about how the wolf and its long-lost kin were seen was true.

It would just have to wait and see.

CHAPTER 8

Eventually, it swapped shifts with its now vaguely wolf-smelling, winged companion, allowing her to prowl about the building as it went to rest.

During that short rest, it routed the metal discharge nerves to mainly go through its right arm, in order to concentrate the shock in one limb, and checked for what had happened to that metal nugget it ate.

The answer was nothing. It had just disappeared, and there was nothing new in [Devourer]. Which was incredibly disappointing, but it wasn't expectant enough to feel sad about it.

After that, they woke up, and it had to impatiently pace around as they gathered up the things the people they killed were guarding, digging them out of stashes and nooks.

Mainly syringes filled with odd liquids, weird-smelling powders, and a bunch of fiddly bits of metal it didn't care much about, until Emhreeil explained that they would explode if the ropelike thing on top was lit on fire.

There may or may not have been a slight panic when the wolf immediately set to testing that and Emhreeil had to scramble for the "bomb" and toss it out into the smog clouds below, followed by a bit of mutual annoyance at each other, her toward the wolf for "putting them in danger," and it was annoyed at her for not letting it see the explosion to understand how useful they were.

Because they were large and bulky, mostly. If they had to cross terrain, the wolf was still by far the best climber, so it would likely be the one carrying a bunch of dust-filled metal balls, in that case. If they weren't all that powerful, there was no point in bringing them.

Also, explosions were fun, and they were leaving anyway.

Still, after a bit more hurried packing and some nice scratches from Scruffy, they set out.

As they crossed the bridge, the humans fumbled their way through trying to explain what they were capable of, both to each other and to the wolf, and vice versa.

Katherine apparently had a Path suited toward guarding people. "Guardian," in human sounds.

The skills she shared were not exactly impressive, however, in the wolf's opinion. Mostly to do with melee combat, and one skill that had to do with awareness. "Vigilance" in human sounds. Some kind of meditative trance where her attention would be laser-focused on watching out for danger, rendering her unable to process words or feel much of anything, some kind of automatic state that, according to the feelings she sent through, felt like a particularly vivid dream of sorts.

That was the sole skill she had that made the wolf feel impressed.

It was a bit redundant with its own senses, what with being able to sense with relative ease for about five hundred feet in all directions, even if the sensations and their detail varied on materials and distances, but extra ways to keep safe were always nice.

Scruffy simply gave an impression of a Path that had to do with fiddling with machinery and using little useless bits and parts to make something that could be useful.

Nothing impressive but very interesting.

When it was time for Emhreeil to explain, she had a lot of skills that were both very impressive and very annoying to understand.

She had some kind of . . . vision that could learn things just by staring at stuff. As far as it could tell, it was nothing too crazy, but there was something of a half lie in the thought. Additionally, the notion that she could just stare at the wolf and learn things made it intensely uncomfortable.

It was activatable, apparently, and overusing it seemed to give her a slight headache, so it let the point go as she further explained her skillset.

One part that stood out was that first, her "haste" skill could be activated through line of sight. Which meant that if she had the mana to burn, she could speed up Katherine enough to keep up with them, even if that meant less speed would be given to the wolf and Emhreeil.

The second was that she would progressively get stronger just by drinking blood, but that also depended on how . . . valuable the blood was . . . ? How pure it was?

It was a fairly strange concept to grasp, especially with how terribly Emhreeil packaged it, but it got the gist eventually, and it could almost taste the hunger in Emhreeil's thoughts, so it eventually just raked its claws through its own shoulder and grunted at her to float the blood to herself to drink.

Her returning glee was filled with a euphoria that made it a tad envious, truthfully, but if it made her stronger, it could deal with the slight annoyance of having a cupful or two of its blood drained every day.

It asked a lot of things as they kept moving. As much as it could think of, really.

They stalked through the housing complex's outside ring, some kind of giant tubelike protrusion of metal cubicles the humans used for shelter, usually some kind of massive structure glued onto any place that didn't have available metal plates to shove homes onto, and had to stop a few times.

The wolf's fault, this time. It wanted to start gathering the light crystals, so it would occasionally send a "stop" order to its pack as it skulked about under a neighboring platform or wiggled its body through some heating pipes to steal a couple, before presenting them to Katherine to put in her backpack.

The humans made an odd snickering sound, quiet and brief, when it explained that it wanted to make a giant pile of the stuff and sleep on it, and it decided not to wonder what the reason they were laughing was as they continued, muttering something about "dogs and dragons."

The grated metal beneath their feet slowly swerved to the left, against a gargantuan wall covered in white letters and spinning red lights, while to their right, spires wrapped in rings spewed flames out into the open air, the scent of burnt metal mixing with the humid air for a quite unpleasant atmosphere.

The path left the housing complex behind, before switching to a big trail of zigzag paths, moving down a colossal wall flanked by gears and pipes.

They continued.

It asked questions about the wider human nest.

Emhreeil and Katherine were both very knowledgeable about the place, both the inside and the flat outside surface.

The outside surface looked almost alien to the wolf, blurry as the images they sent it were, but it was also beautiful. It wanted to go there eventually.

It also learned that the entire place was only four absurdly large floors; they were simply subdivided by countless metal plates upholding all the housing and factories. The place by the burning rivers was apparently the fourth floor, which was interesting enough, and that explained some idle background questions it had held for a while now.

It asked more about who Emhreeil thought it shouldn't eat, and eventually sent back a sense of derision and disagreement.

It understood not eating the weak humans unrelated to the groups chasing after them. It even agreed, mostly, because killing weak humans wasn't really a hunt or a challenge anymore, and it doubted it would level up by hunting useless humans. Unless it was in need of essence or they were being inconvenient, it had no reason to go for them.

For that reason, it could agree with eating the humans wearing certain garments, those who smelled of poorly scrubbed blood, days or weeks old, who smelled of caustic but sweet substances.

The second part she added on, it didn't agree with.

Creatures tended to be protective of their young, so it understood why both Emhreeil and Katherine seemed to get a little squirmy when it blatantly explained that it had no compunctions about eating human pups if it was convenient, but it wasn't willing to budge on some things.

What it ate was one of those things it refused to negotiate on. If it wanted to eat something, it would eat it, end of story. It only agreed to hunt specific groups so long as it was convenient.

It would have been more agreeable to limit itself to hunting only certain groups, had Emhreeil not explained how humans viewed it and its kind. If they hated it so much, if they were so fervent in their previous extermination of its kind, it had no doubt that they would come for its head the moment they knew it existed.

Though they seemed to be more focused on killing and hunting each other at the moment.

They eventually moved on to other topics as they stalked into some kind of industrial lift.

One conversation was a debate on what to do with the various people Ghoul had recommended they see.

One was apparently a group specializing in gaining information and trading it for the metal coin things, another was apparently a very discreet maker of human coverings, another was a weaponsmith, making swords and such, and there were a few other odd people and instructions to do with if they ever needed things like restraints or knowledge of hidden passages into the tunnels below the nest.

That last bit was of particular interest.

Because it needed something to go and kill, but the strong humans were usually tied to one group or another, and it didn't want to broadcast their location too much by going after those. The sewers weren't an option either.

Fighting a metal construct sounded like just the right amount of challenge needed to move forward without getting mangled again. Hopefully.

Since there was even more space below the human nest, nearly all of which had been supposedly blocked off because of the metal constructs that came out from below, it was also a very new place. It wanted to see it.

Despite that, it was very, very interested in general nest information, almost more than the prospect of a place where it could fight one of these golem things, so that was its first pick of a stop for the pack, even if it couldn't exactly be involved.

The "Fox Den." Some kind of cryptic group of people who gave information in exchange for coins.

When it asked what those sounds meant, it was told of what foxes were.

Its opinion soured slightly, but it still wanted to know things. It was so used to just rolling with things as they came, the opportunity to know what was happening around it and why, it was too much to pass up.

Even if foxes were ugly, ugly things with a strange snout and an annoying grin and way too much fur, and apparently they sounded really squeaky and weird.

That eventually, very slowly, rolled into a conversation about supplies, because humans.

They needed so many things.

Katherine needed food and clean water; Emhreeil needed proper clothes for some reason, as if the blanket she was using as a covering wasn't good enough; all three of its humans both wanted to wash up and for some reason refused to let the wolf just lick them clean like normal creatures; and they didn't accept its proposition of clawing a water pipe open for them to do their business.

Frustrating creatures.

Scruffy just wanted something to fiddle with and something that fit the pack's dark colors more. Her dirty coverings were quite light-colored and thus quite dirty by now.

It was generally a bit miffed about it all, but it accepted it as just another inconvenience to do with having human packmates.

Humans were very high maintenance, even if Emhreeil had gotten better about it.

Eventually, Katherine sent thoughts of how humans liked information too, and tended to talk a lot about current happenings, even making giant bunches of papers covered in symbols it found worryingly familiar for the purpose of sharing information.

Symbols they could somehow make sense of. Directly.

It had no idea how they made sense of the weird squiggles they claimed the papers were covered in, especially when they were not sleeping, but the realization that those symbols were the same as the ones in its head led to a very long conversation about what the System was, how it worked, and how humans most definitely had not made it.

As with many things, the stilted, snail-paced conversation actually formed more questions than answers.

For starters, it seemed like the symbols worked on a loose set of principles to do with one's destiny or chosen Path. Activities that had to do with their Path were augmented to be more potent. A fire flinger human had flames that hurt more than someone who had a different Path.

That made the wolf question what [Hound of The Keeper] did as a Path. What did it augment or assist the wolf with? Using the dark stuff?

It wasn't like the symbols told it details whenever it focused on its Path. There was some notion of a claim being put on the wolf, which was mildly grating as usual, and something to do with death.

Not exactly descriptive.

Both humans had paused and stared at it when it asked what its Path might do, which led to Scruffy pausing too, and then the wolf stopped and stared back at them, confused.

That's how they ended up awkwardly staring at each other on a walkway hanging over miles of pipes and flashing lights.

It sent a question; they asked for clarification.

It gave them what they asked for, even putting an image of the symbols forward.

Then the humans stopped using thoughts and began quickly gibbering to each other again, which a quick snarl fixed.

After another few dozen seconds, there was a question of how it got its Path.

It sent them its memories.

The humans were quiet after that, acting strange. Not tense, just . . . dazed? Lost? Fearful?

Understandable reactions to that huge black thing.

They gibbered to each other as they slowly resumed their journey, but it was stilted and with an air of confusion, so it wasn't too interested in chastising them for it.

Besides, the topic of their confused gibberish was obvious. Nothing it didn't know there.

From there, it learned what it had been suspecting already.

The symbols worked on a system based on struggle, effort, and most of all, intent. If it went and shocked itself for no other reason than to increase its [Lightning Resistance] for example, the skill's level-ups would be far slower than if it was being shocked in battle. Which made sense. If continuously casting [Echoes of Oblivion] in its sleep for hours on end gave it a half dozen levels, it could imagine how casting the same skill while in an actual fight for the same amount of time would likely result in far more progress.

The intent of the symbols seemed to be for the creatures using it to act like they weren't aware of it, or at least not consider it when committing actions. Or perhaps some kind of balancing action between trying to increase levels but not spending one's entire day on such things?

Supposedly. Not even the humans were completely sure. Emhreeil claimed it was almost random, while Katherine disagreed quite heavily.

From there, they moved on to less monumental questions.

It was frankly quite relaxing, to just walk and communicate with its pack, not terribly worried about much, if anything.

After moving across space in impossible ways, it really doubted they were still being traced. And that building their prey had been huddling in was pretty isolated.

So it listened in on what the humans were planning to do, idly marveling at the impossible proportions of the human nest around them while the platform slowly inched downwards on the backs of massive spinning gears, pipes twenty feet wide rumbling with gasses to either side.

There was a bunch of machinery behind the wall the platform was jammed up against, so it could only assume this was one of those colossal factories the humans somehow built.

Eventually, the humans settled on some course of action that wasn't terribly dangerous.

Katherine planned to go ask around, buy a few of those "newspaper" things, sell a lot of their baggage, buy some decent supplies, then try to find somewhere where they could all take a bath sans the wolf and change their clothes.

It was curious about the notion of bathing with warm water but found no need to try and insert itself into that.

It wanted to start working on a proper sanctuary, of a sort. Not a nest, exactly, that didn't appeal too much, but something like a main hiding spot within whatever it decided would be its future territory.

It was leaning toward the burning rivers, the fourth floor.

It was a lot more inconvenient for its pack to get and wander around there, but way too safe to settle for anything less. They'd just have to train their [Poison Resistance] or suck it up. Maybe when it was strong enough to flaunt its presence, it could go to the third floor.

Eventually, the platform broke through the smog cloud, and a quiet expanse of warehouses and empty buildings stretched out below them.

It lightly leaned over the railing, head tilting.

It was . . . highly unusual for a place in the human nest to be this empty. Not anywhere but the fourth floor, at least.

A mile of buildings and towers with stairs and walkways in between, all eerily silent.

"The Beaumonts own this sub-district. It's for their workers. Where is everyone?" Katherine asked as she stood beside the wolf, and it let out a low, distracted growl, a wordless request as its head swerved around.

It didn't care for most of the information Katherine sent back almost a full minute later, but it understood that this place wasn't usually this empty.

The platform eventually stopped, the buildings swallowing the world around them like a wired, spiked wreath, a wide cobblestone road stretching out before them.

It took point, antennae flaring as it trotted forward at speed, the humans rushing to follow.

There were still people around. It could feel them patrolling the streets in pairs, sparse, while other pairs combed through rooms in distant buildings, gathering things and throwing them into crates.

It could also feel a lot more activity somewhere to the left, along the edge of its senses. Dozens of people, moving and weaving between giant boxes and chests.

They continued forward, until a pair of humans were close enough to be a concern.

It growled its pack to a stop and sent them a "stay" command as it turned to the glass-covered building to its left and began to race up its walls, claws ripping through pipes and exhausts.

The roof for this building was far too tall, so it turned to the side and shuffled sideways around the corner, until it could get a clear look at the people patrolling.

They wore a vaguely familiar uniform. Hadn't it eaten someone who wore that before?

It thought for a moment, thin shadows shifting around its eyes and claws.

As the humans walked beneath it, closer and closer to the main road, it let go of the pipe it was holding on to, allowing gravity to take it down the fifty feet separating them all.

It wasn't even close to a fight.

One of the guards stopped and whipped his head up, having somehow noticed it, but all that did was make the wolf snap its neck backward with its legs as it fell.

Its tails snapped shut around the second human, one locking his arms to his sides and one pressing down on his neck with careful gentleness, enough squeeze to not let him scream if he wished.

Then it bent down to bite onto the dead human's neck and cheerily trotted out of the alley back to its pack.

Katherine heaved an explosive sigh when she saw it and its cargo, rubbing at her face, and Emhreeil simply stared, one ear flopping to the side as she tilted her head.

Her body language had gotten much easier to read since her upgrade.

The live human continued to wriggle and buck as it dragged him along.

With the telepathic link no longer strained by range, it directed a simple order to its pack.

It would be difficult to put it into succinct words, but the gist of it was an order for them to get the man to tell them what he knew while it ate.

Emhreeil sighed, then turned around a couple times, scouting for something.

It clamped its jaws tight and twisted a bit, pulling the head off the corpse, ignoring the second human's choking wriggles as it began to eat.

Katherine grimaced, looking away.

Emhreeil sent a message, and it raised its head to look at the proffered "shop" just down the street, carved metal and small glass windows revealing empty shelves.

It looked private enough, so it sent back acknowledgment and unwrapped one of its secondary arms to grab onto the human corpse's clothes, the other unwinding to hold the detached head by its hair so the wolf could both move and eat at the same time.

Then it calmly padded forth, dragging the two red-wreathed humans, alive and not, with it.

It could have eaten four humans by the time its pack was done interrogating the hissy man in the red uniform, and its patience was fraying.

Eventually, having gotten most of what they wanted, it decided to just use the tentacle blade to decapitate him, his hissy chattering getting on its nerves. Emhreeil startled in the middle of talking to him, and Katherine jerked in surprise, hand flying to her sword before aborting the motion.

"What the fuck?" Emhreeil hissed, arms half raised in alarm and face speckled with blood. It growled, sending back images of the fourth floor and impatience.

Scruffy dipped a finger into the blood, then brought it to her mouth, only to scrunch her nose up in distaste with a small "eugh" sound, sticking her tongue out.

Humans had no taste.

With a sigh, Emhreeil rose up from her kneeling position, kicked the head aside toward the wolf, and began looting the corpse as the wolf quickly cut the arms off, Emhreeil's weird blood-control ability yanking the blood out of the wounds into a bizarre but beautiful spiral that languidly filed into her mouth.

Its secondary right arm took the arms it cut off, tucking in the limbs against its ribs, and its left secondary arm once again grabbed the head.

Snacks to chew on while they walked.

Eventually, they came across a giant line of barricades accompanied by more of the red-wearing humans, blocking the only bridge leading to a wider area than the couple-mile-wide bubble of buildings they'd left behind.

Emhreeil could apparently use her right arm to dig into steel with contemptuous ease, something that felt eerily similar to its own claws but not quite as potent, but her other claws were not quite that easy to use.

Additionally, Emhreeil's climbing method was loud.

So they had to pile onto its back after sneaking around the edges of the barricades, shuffling around the edge of the bridge into the underside layer.

Even the short minute was straining to its fingers. Templates would help by healing the muscle strain, but it didn't want to keep retracting the progress its teeth were making inside its body, even if the template was reverting to a very recent state.

Emhreeil was just far too heavy now. The massive wings didn't help her suddenly filled-out frame. It felt like it was carrying four full-grown people.

Under the bridge, thankfully, was a long strip of walkway, likely there for repair crews to do work on the bridge's gut, so once they got onto that, they just walked through and around the bridge supports from below as its pack filled it in on what was happening.

Apparently, the pack war going on in the wider human nest had ramped up, and the abandonment happening behind them was one of the packs, the "Guard," relocating a pack to replace it with another they trusted more, essentially kicking people out of their territory to put in a pack that was friendlier to them.

It was quite complicated, and a lot of the nuance flew over its head, but it was enough to sate its curiosity, and it didn't care enough to understand better.

After stalking through walkways wreathed in shadows and flickering lights, the wolf paused and tilted its head, trying to figure out a way to keep going while staying hidden.

That was going to be a problem.

Emhreeil was extremely distinctive, but she was fairly covered up now, even if her wings made her silhouette look like a gigantic warped hunchback under the blanket.

As its current appearance was, it couldn't really show itself without even the most apathetic of humans noticing something was wrong.

Beyond its shoulders and humanoid arms, the second pair of arms was quite visible in good light, as were the odd protrusions at its waist where the spider legs were tucked into their pouch and bulging it out.

That was without mentioning its absurdly bushy and long tail, which was two, actually, and the spikes on its shoulders and forearms.

It didn't care too much, but having just lost its pursuers, or so it imagined, it was reluctant to just pop up into the public. There weren't a lot of people above, but their numbers weren't negligible like before. Not to mention the people in their personal nests, peeking out at the streets from their windows.

After a few minutes of sitting there and thinking as its pack rested, it decided on the simplest course of action.

They'd just split up a bit.

Emhreeil and Katherine could take the green human and go do their business, get more information and get whatever they needed, and the wolf could go get more essence.

Plant matter was still extremely expensive, and it wanted to get a decent stockpile.

It was Katherine that seemed the most hesitant, but after a couple minutes of thinking about it, they agreed to separate and meet back here in two hours.

So it made a path for its pack to follow, sent it over, and then turned around on the walkway and jumped on the railing to grasp onto the floor above, quickly scampering out of sight.

"You all right?" Kat asked, and to look at her, the improvised hoodie making it a tad difficult.

Is concerned. Believes Emhreeil is nervous about being seen by non-hostiles for the first time since recent change. Believes Emhreeil is self-conscious. Wants to offer comfort out of both personal care for Emhreeil and a subconscious desire to draw Emhreeil away from what she perceives as growing inhumanity, trying to bring her closer to a more familiar line of thinking and way of acting that she associates with normal human nature. Subconscious desire partially derived from ideation of Emhreeil's old self and the thought that it is a way to feel less alone in the pack. Feels like her options to bridge the distance to everyone else are either some kind of moral degeneration or monsterhood. Is inwardly scared of such changes but not entirely opposed—

She cut it off before it began to dive too deep, turning her head away to stare ahead as they walked.

The skill was dangerous, creepy, and way too fucking potent.

She was a step away from fucking mind reading, except this skill looked at [Mental Resistance] and started laughing.

Choking down the slight guilt, she thought about what she'd just learned.

First of all, Kat was wrong. Mostly. She felt more proud and confident of this body than she ever felt of her old one. If she was a normal sane person, maybe being self-conscious about being a giant patch-work of scale, chitin, fur, and snow-white skin would be the natural response, but she felt better about herself than ever. She felt good, she thought she looked good, if quite inhuman and fairly creepy.

But there wasn't a way to say that without making it obvious that she was using [Psychometric Vision], which was a bit morally iffy to use on her own friends, so she didn't comment on that.

Even if using it on the wolf sometimes was a bit necessary to understand what the fuck he wanted. Still, considering how cagey he had been about allowing mental links, and from some insight gleaned from the same skill, she could recognize that he would likely take it very badly if he thought she was regularly using the skill on him.

Curious as she was to understand what kind of mental trauma led to his vehement hatred of mind control and subconscious distaste for telepathy, she was pretty sure that asking would make him suspicious as all hell.

He wouldn't kill her or anything, but it would hurt some of that unwavering trust they had built.

That was partly why she downplayed how strong the skill was to her friends. Borderline mind reading was really damn useful in coordination and cutting off problems before they got started, but nobody liked being read like an open book.

She thought about what to say for a moment, then let out a disgruntled sigh.

"Kat, I'm six and a half feet tall at head height, and I think a bit over seven at wing height. I have glowing dragon or demon eyes, or whatever, and a tail that is ninety percent bone, and I'm pretty sure I could kill someone if I whipped it right." She lifted the tail from under the blanket to wriggle in the air in front of Kat, before tucking it back in.

"I quite like it." She shrugged, and Kat turned an incredulous look at her. "But, I am a bit nervous about how much attention I'm probably gonna draw. I'm wearing actual clothes now, even if those clothes are half soaked in dried blood. But still, if lizardmen are an unusual sight in the dungeon, and elves even more so, I'm a bit worried I'll draw too much attention by following you around."

Kat hummed as they kept climbing the steps.

"Then why did you suggest coming with me instead of going with Fleabag? Scruffy could keep me company," Kat said, lifting a hand to rub Scruffy's head, who leaned into it.

"Well, he's going to be picking some odd routes," she started, and Kat snorted a bit, likely remembering how he just jumped onto the railing and slithered out of sight.

"But I also wanted to come, honestly. And I won't lie, I'm not worried about him holding his own, but you might need help if things go awry in the Fox Den."

"Ah." Kat nodded. "I was quite surprised he—it—"

"He," she corrected gently, and Kat sighed but didn't contest her.

"I was quite surprised he cared about what's happening in the 'nest' at all. Speaking of which, isn't it awfully convenient there was a Fox Den front so close to where Ghoul dropped us off?"

"Not really. Ghoul seems to have planned the whole thing for us to some extent, which . . . I guess is nice, but it's also a bit . . . invasive? Feels like he's taking agency away from us in a way." She shrugged. "Honestly I'm too . . . mentally exhausted to think about it too much. Gift horse, mouth, something something."

Kat seemed to think about it for a moment, but whatever she wished to say was postponed by their proximity to the street.

"I'll act like your creepy guard or whatnot. I'll use the demon eye skill and talk to you through telepathy," Emhreeil said as she slowed a bit, falling into step behind Kat, who hummed dubiously.

"I don't think we need that yet. We're just here so I can sell a bunch of loot and get me and Scruffy some food."

"Well, true, but there is that animal emporium on the paper he gave us . . ." she trailed off, and Kat's steps slowed.

"What does . . . you want to grab something for him?"

She nodded.

"Ghoul's a bit of an invasive asshole for writing half a paragraph on every contact on the paper, but he is a really helpful one. He recommended we buy a lyrebird or three. Apparently it's like a parrot, but really good at mimicry. It can mimic engine sounds to a T, for example. No unique magic like phoenixes either, it's purely biological, so the wolf should be able to copy it easily. Suggested it could talk like that if it wanted."

Well, the main point of his suggestion was actually the possibility of the wolf being able to misdirect people and lure them into traps by talking, but she was going to redact that part.

Kat's brows furrowed as her steps resumed.

"That is . . . exceedingly helpful and nice of him."

"Hm."

"I really don't like him," Kat murmured.

"Oh. Why?" she asked.

"I have no idea, honestly." Kat sighed, then straightened as they came out onto the open street.

Em certainly had an idea, considering what her power had just fed her about Kat's subconscious thoughts on the matter of her transformation, but bringing it up would be . . . a bit invasive. And asshole-ish. Like Ghoul was, a bit.

It was fairly quiet as they stopped to let their eyes adjust to the pale yellow light washing over them from spotlights above, just a dozen or so people around the crossroads mingling or cruising about.

As they continued forward, checking signs and scarce markings to figure out if there was a place to buy things from, she would briefly check with her skill for any danger or hints as to what they were looking for, finding none.

Asking people for directions proved far more effective, and before long, they were on a commercial street, nothing quite as expansive as a market, but fine enough.

Selling weapon loot, unenchanted, was only barely worth the time, usually.

With the factories mass-producing decent swords and weapons, there just wasn't much reason to ever buy a used sword rather than one fresh off the assembly line. Weapons were cheap in the dungeon with its factories and endless supply of steel.

To their combined surprise, however, when Kat asked, weapons were almost tripled in price, and so, their short selling trip to get rid of useless baggage turned into almost a full gold coin's worth of silvers.

A mixture of idle chatter and her skill gave her the reason.

The Guard had been aggressively targeting weapon factories. It explained the previous scene of an abandoned neighborhood nestled behind the Beaumont factory.

Not that she knew who those guys were, but if Kat knew them, they were important to some extent.

Combined with the increased demand due to the war, and the fact that the Factory was apparently closed for everyone below the first floor, the price skyrocketed to what most places outside the dungeon would call a "good" price rather than essentially "dirt cheap."

It benefited them now, but she couldn't help but feel the tension, both within and without.

She was frankly surprised the army hadn't already been sent down. Instead, the gossiping shopkeeper thought that they were starting to move guards from the first floor and half of the second to try to push the third one down.

He spewed some drivel about fighting spirit and how it wasn't working, but under the surgical gaze of a demon's skill, his unease and false confidence was as transparent as glass. He was just parroting what people around here would want to hear. A businessman to the core.

While Katherine pocketed the coins and they set out to complete another quick chore, she flashed the enchanted dagger into her hand beneath the blanket and thumbed at its grip, contemplative as she tried to ignore the stares of the other patrons and the guard at the door.

One that she barely fit through. Her wings were too wide and bulky. Strong too, but they were still an annoyance to some extent.

As they spilled back out onto the streets, she reached for the link.

"I'm trying to figure out what to do. Honestly, I'm pretty lost. Any ideas?"

Kat startled for a moment at the sudden voice in her head, then resumed her walk, not even looking back.

"What do you mean? We get supplies, grab a couple newspapers, go to the Fox Den, and ask for a general information package on what's going on in the dungeon just to cross-reference, then we regroup with Fleabag and continue going down until we go to the fourth floor."

"Hmm. I don't mean that. I mean that there's a lot of things to do, but few we can do without drawing attention and danger. We really need to get stronger. Considering how the Snake Eyes were apparently Ironheart's along with whatever other gang he has, and he's hunting the wolf, we're all probably on a kill list. We can't just find a hole in the fourth floor and hide in it. And the war is another issue. I feel like no matter who wins, we'll get shafted."

Katherine scoffed as they brushed past a man walking around with an entire shop on his back, trinkets and supposed "brews" dangling off the bizarre ensemble he carried.

"Even if we tried to hide in a hole, Fleabag would grow restless in a day or two and then go out and start murdering people. Also, I'm not sure telling the wolf about the intricacies of the war and how he will likely live life as a hunted creature no matter the outcome will do anything but make him decide to get rid of all life in the dungeon by throwing points into intelligence and concocting some kind of super plague."

That was . . .

Actually, that was a possibility. Shit. Was it? Could wolves actually do that?

She'd heard about famines and ruined ecosystems in some dusty old history books, but not much about plagues . . .

Why hadn't any other wolves done so? Was it because they were too bloodthirsty to consider that approach? Too dumb? Why was Fleabag so different? She could point to the fact he seemed to have been visited by a god, but at the same time, that was too fucking absurd to consider as truth. It was more likely that he had some kind of delusional dream and the System just handed out a Path based on that, the infernal thing that it was.

"*It's not his style,*" she settled on, eventually, and with not all that much certainty.

"*He'd rather fight and eat. But, point taken. Still, what I'm trying to say is, we should probably go to the unspecified entrance to the Factory. We can't lounge around now that they lost our trail. We should at least head to where Ghoul hinted it's at. Fleabag's got some kind of ground-based tremor detection. He can probably find the entrance easily.*"

Katherine's features tightened in an unfiltered expression of distaste. She assumed it was because she mentioned going into an unexplored or unsanctioned entrance to the Factory.

"*Kat, think about it a little. We're not exactly in a good enough spot to be getting into attention-grabbing fights, Fleabag knows that as well, but we need to fight things, we need to progress. If we kill too many guards, the kingdom notices. If we kill too many of Ironheart's goons, we get noticed and probably reveal our position as well. If we just kill random people, well, me and the wolf might get a tiny bit stronger, but it won't be worth it, and people will start looking out for us. Or for something in general. Since joining the Adventurer's Guild is pointless now that the Factory is closed below the first floor, and since Ghoul claims there are alternate entrances to the Factory . . . we don't exactly have that many options. We can't stagnate.*"

Katherine licked her lips, swallowed.

"I— Wait, how do you know the Factory is closed?"

"[Psychometric Vision]."

Katherine seemed grudgingly impressed. *"Okay. Well, I suppose you're right. And the wolf is a psycho, so he'll agree and be chomping at the bit to get in there if there really is an entrance there. Regardless, to get into the Factory, we have to get to the fourth floor first, so it's a bit early to be talking about it now."*

"Is it? If we can just sneak him onto a platform lift we can probably head straight down to the third floor's bottom level. A day's trip from there to get into the fourth floor, and maybe another to get to the Bone Pits."

The Bone Pits was a rather ironic name for what was essentially a landfill full of broken golems guarded by the kingdom, now that she thought about it.

"If they aren't blocking those lifts because of the war, you mean," Kat shot back, and she frowned as she realized that that was a real possibility.

"Good point. Ghoul's contact list was also accompanied with a lot of extremely unsubtle subtext about how he would only assist us if we put in the work and risk required to progress without him. An assistance but not a savior. He's probably some kind of Struggler's Mantle believer. So, you know . . ." The thought trailed off.

Katherine audibly sighed. *"Yeah, us going into the Factory would show exactly how much work and risk we're ready to go through. Still too early to be talking about this, I think, but I get your point. I'm just . . . hesitant. Lady Anna would sometimes volunteer at some Kingdom Gate barracks, way down on the fourth floor. You know, those parts of the Factory the kingdom keeps private to keep training their army?"*

"Yes, I know what those are."

Kat nodded, eyes roaming store signs and peeking into alleys as they continued.

"They'd teleport us in through the portals, then send us back. The injuries I saw there were . . . I'll spare you the details, but I've seen soldiers that

looked like they got shoved into a meat grinder from the waist down, with too much Endurance to die easily. I imagine you or even the wolf in that position, and my stomach churns."

"Can't be any worse than melting alive," she replied with simple conviction.

If she died horrifically, she died horrifically. That was life.

Katherine winced. After some long, meandering seconds, she relaxed.

"All right. The tailor guy can wait until we need him . . . . Let's just finish shopping, find an inn with a shower room, go to the Fox Den, and then come back and recheck what we plan to do with our beastly leader after. See if they've got some decent information to offer for a trio of total innocents who just want to avoid all the gangs and war," Kat thought with clear sarcasm, and she chanced a snort as her eyes joined Kat in dissecting shopfronts.

"We should get something for Scruffy, by the way."

Scruffy sent back eager agreement, frowning cutely as she tugged the skirt down. More of a pants girl, she guessed.

Katherine immediately turned for a simple clothing shop, and they followed.

It had mostly been focusing on getting around without being seen after snatching some stumbling wreck of a human out of an alley for a quick lunch, both as a game and a precautionary measure, focusing on at least keeping its pack on the edges of its range.

Juggling the task of tracking them with climbing around and between pipes and scaffolding was also an interesting mental exercise. Not hard, due to its auxiliary brains, but not easy either.

What ended up distracting it was a sound it vaguely recognized, some kind of melody that was usually ruined by human gibbers and croons, tinny and croaky most of the time.

This one wasn't. So, overcome with curiosity and finding the sound—highly pleasant, actually—it slowly watched to make sure nobody was watching it and followed the vibrations and its ears to the source.

Under a rumbling cooler, between two rubbery pipes full of wires, and then over a set of thin water pipes, it crawled and stalked its way to the source, the sound increasing in volume as it got closer.

It wasn't sure what exactly made those sounds, but it found them intensely calming, so it sat on its hind legs on the grainy pipe, shoulder and head against the wall.

It was almost always difficult to relax. It just couldn't do it most of the time. Even when sleeping, it didn't rest. It was always listening, always waiting for the next vibration of a step that was a little too quick, a little too aggressive.

Now, it was easy. It was hard not to relax.

Almost like bleeding, it felt background restlessness and worry quickly fading and retreating, replaced with a languid calm as the complex song of varying whining, crooning sounds intermingled with each other.

Then a human walked into the room and began to fiddle with a device on the table, turning a couple knobs on it.

Instantly, the soothing melody drifting out of the green-tinted window shifted into harsh static and croaky human voices, and it felt its claws jerk and tear at the metal they were holding on to, its lightly wagging tails stiffening with anger.

It quickly opened all its eyes and leaned to the left a bit to look around, then double-checked with its vibrational senses.

Twelve feet to its left, a diagonal wall hiding it from sight of windows from the buildings on the other side of the street. The diagonal wall turned into a rumbling mess of vents pumping fumes into somewhere below them, and even farther above, it connected to some kind of hexagonal ball covered in lightning.

It was curious about that one, but it had something more important to do right now.

Below and above to its right, a few dozen stories of the vaguely cylindrical building, stretching on, half the windows lit and the other half either unlit or broken.

The streets below were thin and covered in guarded men and women having hushed conversations while inhaling smoke from some weird smoke sticks, not one of them looking up.

It swung its bottom half off the pipe it was perched on, ignoring the hundred-plus-foot drop below, and repositioned before it raked its nails through steel for a couple of feet, sliding down until it was hanging outside the open window.

It let go and grabbed onto the sill of the window as it fell, before soundlessly swinging into the room, wreathed in darkness.

The human was still fiddling with the machine, back turned toward it as his chair squeaked from the weight. The sound was just getting worse the more he messed with it, before settling on a boring, monotone human voice.

It spent a moment to see how he used the damn thing, then without much preamble, hopped up, snapped its jaws around his neck, and put a hand on the back of his head, pushing him forward as it yanked its jaws back.

The human jerked and toppled onto the floor with his chair, his head rolling in the opposite direction for a beat.

It grabbed the chair, put it back in its place, not trusting the table to take its weight, and hopped on before staring at the odd box.

There were a bunch of scribbles on the front of the wood, with thin pieces of metal.

It would ask its pack what that meant later. Now, it extended two human hands to mess with the knobs.

A shrill shriek rose from the small box, and it flattened its ears as it twisted the other knob, hoping for a different result.

The volume of the shriek rapidly reduced.

Now certain it wasn't going to torture itself with every attempt, it began to play with the other knob, turning it this way and that way, opposite of what the human had been doing with his motions.

Five minutes of frustration later, it heard a similar melody to the first, and its ears shot up. It turned the volume up a little, then hurriedly retracted its human arms and listened.

This one was even slower, varying tones and lengths of something going *plinkdum, plinkdum, plinkduuuuunplink*, adding a vague sense of playfulness to it.

Or maybe this was supposed to sound menacing to human ears, it didn't know. What it did know was that it liked it.

The sound was soothing and alien and beautiful. It had caught glimpses of such things before, but human voices, static, tinny croaking, and a whole host of other things always ruined it.

This, this was perfect.

It jumped off the chair and began to eat its second prey, ears wide open to enjoy the music, dedicating some minor background processing toward trying to find its humans again.

The melody eventually ended, and after ten seconds of silence, it stopped eating, staring at the box with a faint sense of dread.

Did it break the . . . thing? Or did the human do something to activate it that the wolf didn't know about?

Then sound came back in, and it relaxed, going to its meal, slowly savoring it for once rather than just snapping all the bones and scarfing all the flesh down without so much as a bite.

This one used some kind of shrill, continuous note that rose up and down like a wave, some short and some slow.

It wasn't sure it would ever understand human customs, but this one, this one it could understand.

Halfway down the man's chest, unfortunately, a familiar sensation popped up, and its head jerked up, dropping its bite on the floor.

Its pack was in a fight.

It practically dove out of the window.

A moment later, it scrambled back into the room, turned the volume down until it was silent, wrapped its back tentacle around the odd device, then dove back out, hoping its cargo would survive a frantic run.

CHAPTER 9

"Where is Emhreeil?" the man asked Katherine, his gaze flitting from her friend to her.

She blinked at him once, twice.

Then she almost burst out laughing from sheer incredulity but made do with nary more than a cough.

The second man's eyes were laser-focused on her as he pretended to casually lean against the wall a dozen feet ahead.

Glancing behind her at the thin-mouthed alley, then above, where a spinning carousel of neon-lit signs advertised shops to passersby on the level above, she realized that as far as she was concerned, they were the only two people.

Two versus two was a good fight. One she could take without worrying too much.

They probably had some people in reserve, though. Would they run or come and fight?

The bigger question was how they found them.

"I . . . don't know who that is?" Katherine offered, a surprisingly good act, which the man didn't seem to buy, his casual clothes shifting as a dagger slid through his sleeve and into his hand.

Emhreeil made sure her wings were *very, very* still within her cloak, hunching forward slightly to alter her height. She looked to the alley's entrance, and while she was turned away with her face hidden by the flap of her hood, flashed the clawed mask back onto her face.

"I suggest you stop trying to act coy. Where is Emhreeil, slave?" the man drawled, appearing at ease, but his voice was filled with warning as he spun the dagger around his fingers with obvious skill. Puffed chest, straight shoulders.

Like a chicken.

Her lips curled in amusement, even as she cautiously prepared herself.

That was the thing about the System and a world as uncertain as this: You never knew who was truly dangerous until they showed their fangs. So despite her desire to burst out laughing in the bastard's face, she held some caution, because overconfidence would just get her killed.

She activated [Psychometric Vision], focusing on the front man.

Middle-aged. Stat distribution low on Endurance, build and equipment suggests mage-blade or standard assassin distribution, Speed and Dexterity. Not a mage-blade. No spells in his repertoire. Confident, not overly so. Experienced. Is not underestimating his enemy. Not here by choice. Not motivated by money. Has been blackmailed into his current situation. Subordinate to the second man. Is unwilling to fight. Will fight if ordered. Thinks this is a waste of time. Not concerned about Katherine's seeming employer. Katherine's employer has been dealt with already.

She felt the strings of the skill and adjusted them to focus more on information rather than group dynamics and motivations, turning to the second man.

Came here independently, tipped off by unknown party. Hadn't expected tip to be true, is unprepared, came here because of curiosity and a sense of diligence. Has not notified anyone beyond current group. Unknown party is knowledgeable. Unknown party is Ghoul. Ghoul expected Emhreeil to find out. Ghoul sent them to Emhreeil specifically to relay information to her through [Psychometric Vision].

If Ghoul wanted her to know something, couldn't he have just *told her* instead of sending these idiots her way?! She had the communication crystal in her ring—

. . .

A . . . communication crystal that couldn't receive anything because it was in a pocket space. She had *completely forgotten.*

Resisting the urge to groan in self-reproach, she rewound off that frustrating bit and focused on forcing her skill away from Ghoul's nonsensical way of thought and back onto the person in front of her, using [Haste] to give herself time to think, the world slow around her.

Loyal to an ally of House Kervile. Seeking revenge on behalf of his employer. Employer furious over the destruction of House Kervile, blames Emhreeil. Destruction of House Kervile was at the hands of Marquess Irythiel. Knows Emhreeil is Irythiel's daughter. Employer aware of Katherine's existence and attachment to Emhreeil. Has placed a bounty on Emhreeil and Katherine. Bounty is on the Mercenary Guild's board.

Oh, that was just *great.* It wasn't like half the dungeon was already hunting them down or something.

Sarcasm aside, what did she have to do with House Kervile? Who even was that?

It took her a few moments of baffled confusion to realize that was Lady Anna's family. Kervile. She vaguely remembered that.

She cast [Haste] again, stronger, forcing the world to slow down as much as she could. What the hell did "dealt with" mean? Destroyed?

Had they killed Lady Anna?

No, she knew her mother. She didn't kill Lady Anna, she probably killed *everyone,* down to the last man that had been in the vicinity of that manor, after interrogating them. That meant that . . . that she had indirectly killed Lady Anna. And everyone in that manor.

She felt her gut twist in that familiar guilt she'd grown so accustomed to but could never seem to find a way to escape from.

Some part of her noted how much easier it was to deal with that guilt, faintly concerned from how muted the emotion was, while the other parts were struggling to compose themselves.

Fuck.

Katherine opened her mouth, and she cut in.

"My little friend's acquaintance is dead." She spoke slowly and calmly, deepening her already deep voice to something only *vaguely* feminine, casually extending a malformed hand out of her cloak to put on Katherine's shoulder.

Both men's gazes snapped to her, lingering on her seemingly gigantic hunchbacked figure, her left arm drawing their gaze.

Microexpressions indicate disgust, unease. Unknown variable is alarming to both. Previous assumptions toward Emhreeil's current persona were something akin to a mindless brute hired as muscle. Katherine was expected target.

So Ghoul hadn't told them she was still alive. Smart man.

Her yellow eyes glowed like little lanterns from within her dark hood, and she slowly tilted her head.

"She is gone. She had a brain injury after getting into trouble with Snake Eyes, and without healing magic or regeneration, the potions did nothing. She died. My friend here cremated her," she continued, eyes on the leader, ignoring the first man.

Shift of shoulders and demeanor indicates mild unease, alarm. Is confident you're the biggest threat. Is unsatisfied with answers given. Will seek confirmation. Driven by a sense of pride and accomplishment. Seeking personal glory. Will dig for information on Emhreeil's current persona. Personally invested. Will not be persuaded out of violence.

She reached out through the link and directed Scruffy to try to sneak out of the alley and relay whatever she saw to her.

To cover her, she straightened a bit, drawing attention to herself as she, in their eyes, grew half a foot taller by a mere adjustment.

The familiar body language of a person who was learned and refined draped over her, no doubt incongruent with her odd, dark appearance beneath this giant, shredded blanket of a cloak.

Her eyes moved to the first man.

Unsure of what happened to House Kervile. Assumes dead, vanished, swift operation standard with his usual experience. Doesn't truly know. Isn't invested.

Then to the second.

Knows what happened to Katherine's employer. Reducing his tells, consciously shifting body language and expressions to deny information, feels like Emhreeil's gaze is too discerning. Feels as if he is being read. Is correct. Is confident his [Mental Resistance] will protect him from psychic readings, assumes genuine skill is being used rather than anything else.

"You won't be getting your employer any revenge today," she stated simply, staring at the second man, who stiffened even further. The first backed up a step, glancing to his superior.

Unsure. Nervous. Wishes to attack first before he is placed on the backfoot by allowing someone to set the pace of the fight. Looking for a reason to attack. Silently asking for permission.

Her gaze moved to the second.

She turned the skill off to take a deep breath.

Her chest felt tight, her gut heavy.

Lady Anna and their entire *house*, just *gone* like that, because she happened to pass them by. How the fuck did her mother even know? Had they been tracking her already? Did her stunt with those two guards really draw that much attention?

She turned the skill back on as the leader of the two stood up straight.

"May I ask how you know that? Or perhaps your name?" he asked with tension in his voice, clashing with the polite tone he was trying.

She let her eyes lower, just a bit, making the orb lights the man saw thin out a tad, the slit of her eyes narrowing.

"You may. I believe it's courtesy for one to introduce oneself first when asking, however," she said mildly, mentally preparing spells and fields as she spoke.

Her head felt a bit tight from this prolonged concentration. Or maybe she'd already overused [Psychometric Vision], though she doubted it.

Scruffy noted a third man ducking into the alley and sent an image of a lanky, middle-aged man with his hands jammed far into his pockets.

When had they called him? Did she miss it because she shut off the skill for a few moments? Or because her skill had certain holes in it? Did he come here because he felt like it?

The leader nodded, gesturing to himself dramatically as his jacket shifted.

Weapon on left side, under ribs. Six-inch dagger. Needle below, filled with paralytic. Has more weapons. Has more concealed weapons.

"My name is Jack. What's yours?" he asked, an easy, charming smile on his face. He would have been handsome if she could register him as anything except a talking bag of blood that she *really* wanted to rip apart.

False name. Real name starts with J. Real name starts with "Ja." Real name is Jax.

"Ah, hello, Jax," she slowly intoned, tasting the words.

He twitched, stiffening to the point it was obvious, his expression crumpling *ever so slightly.*

"How the f—" he started, dropping the act for a moment, and she spoke over him.

"I simply know things. Usually things I shouldn't. I know, for example, that Emhreeil died penniless, weak, and without any personal belongings, despite not being there myself," she said simply, and spread her lips wider. In a funny way, she wasn't even lying. "And my name is—"

For a moment, even as her mouth moved ahead, she considered.

What name to give? Not that it mattered, but still, she was buying time to charge and form her attacks.

She had an alternate adventurer name picked out, made up of idle thoughts while keeping a lookout or resting and dreaming of simpler days.

And what better name for someone and something like her, than— "Ramuel."

It just fit too well. Ramuel, Second Wing of Seven. The parallels in their stories were almost shockingly numerous, despite the religious connotations to the name.

Once a mortal, pure and innocent and curious, turned into a creature with mangled wings that would never fly, a twisted form whose legend first began when it bathed in blood the first time, and whose legend ended in uncertainty and mystery.

It was a name that fit her like a glove.

When he came up behind them, she shifted to have the third man in her sight as well.

Stance and bearing suggest something is in their pocket. Right pocket. Something powerful. Size suggests magical nature. Is wearing a magical ring, bound spell. Incapacitation spell. Sight based, low range. Two uses before extended recharge time. Doesn't like being so close to the action. Doesn't like being so close to you. Is unprepared for confrontation. Prefers long range. Main use is connections and discrete assassinations using poisons, long-range executions, and traps. Can fight. Doesn't like to.

She wanted that ring, and she wanted him and his connections to spread the word of her supposed death.

Her fields adjusted.

The second man tried to maneuver to the side as much as he could, as if to get an off angle on them, though Katherine easily matched him with a challenging glare, well aware of the game.

Jax hummed, easing his shoulders in a casual tilt as he examined them, reapplying his mask, a hauntingly familiar smile on his lips. He opened his mouth.

Frustration and annoyance at this stupid game they were playing peaked, her chest feeling too tight, his fake smile reminding her too much of Ghar's grin, her blood too hot in her veins.

Before she could second-guess the impulse, she activated the mana construct to her right. It snapped to life with a muted *thwoom-pop* and a sudden rush of air, followed by Jax's face becoming the back of his head with the sound of a sharp, fleshy crack.

His corpse spun once to land on its chest a few paces away from its original position, and sweet, *sweet* blood filled the air like the scent of honey as his nearly decapitated corpse spasmed once, then went still.

Another repulsion field threw the man with the magic ring onto his back before he could react, and she spent a large portion of her mana on boosting Katherine, her hand on her shoulder tightening to still her as she reached through the link.

"Man behind you, line-of-sight spell in his ring. Either cut off his right arm or blind him, I need him awake and capable."

Katherine burst into motion, slipping out of her grasp.

The second man was faster than she'd expected, managing to actually unsheathe his dagger before her right wing uncurled from her shoulder and devoured his head in its hand and fingers, the oversized hand easily curling around him despite the last joints tapering off into swordlike blades.

A middling [Sparkburst] coming out of her wing's hand as it squeezed was enough to end him, gore and viscera practically turning to mist in her hand as it clenched shut.

She stumbled back and shook her wing's hand clean as best as she could, drawing the blood toward herself.

Her throat was tight.

Her emotions felt so chaotic. She didn't know if she wanted to growl or cry. And she wasn't even entirely sure why she felt this way.

The only surviving of the three continued to gag and choke and cough as he writhed on the floor, Kat standing over him and tying his arms behind his back.

"*Kat?*" she asked through the link.

"*Em?*" Katherine questioned, concern plain in the voice that echoed in her head.

"*I'm so sorry. Lady Anna. Irythiel found out about them helping me. Tortured and killed them all. I don't know what her assumptions or motives were for such drastic action, but . . . they're dead. House Kervile is gone. I'm sorry. I'm really sorry,*" she sent, voice far steadier than it should be with the lack of involuntary bodily functions to make her stutter and choke on her guilt.

"*How certain are you?*"

She felt her chest compress, like she couldn't breathe in deep enough, and idly realized that she was on the border of an anxiety attack.

Why? The fight was easy. She hadn't known Lady Anna much, if at all. So why?

"*Fairly,*" she finally said. "*My skill told me. These guys were after us because House Kervile had allies who blamed me for their sudden demise. Ghoul told them where to find us to tell me about it through my skill because I forgot that the communication crystal can't receive anything in a pocket dimension. So . . .*" She trailed off.

Turning her head, she watched Katherine take a deep, shuddering breath as she finished tying up the assassin's broken hands together.

"*It's not your fault. It's mine. I was way too obvious with getting you to them. I raised too much of a fuss, because I was panicking and thought you were going to die. This is on me. You weren't even awake. I'll go now, he's all yours. I need a moment alone,*" Katherine sent, and rose, eyes blank and face expressionless as she walked past her.

"Okay. All right. I'm sorry, again," she repeated.

Her wing's fingers flexed as she quickly shuffled the wings back under the torn-up blanket she used as a cover, and after another moment of breathing in the scent of blood and death and choking on its taste, she turned to the only live man on the floor, struggling to squirm upright, half-healed eyes turned skyward as a mixture of blood and healing potion residue trickled down his face, breathing hard and fast.

She shook herself like a dog, physically shaking off her thoughts, and walked to her writhing captive, hoping that a healthy dose of intimidation and mystery would make him do what she wanted.

With [Psychometric Vision], she could probably just ask him questions about anything and watch his reactions to wheedle out enough information to make him think she was a mind reader or something.

It didn't escape her notice that her skill consistently learned things mere deduction and attentiveness could never glean, but she was mostly going to operate on the constant part of the skill rather than the inconsistent one.

A skill from a demon sounded like the exact kind of thing that would be frustrating to make sense of.

It was a frustrating trip back, because while the human nest was exceptionally three-dimensional, there were plenty of spots where there just wasn't a fast *and* sneaky way to move.

Combined with how the fight stopped almost as soon as it began, it ended up slowing down a bit, torn between believing that its pack could handle itself and their chronic inability to do so until very recently.

After briefly killing some lone human sleeping in an alley to steal his patchy blanket and drape it over its back, it sped through crowds, its two humanoid arms keeping the blanket in place while it sped forward, choking its curiosity down as it rushed past places full of light and life and bizarre scents.

When it finally got to the place it felt the fight, nowhere near where they'd agreed to regroup for this Fox Den place, it leaned over the railing of the walkway and stumbled onto a strange situation.

Katherine and Scruffy, sitting on the floor at a nook within an alley, while deeper inside, Emhreeil seemed to be talking to someone she'd captured, occasionally glancing about.

None of them looked or moved like they were injured, and it was a bit of a sudden realization to have, suddenly facing the fact that its pack was . . . actually quite strong, as far as it could tell. They could handle some trouble on their own.

It briefly mourned leaving *two* perfectly edible people behind, and hopped up on the railing to reach the nearest pipe. It didn't bother shrouding its descent, jumping and allowing the screech of metal to announce its arrival while it slid down, being careful not to jostle the melodious box too much.

Emhreeil's head snapped up to it, then she relaxed.

Its feet met the floor. A harmless prod at its mind followed as it curiously trotted up to her, and it lowered its walls as she slowly explained what happened here, eerily staring down at the man on the floor as he quietly trembled.

Something told it she was using that reading-eye skill, so it inched a foot away from her target of attention, slowly dissecting what happened and the background explanations.

It took a while, and by the end of it, it had learned something.

Humans and their relationships to other humans were *bizarrely* complicated and nuanced. And for some reason, Emhreeil couldn't see the simple solution to her problem.

Why not just kill her mother?

She paused when she parsed what its message entailed, making an odd facial expression.

Her late but significantly faster-than-usual reply was that her mother was on the surface, too far out of the way of their objective, and it conceded defeat on that front. For now.

Once they had someplace they could be safe and rest, as well as some kind of mode of transportation, they could go up on the surface to kill her. Simple.

Emhreeil seemed terribly amused by the simplicity of its plan, but agreed to it.

Humans had the tendency to make things way too complicated for no reason.

Another ten minutes passed as she resumed talking to the man on the floor, simultaneously forming an explanation as to what was wrong with Katherine and pushing it over to the wolf.

It wasn't quite sure it understood or that it could empathize the loss of such a distant figure, but it didn't like the idea of one of its humans being sad and mourning. It also wasn't sure what to do about it, but after a few seconds of idle thought, it came up with a simple plan.

It told Emhreeil to link it to Katherine, bit an arm off one of the corpses, and padded over to her slumped form.

Scruffy didn't react much as it sat next to Katherine's free side and curled up to eat its snack, but the human in question did, startling a bit then slumping back down.

It slowly worked through the arm, down to the forearm, one of its human arms stabilizing its food and shoveling it into its maw while it made sure to subtly wiggle into Katherine's personal space, until its side was pressing into her right leg and hip.

Then it began to push simple feelings toward her, the fluttery warmth of companionship and comfort. It wasn't as easy to picture and form and bundle as other feelings, ones it was much more familiar with, but it was what it could do while Emhreeil worked on a convoluted plan to make the humans think she was dead.

As it got to the wrist, she finally reacted for the first time, in the form of tiredly putting a hand on its head.

It paused and turned to look at her, curious if its plan to make her less scared and squeamish of it had worked.

Her eyes were half lidded and a little wet, but she stared back placidly.

Her hand slowly stroked between its ears.

It cautiously wagged its tails a bit.

She kept that same dead-eyed look, but her hand alternated its patterns until she was using her thumb to massage the base of its ears in a way that made its eyes slip shut and its head to lean into her.

Inwardly, it preened in pride, while outwardly it grumbled in pleasure and decadence.

Its genius plan had worked.

It tore off a finger and presented it to her—an offering.

She made a scrunched-up face as she leaned away, sending back pure disgust.

Humans had *zero* taste. It popped the finger back into its mouth, then curled its human arm back under its ribs.

"Why is there a box on your back?" Katherine wondered, and after a growling chuff of reproach, she asked the same question in a way it could understand.

She still seemed tired, but she wasn't moping anymore, so it decided to try and explain itself until Emhreeil stopped gibbering to their captive.

Katherine stared down at the wolf as its head jerked around with its ears, its monstrous form hidden by a thin, half-torn, dirty blanket that barely covered it up to the back of its neck, where that eye was.

Then her gaze wandered to the softly singing radio she was holding in her arms.

She tried to tell the creature that they couldn't afford to lug a radio around, but it wouldn't listen at all, shoving it into her arms over and over again until she gave up.

Their backpack had plenty of room now that they had gotten rid of so much stuff, despite the food cubes and water purifier she got, but between the canine kleptomaniac's bizarre obsession with light crystals, its new odd fascination with *classical music* of all things, the bombs, and the supplies they were picking up along the way, she began to think it might be best if they got another backpack.

Added onto the not-yet-blunt realization that Lady Anna and her entire family were slaughtered *because of Katherine*, she just didn't have the energy to argue or . . . or feel anything, really.

They wandered around Lord's Market, bobbing and weaving out of the path of Enforcers who seemed oddly uncaring of their rowdy group, Emhreeil and the wolf seemingly determined to drag her along on a superfluous trip that was . . .

Suspiciously harmless.

She didn't know if he and Em decided to try and cheer her up or if the wolf was just curious and was using them as cover to go around figuring out new experiences, but either way, it was a . . . nice distraction, she supposed.

She wasn't sure if they could afford to be leisurely strolling along the market, but she wasn't the shot caller here, the wolf and Em were. Mostly the wolf. She didn't think that was a good idea, personally, but it was the drawback to having a friendly wolf on their side, she supposed.

She watched the canine's wide, curious eyes as it shoved its snout into a small passing cart of mushroom bread and watched Emhreeil startle before lunging forward to pull the ravenous thing off the flabbergasted old man's wares, apologizing profusely while the wolf inhaled a loaf of bread like it was made of smoke, largely ignoring her pulling hands with faint grumbles before raising its head to sniff at the air again.

She couldn't understand where he was putting it all. He was huge enough to make most people do a double-take, but still, it didn't make sense.

Scruffy leaned on her leg, yawning, and she glanced down for a moment before shifting the radio a bit as it dug into her forearm.

There was just something about this whole situation that didn't really compute. Like a faulty wire that refused to connect in her head.

Just an hour ago, she had watched Emhreeil brutally execute two men with a sneer on her face, before threatening the third to do as she told him before tossing him down the alley.

Now she was watching her friend hurriedly throwing thoughts and feelings at the wolf to try and get him to understand that he couldn't just shove his head into people's stalls and eat things without losing their "shiny metal bits" while she paid the man for the loaf he'd lost.

Said wolf had also been casually eating a man's whole arm next to her, just a bit ago, before graduating to inhaling as much of the two men as it could handle until Em was done.

Now it just looked like a really wide-eyed curious puppy the size of a person and a half, ears twitching all over the place and dragging their entire group by its snout to whatever scent caught its interest, gazing around the market with open wonder. Its appearance was especially helped by the patchy blanket covering most of its grotesque mutations, only its head and entwined tails easily visible.

Considering its ignorance to so many things, it really *was* a puppy, but that image was too incongruent with the monster hiding under that thin wool sheet, so she put the thought away.

Their group didn't seem all that out of place, surprisingly.

Of course, they were a bit dirtier than the usual around here, but Emhreeil had the uncanny ability to just wave her hand and get all the blood off, so they just looked like a duo of weirdos with a pet and a goblin slave rather than a psychotic vampire, a genocidal monster, an armored maid, and a mechanic-wannabe goblin.

What a group they made. Going from casual murder and torture to a shopping trip at the drop of a hat.

The absurdity and whiplash was probably contributing to the numbness she felt.

She watched Fleabag impatiently pace behind Emhreeil as she hurriedly bought some impaled candy from a little shop in the wall that reeked of sweet herbs, and momentarily felt her shoulders go lax as the warm scents and lights slowly soothed the chaos in her head.

The music helped a bit, even if she could only barely hear it.

They walked on, Scruffy holding the stick in front of Fleabag's snout as they walked, its tongue endlessly lapping at the green-gold candy ball.

Then it smelled roasted meat and its head shot up, pivoting their path.

Her lips momentarily twitched in amusement, before a heavy weight replaced that levity.

It felt wrong to be happy so soon after realizing what she'd inadvertently done.

She couldn't cry, but she couldn't smile either.

She walked on, occasionally comforted by a hesitant, concerned smile and a hand on her shoulder by Em, or amused by the wolf's demands of volume control to his favorite music, depending on how much it could hear through the ambient noise around them.

Right now, she was content to just bask in the presence of their group as a silent companion.

The tailor shop was so hidden Emhreeil would not have even noticed it if Ghoul hadn't left very specific descriptions.

At the far edge of the market, tucked into the side of a tiny alley that led down a steep cobbled slope, was a singular metal door with a stylized engraving over it.

She summoned the paper back into her hand, comparing the design, the location, glancing around.

Katherine stood watch behind her, Scruffy nibbling Fleabag's remaining candy ball while said beast was hunting rats in the sewers a couple dozen feet below. In its own thoughts, they gave it "change-power," whatever that meant.

They really needed a way to communicate at long range. Maybe Ghoul had another crystal to spare, though considering their price, she doubted it would be given for free. Still, Fleabag was surely smart enough to learn how to use one.

She flashed the paper back and knocked on the door in a specific pattern, then pressed a button on the left side of the door for three seconds.

A crackle of static sounded out from . . . somewhere, followed by a throat clearing.

"How may I help you?" a voice said, gravely and weathered with age, calm.

"A corpse told me you make good coffins," she said, feeling a little silly as she fiddled with her new magical ring, its effects completely unknown until she found someone to use it on.

She flashed the paper back to her hand to confirm she said the password right, and resisted the urge to snort as she flashed it back into the storage ring.

Really, who used verbal passwords for *tailoring*?

"Ah," the man said, and the door clicked open, some mechanism on the top of the door pulling the it open with a light rattle.

A short, spacious hallway presented itself, covered in bright red, and after a brief moment of wondering if this was really a good idea or if her claustrophobia was just piping up again, she walked in.

The hallway lowered to a small staircase, which she went down on, pulsing mana freely to relieve her unease.

Then the staircase bent around and opened to a view that had her pause, brows raising.

The underground of this shop was at least a hundred feet long and eighty wide, and this staircase allowed her to see most of it.

Racks upon racks of fabrics, sewing supplies, carpets and tools and entire buckets of tiny metal bits she had no idea the purpose of, tubs and jars of liquids sitting in the corners, lacy fabrics and leathers and feathers and everything in between, all held within a room lit by simple light bulbs and four equally red walls.

Her steps resumed, and before long, she was standing awkwardly in a corner next to an empty . . . reception desk of sorts, surrounded on all sides by racks of clothes and supplies, blocking her view of the labyrinth beyond.

The tailor slunk through what looked like a lacy curtain.

He didn't look like much.

Vaguely dark-skinned, a lanky figure in a tight but flawless suit, a cleft chin and pronounced brows, with a thick white mane of hair. Straight back, professional dress shoes.

He paused as he looked at her, dark brown eyes squinting.

She resisted the urge to glare.

He lifted a hand to point at what she had grown used to pretending was a severely hunched back, his other hand still behind his back.

"Are those wings?" he asked, his voice sounding oddly excited.

To humor him, or perhaps because she felt like showboating a bit, she shrugged the wings and let go of the blanket to drop it, revealing the tight and hastily cut-up pants she wore, the bloodied and lightly torn shirt, and most importantly, her "wings."

Lacking membranes or supportive bones, more akin to spider legs with an oversized humanoid wrist glued onto where the sharp tip should be. Positively horrific in appearance.

The man's eyes widened, and she was fairly sure she could see stars in his eyes.

He grinned.

"Oh, Ghoul, you magnificent gatherer of freaks," he muttered almost reverently, and she wasn't sure if she should be glad he seemed so interested in working with her or creeped out.

"How would you feel about rings for those?" he asked, and pointed at her wing's hands.

She turned to stare at said hands.

Dark-black patchwork, absurdly oversized yet gaunt, and tipped off with foot-something-long blades at each fingertip.

Why would she ever *decorate* these things?

She shook her head.

"No. We have a strict budget."

The man's shoulders lowered in disappointment.

"So uninspired," he sighed quietly. "All right, come in for measuring and tell me what you need and for what purpose, we'll work the price out depending on how long this takes and how interesting your needs are. Shouldn't be too long. I've made masterpieces in an hour," he boasted, and waved a hand lightly. She felt mana in the motion, a monstrous amount of it, and stiffened, spells ready to be cast in her mind.

She watched tape measures, needles, scissors, and a dozen individual threads of string pick themselves off the shelves and float to hover behind him, orderly and perfect, as if sitting on an invisible shelf.

She spent a moment gaping.

If he was a telekinetic, what the *fuck* was he doing making clothes?

If he wasn't a telekinetic, what the *fuck* was he doing not being an archmage and rolling in gold inside the royal palace? The amount of fine control and concentration needed to lift up so many things, so many *tiny* things, and hold them in place while individually moving them, was ridiculous. Emhreeil could probably manage five needles at best.

Unless this was some other kind of bizarre Path and he was bluffing.

"Do you sew using telekinesis too?" she curiously rumbled, genuinely puzzled.

The man's smile turned positively predatory.

"Of course. Young miss, there is a reason I do not need protective detail despite making garments of all kinds for leaders and creatures of all kinds. More trouble than I'm worth. Now, come. Let us not share too much information. Bad for business. What exactly do you need?"

She stepped forward, followed by Scruffy, and just in case, prepared a few spells in advance.

Something about stepping into a giant sphere made of silk lines and tapes and scissors and a hundred needles was uniquely discomforting.

Ghoul, where do you find these people? she inwardly hissed in disbelief.

She looked down at herself, twisting her torso this way and that to marvel at herself.

It was . . . something akin to a skintight black body sleeve that ran from her ankles to her neck and upper arms before cutting out, made up of some kind of silky string material that was stretchy enough to qualify as high quality rubber, most likely. Putting it on alone was quite the challenge, but doable, helped a lot by its stretchiness.

It wasn't silk, she was sure. Silk didn't stretch at *all*.

She'd even done some mock-fighting with this thing on, at the tailor's insistence. Darting about and throwing punches and *very* clumsy kicks.

All came with ease.

Well, as much ease as could be feasible after spending three hours being used as a mannequin for her own clothes, even as his armada of needles sewed a garment *right in front of her*.

The man was terrifying.

Sewing.

With *telekinesis.*

With something like two hundred needles. Working on two different pieces simultaneously.

It still boggled her goddamn mind. The old man was either bluffing hard with some convoluted enchantment setup or deserved his own *academy*. She was sorely tempted to ask him to teach her, but they just didn't have time.

The end result of his work was as incredible as his skill.

According to him, it was waterproof, fire resistant, electric resistant, tough to puncture and cut, at least for regular blades without esoteric or exotic effects on them, like enchantments or whatnot, its color was a glossy black, and best of all, it was *extremely* comfortable and quite warm while still being breathable.

She still wore those torn dirty clothes over the bodysuit, which seemed to uniquely disgust the tailor, but she had no desire to let this suit get scuffed when something less valuable could take the damage.

Another factor was that this thing looked *expensive*, so she had to counteract the look.

Expensive was not a good thing in the dungeon. It got more attention than a giant hunchback with a clawed metal mask did.

Her new cloak was less impressive, but much more comfortable than a shredded blanket.

Tougher and sewn like some kind of segmented coat with a hood, while also being fairly light and *very* large. Just a foot below where her wings' points sat at a resting position, about where her shoulders were, it split into thick strips of fabric, so with a small push and shift, she could free her wings and get to work.

Scruffy's clothes were much simpler, and he didn't even have to tailor anything for her. Her proportions were standard for children's clothes, and she had some cheap but tough and comfortable clothes within minutes, picked out of his ready collection. Dark-gray denim pants, standard with factory workers for the fabric's toughness, and a criminally adorable brown shirt and poncho combo.

No skirts this time, thankfully.

As Katherine finished payments behind her, she focused on Fleabag, about two hundred feet below and to the right.

Still hunting rodents.

She wasn't sure *why* he was hunting so much, or where he was putting all of it, especially after desecrating several stalls and carts by impotently stealing food from whatever he could stick his snout into, but it didn't feel like he was in trouble from the way he moved. It looked more like he was playing.

Katherine walked past her, and she pushed a wordless question toward her friend as they made their way back outside.

"*More specific?*" Kat replied.

She sighed.

"*Trying to get used to speaking in a way he can understand. Kind of important for the leader to be able to understand us, you know?*"

"*Mmm,*" Kat said affirmatively. "*Practice can wait. I don't have the brain power to bother at the moment. What was the question about?*"

"*Well, firstly, you. This is going to sound kind of hollow, but are you all right? How are you feeling? Any request or . . . something we could do to cheer you up?*"

Kat made a sound.

"*No need. Your earlier attempt was . . . nice. Thank you. Anything else?*"

She grimaced a bit as her wing scraped the wall and tightened them against her back.

"*Well, uh. How much did we pay, exactly?*"

Katherine made a dubious sound. "*Frankly, I'm not sure. One gold coin and whatever that small bundle of drugs we kept from that ware-house was worth. I'm not sure why he took that as payment, but I wanted to get rid of it, and he was strangely interested in taking it, so it worked out well.*"

It took a moment to remember those syringes of glowing green fluid that they'd packed on the bottom of the backpack.

She frowned.

A gold coin was quite hefty for something without enchantments on it. She dreaded to think the price tag without his supposed discount.

"*Might ask Ghoul's crafter teammate if she can add something to this for free. I'll call him sooner than later. Assuming Fleabag agrees and isn't scared of him anymore.*"

"The fact a wolf is scared of him rings every alarm bell I can think of. Frankly, I don't trust him at all," Katherine sent with a mental . . . sigh?

"Well, when we met Ghoul the first time, Fleabag was about half his current size and a third as strong, I'd say, so . . . I don't know, take it with a grain of salt. I don't think Ghoul is invincible or anything. Just way too damn knowledgeable. Can't blame you for distrusting him either way, but I have trouble doing the same. He's frustrating, but he's helped a lot. And I think I'm rambling straight into your brain, sorry. Oh, and do you want me to ask questions about House Kervile at the Fox Den?"

Kat's steps stuttered for a moment before she resumed, gracefully opening the door and coming out into the quiet, sloped path outside, holding it open for her.

"Is it useful for me to know?" Kat asked pointedly.

She spent a moment to think about that as Scruffy squeezed through their legs to walk out onto the alley and fiddle with her new clothes, smiling and miming punches with her personal sound effects, like a little kid playing.

"I don't think so, honestly."

Katherine took a deep, hasty breath as they stood there.

"What are we going to do about Irythiel? We can't just let her get away with this. We don't even know if she'll keep sending people for us," Katherine rushed out.

She raised a hand, placing it on her shoulder.

"She won't get away with this. Fleabag's first suggestion when I explained was literally just 'Why are you thinking about this so hard? Just go and kill her.' I happen to agree. Once he's done looking for a place we can rest and regroup at, we can think of going for her."

"Hmm." Without much else to say, and Kat's understandably dour and blunt mood, she bent forward, and stomped, rhythmically.

Stomp, stomp, stomp-stomp.

She felt Fleabag's head jerk toward them in recognition, before turning back to assumedly wrap up his snack-gathering session.

* * *

The Fox Den front Ghoul had jotted down was absolutely nothing like what she was expecting.

She was expecting some kind of shady window in a wall or something, or a derelict building full of scar-faced muscle. Maybe some kind of seedy establishment like a brothel or a casino.

She hadn't been expecting the back door to a high-end tea shop.

That was likely the point, of course.

All it had taken to get past the veritable *giant* guarding the back door was some honesty.

She glanced up along the dark edges above, fully aware that Fleabag was stalking around up there in the darkness somewhere with Scruffy on his back feeding him candy, waiting to pounce should a fight erupt, and that helped her swallow her nerves down enough to duck into the building.

Katherine was off buying lyrebirds for him, having surprisingly volunteered for the duty rather than come with Emhreeil.

She'd never been in the back of a shop before, but she could gather that this was likely what they looked like. A couple storage rooms, a giant metal box covered in preservation runes, a wall of cabinets, and finally, an office at the end of the hallway, which a man relaxing in a chair quickly gestured her toward.

It was plain, and sparsely decorated. Gray walls, gray metal desk, a pen and a couple pencils, a stack of papers, and a rolling cabinet on the side that seemed to be locked with something magical she couldn't quite identify.

Behind the desk, a fat man slouched in a soft chair, wearing a striped suit, his eyes cold behind the metal fox mask he wore. Black curly hair pulled back in a ponytail, and a *very* bushy beard that suggested laziness or high Endurance.

It was hard for someone to shave when they needed enchanted bolt cutters to even trim their own hair. That was a bit of a known budget problem for high-end adventurers.

Her head still felt tight and vaguely raw, so she refrained from popping [Psychometric Vision] just yet.

The seats in front of the desk were like two tall backless armchairs, the only things with any real color in them, a brown-red rusty velvet, something her wings and tail greatly appreciated.

She sat in the chair closest to the door, recognizing it for the olive branch it was.

The man paid her no mind as she got comfortable, hurriedly signing a paper, even as he opened his mouth.

"What kind of information are you looking for?" he asked, voice deep and rumbling in the way that suggested heavy smoke and alcohol use.

She cracked her neck and spoke.

He breathed in, hands clasped in fearful, wishful prayer as he woke up from his fall. A soft willowy hiss of inflating oxygen cages echoed faintly in the strip-lit darkness of the alley, rancid air dragging through the filters of his chassis.

It hurt, once.

It hurt now as well.

Like a fingernail chewed a bit too far, a muscle strained too much, something horribly painful but deep down, satisfying, for no seeming reason. Such mortal sensations, he'd almost forgotten them.

He breathed out, feeling the oxygen cages blow the air into the furnace nestled against his spine where a stomach used to be. A soft hum warmed what little remained of his flesh, followed by the soft hiss of steam release.

He had no mouth, yet he imagined himself forming the words, whispering the prayer even as his hands unclasped and he forced himself to take stock of his broken body and turn over to crawl to salvation.

A sinner within the church was he, a monster in the confession booth, waiting for the priest to lovingly clasp the cage around his mind and bring him to Its arms.

A faithful pawn to perfection.

A mere Eye, looking for Its perfect creation, last of millions.

And he had found it. Thousand others in the tomb had failed, but he had not. Chance or providence, he had served.

The pain reminded him of his purpose, of his weakness, of his flesh. One and the same.

His cloak held the symbol and the gateway, a painting of a glaring eye within a softly clicking gear, in red paint. He couldn't find It no matter how much he looked, so he continued on.

He missed it. He felt empty and cold without it. Archbishop Varmond would give him another. He just had to make it back. He just had to crawl forward, ignore the broken, twisted metal, and hiss prayers to perfection.

The pain was secondary. The pain was good.

Through pain only, will he shed his flesh. Through devotion alone can eternity be grasped, and through reverent prayer soothed to tears will a lowly man like him witness the End and march alongside his brothers to eternity within the blessed machine.

The vent he found was large, reminiscent of home. Yet the air was still too thin. Too clean.

Grease and dust had conjoined into an oily mud, coating the vent, inches thick. He crawled forward, trusting Archbishop Varmond's mastery of form to keep his ruined body functional.

He crawled and crawled, guided by the whispers and whimpers within his mind, and pushed forth.

It was watching, It was always watching, and It was always guiding.

He brought his hands, metallic and beautiful and timeless, before him, and continued to claw his way into the tomb's wall, even as the steam engine inside his shoulder hissed and spewed superheated vapors into the air around him, a cacophony of cracks and metallic clicks singing of his broken body.

A trickle of water, a rattle of thin steel, the scrape of his iron spine against the floor.

But he survived. He had succeeded. He found it.

The edges of his vision played like dark shadows, and he wished to moan in effort, in penance, in triumph.

Fingers made of centuries and maddening croons pointed him forward, a voiceless voice vibrating through his every plate and pipe, pushing him, telling him where to go.

The distress signal was beeping away, but the tomb was big, his brothers few. He would get help, but it would be long before that happened. Yet It would come.

Time was meaningless to a true believer, to an Eye. He would last.

Despite the thermometer at the edge of his lens telling him he was overheating, he felt cold. He was always so cold.

Yet whenever the faint mortal urge to give up reared its head, It was always there.

When It spoke in words that weren't words or sounds at all, he felt warm, felt phantom sensations wriggle in his body, begging him to giggle in glee and shudder in ecstasy, for he was seen, and he was guided.

His inhaler hissed on and on in the darkness, and he dragged himself through the greasy mud, deeper into the tomb, awaiting for his kin to find him. Time slipped, unsure, leering at him with puzzled eyes, unsure of what to make of him.

One final step, a scrape, and a faint, familiar rattle of chains echoed comfortingly up the pipe. The vent? He was not sure where he was. He did not care. It had guided him here, and thus, this was the right place to be.

He had no mouth with which to call for help. He did not need one.

As the stripes of light behind him faded, he heard the chains again, closer.

The vent was large, but not large enough to stand in, even if he did have legs. So he continued as he was, toward home.

And eventually, a scraping form of cables and gears and interlocking ball joints tumbled into sight, legs like spiked rods, hundreds of feet down the pipe, a dozen lenses peering around, chains dragging behind it.

He turned his lens off, then on, then off and again.

The Seeker saw him and scrambled into motion, misshapen and imperfect as he, thundering its way up the pipe like a metal centipede, and so he finally stopped moving, clasping his hands before him in reverent prayer, pleased to pay back a fraction of Father's love.

He had found It.

CHAPTER 10

Katherine was off buying a feathered blob for the wolf to eat.

The mental image was too chaotic to tell what it was.

It had a feeling that beyond a name, Katherine didn't know what it looked like either.

And while it didn't particularly mind her doing that while Emhreeil updated herself on what was going on in the nest, after the first thirty minutes of waiting for Emhreeil to stop talking to the fat human and just *go* already, it was too impatient to just sit guard.

Besides, it didn't like being *defensive*. It was an annoying mindset.

So it took the blanket back from the little green human, threw it on its back, covering most of its mutations except its arms and the spikes on its forearms, which it did its best to hide by puffing its fur up and pinning them to its skin as flat as it could get them, and descended into an alley before walking out into the open again, Scruffy hiding in its shadow, her head barely as high as its shoulders.

And while the fact that it was as big as Emhreeil on all fours before her upgrade and almost twice as wide certainly drew quite a few looks, which was as mildly alarming every time as it was the first time, the wolf was not even close to being the most eye-catching creature or object in this "market."

There were people with floating . . . vaguely animal-shaped blobs of light ducking and mucking about their heads, people in strange distinctive armors, a giant scaled creature on a leash that was *almost* as big as the wolf itself, and that was without counting the bizarre objects and devices strewn about the place and stalls. It even saw something covered in multicolored feathers wreathed around a green beak, which was a sight so genuinely awe-inspiring it stared at the thing until its keeper started giving the wolf suspicious glares.

It even saw some *things* that blurred the line between animal and human so much that it wasn't sure what it was even looking at, a giant scaled biped with a snarling snout, a man with a beak and feathers all over his body, and even someone with feline features and fur along their hands.

So, while a proportionally giant canine with glowing eyes was quite eye-catching, Emhreeil had been right.

There were a *lot* of eye-catching things for people to stare at in the market that weren't the wolf, and with the blanket and the green human by its side, most people just took a second glance and kept moving.

Some glances were much more covetous and shrewd, but it mentally marked those people and did its best to avoid them rather than disemboweling a human because they tried to control it again like that woman with blue hair had tried to ages ago.

Following Katherine from a couple hundred feet away while incessantly checking for any creatures it could eat yielded many interesting results, but few that it thought would help with its current goal.

This trip through the market wasn't for leisure and curiosity like its first one, no matter how much it wanted to grab another "chur-ball" and taste sweetness again. It had a concrete goal to accomplish.

Upgrades.

Considering its growth hormone hadn't been tuned down yet, it would keep growing bigger, and it wanted to have more options, mutate further. To do that, it needed things to copy from.

The wolf was reasonably creative, but its best personal creations were more . . . strokes of inspiration than a consistent thing. It needed something new.

Eventually, however, as it passed by a stall, its eye was drawn by a beautiful colony of little lights.

Had about a dozen of them not suddenly begun to shift and scuttle about, it would have walked right past them.

It paused, resisting the urge to open additional eyes, and slowly stepped forward, ignoring the way the crowd awkwardly shifted around its form, the flow of traffic changing to accommodate it with muffled hisses from disgruntled humans.

The lights were moving.

It tilted its head, stepping closer to the glass tanks.

The lights were skittering around. They were . . . insects. Of some kind. All glowing.

One tank had orange-red bugs, while another had green like those flies that lived by the burning rivers, and one even had blue ones, which were covering their enclosure in some kind of vein-patterned glass.

It wanted them. It wanted *all of them*.

Problem was that if it just walked up and threw the bugs into its mouth, it was pretty sure the humans would get angry again about not getting their shinies for what it ate. Then the people chasing them might hear of it.

Hm . . .

It turned and slowly squeezed around the back of the stall.

The stall's structure was more akin to a box of mechanical joints and thin metal sheets that unfolded to make a square metal tent when fully expanded, and since the more solid constructions were gener- ally large and surrounded the more open spaces, the stalls were tightly wound together, forcing the wolf to squeeze between them and position itself so the little human could somewhat follow.

Then it spent a moment mapping out the stall itself. It was about twenty by twenty feet, with one corner dedicated to some wheeled cart of sorts, presumably to carry their things away when they were done sitting here.

But the back of the stall was covered in jars full of liquid and tons of other tanks, inside which it could feel the tapping or bulbous forms of its chosen prey.

It wreathed its claws in silence and cut a relatively round hole into the back of the tent, gingerly taking the resulting piece of metal and laying it on the floor when it was done.

It pointed to the green human, then down at the ground to indicate she should stay, and after she did the head-bob thing that humans did to indicate agreement, it slithered into the back section of the tent.

Forcibly stilling its wagging tails before it knocked something over, it took a quick glance at its choices.

Lots of small skittering things glowing softly in their containers. Their variety wasn't tremendous, but the sheer numbers guaranteed some fairly in-depth knowledge of its prey.

It carefully felt for the two people in the stall, antennae wriggling around its legs and arms to brush against the floor, and after making sure that neither was looking in its direction or moving much, it picked up a small tank with its secondary arms and lowered it to the floor off its jointed shelf.

After a moment of fiddling with the glass to get the top off, it reached inside, and without much caution nor delay, grabbed a giant fistful of the luminous orange bugs and tossed them into its mouth, hurriedly chewing and swallowing.

It had to cover itself in darkness from head to toe to release a startled snarling cough when the sheer *heat* emanating from the bugs' innards began to boil its throat, and it hurriedly swallowed them all down, using a stumpy thumb to massage its throat, lips pulled back in a snarl.

That had to have been at least a dozen, so it quickly flicked the ones trying to escape back into their place, closed the top, and put the diminished tank full of angry insects back on its shelf, and carefully reached for the blue ones.

It had no idea what a blue glow meant, besides electricity. Which it had plenty of already, but it wouldn't hurt to check.

Assuming these ones were of a similar nature to the orange ones, it was careful about not biting down, if only to save itself the bruised throat. It carefully swallowed one whole and blinked at the soothing cold that passed through its tissues, before the bug dropped into its stomach and vanished.

After a brief shiver born out of the inherent discomfort of swallowing something that was still squirming and wriggling, it powered through to scarf them down, one by one, until it was done.

The moment it was about to reach for the green ones, it felt one of the humans get up and turn halfway toward it.

It didn't bother putting anything back, instantly turning around, using its human arms to grab onto the blanket again and jumping out through the hole it had made, jogging away as Scruffy followed.

The experience made it realize that while it could feel a *lot* of things through vibrational senses, knowing the shape of something, even if in-depth, was not quite the same as knowing what it was, so it slowed down a bit to manually check any interesting places it could steal some progress from.

There weren't many, truth be told. Not because they weren't *there*, but because it couldn't really find a way to steal and be sneaky about it. Too many eyes, too small of a stall, too well-lit, not partitioned, so on and so forth.

The only place of interest was a shop that Scruffy seemed to get excited over, some kind of edible plant collection from what it could see. It wasn't sure what context made her give this shop in particular so much attention, but she was practically bouncing in excitement over it.

This one was thankfully inside a building rather than an open stall, so it wasn't terribly difficult for the wolf to send Scruffy in to make a distraction while it went and ate whatever it fancied from around the back.

The variety was extensive.

And very pretty.

And it smelled *incredible*.

Its only complaint for a while was that some of the plants were alive and *feisty*. One shimmering one turned into glass in its mouth which it eventually decided to just swallow down anyway, another *hissed* at it and ineffectually tried to bite its tongue off even as the wolf chewed on it, one burned its mouth with a sensation that wasn't similar at all to fire, just . . . warm *pain*, and the last one it had tried before deciding to go for some of the more mundane ones was a plant that grew spikes out of everything when damaged and excreted something that tasted *horrible*.

The spikes didn't even tickle, but it was still terribly uncomfortable to swallow.

It would have gone on to try some of the more tame and more numerous plants, had it not felt one of the human guards of the shop reach down to slap Scruffy.

It hadn't been paying too much attention to what kind of distraction she was providing, just enough to keep track of Katherine and the guards, but the sudden vibration of the strike worked to yank its attention to them.

After a brief thought of jumping on the guard and yanking his spine out of his ass, it took a deep breath, ran quietly around the racks of plants to jump out of the back window again, and went around the front of the store, where the guard was dragging a struggling Scruffy by the hair, glancing around the entrance of the shop as if looking for someone.

It turned the corner, the snarl it let out more akin to a chainsaw, making the human startle and let go of Scruffy, who quickly scrambled up and ran to its side, eyes shining with . . . water?

Why was she leaking water?

After a brief sniff for any blood and a jaw-to-hair lick of its tongue to get rid of the oddly salty fluid, it glared at the guard, who hurriedly backed up, each regarding the other for a moment.

Humans all looked the same to the wolf, so it wasn't sure it would ever remember his face, but his scent? It would stay for a while.

Ignoring the urge to shoot a spike through his throat, it instead turned around and left, its human arms vibrating in rage it didn't care to show to the world, clenched in fists against its ribs, holding the blanket closed.

It wasn't all that angry about Scruffy getting hit; it was more angry about the fact some weakling dared to do that to someone in its pack, and the fact it hadn't done anything about it.

Turning away like this, it felt like it was surrendering, or admitting weakness.

It hated being weak. No, it *wasn't* weak, but it didn't want to bring more trouble to itself now, so it kept walking away.

After another couple minutes of weaving in and around crowds, it found a decent route with little to no traffic and swung Scruffy onto its back before using its slime and claws to scramble up a crystal light pole and jump off its top onto a pathway made of equally sized pipes spewing some kind of green gas, meters and devices clamped along their length.

It was a great shortcut because it mostly went *over* and *through* the market, and the market was a pretty open space, meaning that it could skip weaving around buildings and people to just follow the pipes.

Another ten minutes of squeezing itself and its human into the gaps where the pipes squeezed through and over, and it had Katherine in sight, talking to someone who was glancing around and gesturing to their left, each of them bobbing their heads every few seconds.

Five more minutes of tailing Katherine, and it watched her go inside a building eerily similar to the one it had escaped from when it had been separated from Emhreeil, full of cages and animals.

The temptation to jump in through a window was there, but the entire place had too different a structure for the wolf to do anything without being noticed.

For starters, there was no stage or seats. It was just rows of cages on two floors, and humans could freely walk around them and pick whatever they wanted to take with them.

For most, that is.

The ones that didn't have such a treatment were the large, likely dangerous ones, which were held in a more exclusive room in the back, but even if it wanted to go for those ones, there were people there as well, and it would take quite a while to eat them.

Begrudgingly, it pushed down its greed and sat down to wait.

She glanced down at the little cage containing three lyrebirds, just in case the wolf needed a . . . sample size?

Katherine frankly wasn't quite sure why Em hadn't given her any ideas as to other things the wolf could eat, considering they had a decent enough pile of coin, but she was bit too mentally preoccupied to concern herself with the question.

Mostly trying to get herself to accept what she'd heard and *feel* something about it.

She was used to death and losing people. She was torn out of her family's arms as a child, and then out of her slave group to be shipped to this godforsaken island at the behest of Emhreeil's mother, and then she had to get used to having the staff around her rotate or disappear beyond a specific few, her included.

She was *very* used to losing people, whether through death or estrangement or separation.

It was all the same in her mind, really. Did it matter if someone was alive out there if she would never see them again? It was pretty much the same thing to *her*, as far as *she* was concerned. Someone unseen was someone dead.

That had been why she'd gotten that coin necklace of Emhreeil made when she stumbled upon that old artisan. She never believed she'd see her again.

The first time she lost her family and home, she'd bawled and wailed and screamed.

The years that followed, she'd cried a few times.

The first time, after seeing a kind gray-haired man, who'd smiled at her, gutted in the hot sands of the arena and being forced to clean up the rust-red sand he left behind, going through the sand with a sieve to gather whatever teeth and bits of gore had ended up within the golden dust, late into the freezing night.

After coming to Carmera, outside tears of pain, involuntary, she only ever cried after she'd watched Emhreeil's figure retreat into the distant crowd for what she thought was the last time.

Two years ago.

This numbness wasn't new to her.

But it felt like she *should* be feeling something more, even if just to make right by Lady Anna and her father. The people who gave her the chance to learn to fight instead of endure, the chance to learn how to read instead of looking for symbols in every sign she looked at.

If only so she could abide by the comforting idea that people mourned others when they passed. Even a fraction of the grief that forced tears out of her eyes back then, like squeezing blood from stone would be enough, but all that came was an exhausted, vague, accepting sadness.

Her first thought was that the news was too *impersonal* and just hadn't felt or become *real* yet. It was too sudden, out of nowhere. They were beating up some of Ghoul's involuntary messengers, and then she learned her only real connection since Emhreeil had been killed.

Mentioned like an afterthought.

So she'd snatched a couple newspapers on the way, and beyond the first page, she found it. There was even a skilled needle-sketch of the ruins, the press machine distorting the image but leaving enough to see the outline of crumpled ruins.

The words were few.

It read like a eulogy spoken solemnly before a casket being lowered into the incinerator.

The papers went into a trashcan on her way to the store.

The idea to visit the place was there, but she wasn't sure what purpose it would serve. It was too out of the way for where they were heading.

The lyrebirds inside the cage repeated random sounds as she began to walk back to their designated meetup location, and she quickly affirmed what she'd known about these birds when one began perfectly imitating a rumbling steam engine, even down to the creak of metal and rattle of a startup failure.

It was *uncanny* what kind of noises they could make.

The thought of the wolf's voice turning from the broken mess of snarls and rasps and whistles it currently was into whatever it wished was quite appealing. She would like to feel a bit more at ease with the mythical monster that was leading them.

A mental image of the wolf speaking in a perfectly enunciated seductive drawl came to her mind unbidden, and she shuddered in horrified disgust, discarding the thought.

At least it would be more legible.

Maybe—

A rough, snarly scoff came from behind her, *right behind her*, and she dropped the cage on the floor to jump forward then whirl around, hand flying to the handle of her recently looted enchanted dagger, only to freeze stiff when her brain caught up to notify her that the sound was a *chuff*.

The realization was accompanied by the sight of the wolf staring at her nonchalantly, Scruffy stumbling in place dizzily beside it, holding on to the blanket.

Speak of the devil, and he shall appear.

No, *it*, it shall appear.

Em might think the wolf was a person, or an individual, or perhaps an equal to a human, but she was hesitant to think the same, even if she could admit to warming up to the wolf significantly during the past week.

The lyrebirds suddenly began screaming and making every threatening noise they could think of while they uselessly fluttered and scrambled about their cage, and she winced at the volume.

She let go of the dagger and took a deep breath, closing her eyes momentarily as she straightened her trench coat.

The noise from the birds suddenly cut out, and she opened her eyes to a familiar ball of smoky darkness, taller than her and just as wide, the cage by her side nowhere to be seen.

Scruffy's hand peeked through the ball of darkness, pawing at the air before the goblin stumbled out of it, blinking before finding her and giving her a smile.

The darkness receded, revealing a shredded cage on the floor and bloodied feathers on the ground.

The wolf chuffed at her, mild gratitude in the sound. Then it yawned, wide as it could, and she unconsciously took a step back as she goggled at its teeth, snow white and perfect, with canines more akin to small knives with how large and long they were.

Its mouth clacked shut, and with a toss of its head, it walked away.

She sighed and followed.

She wished they had some concrete goal to follow. Something more than just "find a safe space to rest and go from there." Maybe this would feel a bit less like wandering, then.

Not that it was a bad plan, all things considered.

Just too abstract.

The wolf was likely used to this method of living. Small simple goals with unknown paths to acquirement. Get food, get shelter.

She was used to far more order and certainty than this, however.

Not for the first time, she wished that Em was the one leading the pack, but she reasoned to herself that if it wasn't for the creature in front of her, Em would likely be long dead.

And she couldn't deny that the wolf was learning about the world *fast*.

She mutely followed, turning on [Vigilance] and letting her mind scatter to the winds as the world stripped itself of context and reason around her, sinking into her defensive fugue like dropping into a soft bed.

It was a terrible coping mechanism, but she didn't have much else.

Emhreeil sighed as she stepped out into the alley, ignoring the man who brushed past her to enter the building she just left.

She massaged her temples, resisting the urge to whimper in pain as the migraine continued pounding through her brain, as it had for the latter half of her conversation with the man.

After a few seconds, she began to trudge her way to the corner they agreed to regroup at, trying to organize the information in her mind.

She learned a lot.

None of it was good news, not really.

The information package she paid for wasn't very in-depth, because she could save money by using [Psychometric Vision], but it covered a very wide variety of subjects, out of which she squeezed as much info as she could. Probably too much.

The Grate, where the second floor turned into the third, was now a war zone between the newly formed Syndicate and the Guard. It was escalating enough to make the kingdom teleport troops down into the second floor, which were currently marching down. Open warfare was starting, and sooner or later, it would stop being melee combat and bombs and turn into magical devastation once the kingdom pulled the Crimson Guard out of wherever they kept their resident demigods.

Or so she assumed through simple logic, really.

In response, the gangs had apparently seized control of all teleporting stations on the third floor and were fortifying them as heavily as they could. The adventurers from the Adventurer's Guild were sort of turtling at their local branches, waffling between helping or keeping their head down and between their shoulders.

House Kervile had "mysteriously" burned down, which she already knew.

Then she learned of the dozen gangs operating on the third floor, in a spew of information so dense she was starting to forget their names already. Mostly because if there was a Syndicate, and if Ironheart was a part of it, that meant he had multiple gangs under his thumb, and she wanted to know exactly which people to kill. Or avoid.

Intellectually, she knew there were a *lot* of gangs around. Of course there were, people could literally starve to death here without an ounce of pity, and the churches could only give so much, so people had to feed themselves somehow.

Still, hearing about all of them was a slight wake-up call on their sheer number and complexity, as well as the simple fact that some people really just didn't have a choice. Gang members, for all that it mattered.

There were the Dockside Merchants, closest to their current location, and apparently the people they'd killed just a day and a half ago were part of them, according to her skill. They had roots in Carmera's dockworkers, about 160 something years ago, before the leviathans decided that they liked the Black Ocean and moved in.

The Dockside Merchants were apparently just small-time drug peddlers now, and some of the most chaotic of the bunch. Their only stable holdings were nightclubs and seedy bars around the walls. Their leader was some crass man whose name she didn't care to remember.

There were the Snake Eyes, Ironheart's apparent lackeys, judging from what Ghoul had said, mostly dealing in protection rackets and services for the dungeon barons, like protection rackets, peacekeeping, debt collection, gambling, intimidation, and the occasional "hit."

She wasn't familiar with the slang of these circles, but she assumed that meant assassination.

In short, they were pseudo-mercenaries. Their strongest group were the very same people that tried to kill her and Katherine, called the Butchers, a name that she found both stupid and arrogant, personally.

Their general territory was less of a sprawl and more of a cylindrical area going from the middle of the third quadrant of the floor all the way to the top of the fourth, which was not terribly far from where they were at the moment.

There were the Enforcers, Baron Simian's attempt at recreating what Ironheart did with Snake Eyes, mostly localized around the more "high-class" areas of the third floor, like the very same market they'd been blindly prancing through in Fleabag's quest to satisfy his curiosity, but they weren't so much a gang as they were Baron Simian's law enforcers.

Specifically, *his* laws. The man's ego could rival a king's, considering that was what he was trying to be.

A petty kingdom of thugs and druggies. How grand . . .

Thankfully, he had an openly antagonistic relationship with Ironheart, so she wasn't terribly concerned about them being buddy enough to have Simian run to Ironheart the moment something black and canine walked into his sight.

The Beakers, a group of doctors, scientists, and miscellaneously skilled people and craftsmen who banded together to try and stop the forceful recruitment of such individuals going on by Tillenhall and the gangs.

They were the least evil from what she'd gleaned, mostly doing black market products and magitech trading, regular old drugs but with a twist of alchemy, and providing discrete medical aid without having to worry about someone hearing about it. They held a small amount of territory but had it locked down *tight*, and were almost anarchistic beyond that, operating in small mobile pockets across the more peaceful or uncontested areas of the third floor. Only those in the know would hear of their new black market, and anyone going to investigate or wreck it would find it gone in a few days.

Lady Lauren's Mice, or the Mice, were a seeming oddity, a gang mostly made up of children picked off the streets and used for low-tier espionage. They were slowly groomed into being drug movers and muscle for the gangs once they came of age and "graduated," so the gangs mostly left them alone. If the kids failed in being useful before their "graduation" and weren't good enough to be sent to a gang, they were either sent to brothels or other disreputable pits of villainy, or sent to Tillenhall for "rehabilitative stay."

Much as she wanted to go burn this Lady Lauren alive, she doubted Fleabag would give a shit about human children.

Red Spring was another minor gang, which mostly ran dog fighting rings, where canines as well as anything with legs were thrown into a pit to die and kill for entertainment. It was led by a very powerful beastman who took the racial stereotype of a feral melee fighter and ran with it, and it was with his strength alone that his gang had any foothold in the cliff race. He'd fought against the Butchers and won, apparently.

The feat didn't sound that impressive because Fleabag *destroyed* them, but for normal people who weren't nigh-mythical beasts of carnage, the Butchers had earned their name.

There was a group of informants around the bottom of the third floor, and some people who specialized in moving people and objects for long distances, discreetly.

It was the latter that really drew her attention.

Fleabag's simple solution echoed in her mind.

If she hated her mother so much, she just had to go and kill her.

The group that moved people for a fee was called the Railroad, and was centered around a man called Reeman, with presumably few members.

Whatever or whoever Reeman was, he had some kind of ability that allowed teleportation of tagged objects whose mana cost did not rise with distance, and he did not like people telling him what to do.

That was who she wanted to meet, but the price for that information was too much, and her skill had so much crap to work with that she could barely wrangle it in the Railroad's direction enough to tear the knowledge of their general whereabouts from the man before she felt warm blood trickle down her nose, at which point she had to stop and loudly sniffle before she gave the game away.

There were more players in the criminal underworld, many more, but most of them were so small time or disconnected from their needs that she couldn't really find it in herself to try and remember them.

The more immediately concerning part was almost an after-thought, a mere mention of "lamp-heads" prowling around the fourth and third floor, half-said in jest. After a bit of forceful prodding, she got an elaboration, likely because she had the potential to be a good client in the man's eyes.

Whatever that golem with the cloak was doing, it wasn't alone. A lot of folks had spotted a *lot* of "people" with giant lenses and bulbs for faces prowling around the dark alleys, and even more suspiciously, not one of them had been caught.

Rumor on the street was some kind of augmentation-based group that was just starting to go crazy from putting too much metal in their bodies, letting the dungeon have too much influence over their forms and minds.

It was more plausible than a nonaggressive golem; she could agree with that.

Two maps and a couple of vain pleasantries later, she had everything they needed to get the hell out of here.

There was a lift along the edge of this plate, and the route to hitting the bottom of the third floor wasn't nearly as timely and convoluted when there was an entire network of lines on paper for her to show to Fleabag. There were also a couple of marked inns along the way where they could finally get a proper shower in as well, which was very appreciated.

When she finally got to the meeting point, a little corner next to some kind of industrial chem compressor, she found Fleabag half sprawled across Katherine's lap as she hesitantly petted him, Scruffy having no such compunctions.

The sight filled her with something warm and fuzzy, and she smiled before the migraine took the expression away from her.

An eye on Fleabag's hip opened to stare at her, and with a long-suffering groan, he got off Katherine and stretched with a wide yawn.

She linked their minds again.

Question, the link immediately sent, flavored and presented from the wolf, followed by clarification of knowledge and a mental image of her speaking to a vaguely human figure.

As they began the long, *long* walk to the lift indicated on the map, she filled the silence with careful recollections and translations of everything she learned, while the wolf focused on navigating them around areas of trouble and conflict by using its vibrational senses.

The walk was slow, both because of relative exhaustion from her and Kat, and because they constantly had to dodge armed people the closer they got to the local Adventurers Guild branch.

She only barely got to explaining some background context needed for the wolf to comprehend what exactly a gang was and why it was *not* a pack, when a distant light suddenly bathed everything in yellow-orange hues, making them all startle and whirl in its direction, tense and confused.

Far above and somewhere behind them, she could see the source of that light peeking through smog and pipeworks to cast light down on them like a strange sun, but not the least bit as stable. It sure felt like she was staring straight into the sun, especially with how unused to bright light her eyes were. She could barely see anything through the squint.

She walked forward to peek out of the alley, hearing distant screams and gasps, and saw nothing but a rapidly approaching wave of shattering debris.

Wide-eyed and frozen in confusion, her new eyes were only saved by the tails that suddenly yanked her back into the alley as the shockwave passed them, slamming into everything like a wall of roaring thunder, deforming the alley itself as the building's foundations cracked and snapped with whirring shrieks of metal, starting to topple over them.

The world spun, and then they slammed into something, someone. Arms snapped shut around her, and she only managed to stop her motion enough to see Fleabag shove all three of them under his chest, one arm covering his head and the other supporting him as they were showered with broken glass and a torrent of broken metal, sheets of metal thudding against his back with tiny grunts.

She hurriedly curled her wings in, closing them around their makeshift pile.

Even through the screaming ring in her ears, she could hear the calamitous groaning of something distant bending under pressure.

She leaned out of cover for a moment, staring up at the suddenly smog-cleared sky, only half of it visible due to the building to their right tilting heavily over them, and watched countless structures and towers all tilt bend and break under the concussive shock wave, tumbling down like dominoes.

One of said dominoes was slowly falling right on top of them, a monstrosity of steel spewing wheezing steam and lightning as it crumbled. A factory's spire, a pipe, she couldn't tell what it was. She could only tell that it was wider than the buildings on either side of where they were currently cowering.

The eye on Fleabag's neck likely told him before she could, because he jumped off and sent her a mental sense of urgency.

She didn't hesitate to buff Katherine and herself with [Haste], use her wings to throw herself upright, pick Scruffy up, and run.

She vaulted over piles of brick and followed in Fleabag's steps as he barreled through the doors of fallen buildings and ran on walls turned to floors, through a stretch of jagged obstacles made up of overturned walkways, grates, pipes spewing acids and pink gasses, buildings crumpled like tin cans, navigating the maze of a broken city all around them as blood ran down her face from her bleeding ears while an insistent whine rendered her as close to deaf as she'd ever been.

She could smell the blood, could see the suffering of innocents all around her.

This time, she hardened her heart and ignored it.

Another mental tactile image came from Fleabag, one that made her newfound confidence after the ritual crumple like wet paper.

Buried underneath the mind-jolting impacts and vibrations, deep underground, blobs of motion and metal were surging upward with a horrifying speed in all directions.

Including theirs.

ABOUT THE AUTHOR

SomeoneToForget is a LitRPG author whose debut series, Fleabag, was originally released on Royal Road. He writes to inspire in his readers the childish glee and wonder he has always felt upon discovering and immersing himself in new stories, and hopes his own stories will not soon be forgotten.

RESPAWN YOUR CURIOSITY

follow us on our socials

podiumentertainment.com

@podiumentertainment

/podiumentertainment

@podium_ent

@podiumentertainment